# NAPOLEON MUST DIE

A Mme. Vernet Investigation

# QUINN FAWCETT

AVON BOOKS · NEW YORK

If you purchased this book without a cover, you should be aware that this book is stolen property. It was reported as "unsold and destroyed" to the publisher, and neither the author nor the publisher has received any payment for this "stripped book."

NAPOLEON MUST DIE: A MME. VERNET INVESTIGATION is an original publication of Avon Books. This work has never before appeared in book form. This work is a novel. Any similarity to actual persons or events is purely coincidental.

AVON BOOKS
A division of
The Hearst Corporation
1350 Avenue of the Americas
New York, New York 10019

Copyright © 1993 by Bill Fawcett & Associates
Published by arrangement with Bill Fawcett & Associates
Library of Congress Catalog Card Number: 93-90114
ISBN: 0-380-76541-1

All rights reserved, which includes the right to reproduce this book or portions thereof in any form whatsoever except as provided by the U.S. Copyright Law. For information address Bill Fawcett & Associates, 388 Hickory, Lake Zurich, Illinois 60047.

First Avon Books Printing: August 1993

AVON TRADEMARK REG. U.S. PAT. OFF. AND IN OTHER COUNTRIES, MARCA REGISTRADA, HECHO EN U.S.A.

Printed in the U.S.A.

RA 10 9 8 7 6 5 4 3 2 1

# NAPOLEON MUST DIE

# Prologue

❖

UNDER THE CANVAS tarpaulins, darkening as the desert sun set in its now familiar rapid manner, lay the lion's share of the plunder. The Battle of the Pyramids had given up a rich harvest to the French, and their commander, General Napoleon Buonaparte, had taken the best of what was available. The loot had been left behind at the original French encampment by Napoleon, and was worth more than all of last year's Directoire budget.

"We must protect this booty Lavallette has delivered to us. He personally sorted the most valuable of it and brought it here," said Louis Alexandre Berthier to the three officers with him. One was a grizzled marine captain off the *L'Orient,* one of the ships anchored a few miles away. The second man was the commander of half of the army's cavalry. His left arm was in a sling because of a slight sprain garnered not in the recent battle, but while lifting a horse that had fallen on a trooper the day before. He wore a uniform that was lavished in gold braid and silver thread. It was still covered in dust from the long ride back from the main army. The neatness of the third officer's uniform annoyed Berthier. Napoleon's aide, Major Lucien Jeannot Vernet, was the type of man who wore the stiff, high-necked collar of a staff officer and seemed to enjoy it. It was late and they all had worked hard all day, but somehow Vernet had taken the time to change or brush his blue and yellow gendarme's uniform clean. Vernet had befriended Napoleon during the decisive battle where the young Corsican officer had gained fame for his "whiff of grapeshot" that had been fired into the rioting mobs. As always, Berthier resented anyone with whom he had to share the young general's regard. "It would not be wise for any of this to wa ... wander. The general promised in his last letter to present the scepter and other pieces to the Directoire." Everyone knew which general he meant, Napoleon Buonaparte. He looked from one to the next, the lamplight making a halo of his frizzy hair. "There are English spies everywhere."

"There are Egyptians everywhere," said Major Vernet in his calm way. "They've more reason than the English to want the treasure."

"But we're not allowing any Egyptians but water carriers into the camp. Even if they sneaked in, surely they wouldn't dare risk taking any of these riches." Louis Alexandre Berthier spoke with the confidence of a man who knew that in the order of the world, France led in civilization, culture, and politics. "How many of your fellows are standing watch here?" he inquired of the marine sergeant who stood by the tent flap.

"Four, sir," answered the sergeant. He appeared uncomfortable in this exalted company. "We stand two watches each, one during the day and one during the night. Our watches are three hours. I stand mine at noon and for three hours after sundown." Even before the losses at the Pyramids, the French army was stretched thinly. There were probably only two hundred men capable of fighting in the whole camp, and most of those were officers and so unwilling to stand any watches. The four marines had been all the men Vernet had been able to dragoon for guard duty.

"It's very tempting, with only a tarpaulin and a tent to protect it—and a single guard," said Berthier, his frown deepening. "There's so much wealth here. Gold, rare stones ..."

"What about that magnificent scepter?" asked General Joachim Murat. The cavalry general wore a uniform that rivaled the splendid treasure. Beneath his carefully kept curls and sensitive eyes, the man wore a hussar uniform with a few touches of his own. Among these extras were two rows of buttons made of emeralds and a sable lining. Vernet wondered if he wore the fur during the afternoon heat. The general was directing his question to the sergeant who had stood guard over the loot for a third of the last two nights. "Might they not risk something for that scepter?"

Berthier looked nervously at the tarpaulin, then took his snuffbox from his waistcoat pocket, his most recent attempt to keep from biting his nails. As he inhaled a little pinch, he said, "It is our duty to see they do not get it. Or any of the rest of the treasure."

Inspector Vernet glowered at the tarpaulin. "It would take one or two mules to move the golden chairs, but that scepter doesn't weigh so much that a water carrier couldn't bear it away." He went and lifted the edge of the canvas.

"Look. He wouldn't even have to search for it."

In the lamplight the golden flail gleamed, and its porphyry bands along the handgrip took some of the fire, glowing; it was very old, coming from the time of the Pharaohs and passed through the hands of Egyptians and Nubians and Greeks and Romans, Greeks again, and then into Muslim Egyptians, a symbol of the durability of the country, and a last token of the authority that had raised the Sphinx and the Pyramids. The scepter was made of gold and half again as long as a man's arm. Precious stones ringed the top, enmeshed in finely wrought designs of silver and turquoise. Of all the booty under the canvas, none was so indicative of Egypt's subjugation to the French as this glorious scepter that never had beat grain.

General Murat rubbed his sore arm, his handsome features haggard just now from lack of sleep. "You've got a point, Vernet." He patted the tarpaulin. "We'd better get this all into a more secure place. Perhaps in the hold of the flagship, though I mistrust the scum manning those ships almost as much as the Egyptians. Safer there though. First thing tomorrow, Berthier, what do you say?"

"I was told to keep the treasure here, under Vernet's watch. If Napoleon orders it, I'll store this treasure wherever he decides is best. Otherwise, it will remain where it is, with its marine guards," answered Berthier quietly, his dedication showing in the way he stood, the way he spoke Buonaparte's name. "He's only a hard day's ride away. You may warn him, if you think it necessary."

"Fine, a most correct attitude," said the handsome, olive-skinned Murat, who, while tired, was already growing impatient to return to the campaign. "We'll tend to it at dawn."

"Very good," said Vernet, giving Berthier a hard look. "In the meantime make sure the guard is fully armed and his weapons charged. I don't trust the English or the Egyptians. General Buonaparte has placed this treasure in my charge and it is my duty to ensure its safety."

"Very wise, I'm certain," said Berthier with faint, damning disgust. "Your wariness does you credit, Vernet."

General of the Cavalry Joachim Murat glanced at the young Inspector Vernet. "Quite a duty for so young a man, and already a major in the gendarmerie of the Republic. Aren't most headquarters' companies commanded by a colonel? You must be considered most promising." Both Murat and Berthier were generals and only a few years older than the gendarme officer.

Lucien Vernet's color heightened but he knew better than to answer back. After a pause he answered in a flat voice. "I'll report to you after we change the guards an hour before dawn."

"Report to Berthier, as you're supposed to do. He likes the morning sun. I hope to slumber far past the dawn for a most exquisite change," answered Murat, making light of it now that he had taken a jab at the young Vernet. Then his voice grew somber. "Unless something goes wrong."

Murat crossed himself as if he were still a seminarian.

"I shouldn't even joke about it. If any of this treasure disappears, as definitely as could be done by Madame Guillotine, it will put paid to the career of the man who loses it."

# 1

✦

VICTOIRE HEARD HER husband rise from his camp bed and make his toilette before getting dressed. It took a moment for her to accept that the night was over. The memories of her husband's firm body pressed against her, his face buried in her neck and his breath warm and fast as their pleasure grew, were still too fresh. Naked beneath the soft sheets that had, until recently, belonged to a Mameluke noble, Victoire Vernet was still too relaxed to even sit up. Her husband was trying to be quiet, but she could not help but hear the soft clatter of his sword, the rustle and slap of his boots. She turned on her side and opened one of her sapphire-blue eyes. "What time is it, Vernet?" she asked.

"Too early," he answered softly. "Go back to sleep." He was very handsome, even in the dim light of a single candle, freshly shaven and his uniform crisp.

"Four-thirty? Five?" Victoire stretched once, reaching out to brush his hand with her own. Once again she felt her good fortune at securing the affections and the name of this splendid officer, for she was not so wealthy or so beautiful that she could have secured a husband with the crooking of her finger. Her fortune was modest, her fair beauty unfashionable, and her advanced education was seen as a disadvantage by many. The young wife was glad of her decision to take the chance of booking sail on a merchant ship to Athens and then Alexandria in order to be with him.

"Four-thirty." He bent down and kissed her forehead.

His gentle, firm touch thrilled her and she wished he didn't have to go on duty so soon.

"I'm to meet the seamen. We're getting more supplies off the ships, thank goodness. I didn't mean to disturb you."

"It's all right," she said, her yawn turning to a sigh. "I want to rise while it's still cool." She stretched her arms, wishing she had more wool fat to rub on them. Between the sand and the heat her fair skin was dry and fragile as paper, and her pale hair had faded to nearly white.

"I'll be back in an hour or so. We will have breakfast together," her husband warned affectionately as he lifted the tent flap and left. "Be careful, little wife."

"You as well, Vernet," she said, beginning the routine of rising.

Dawn came suddenly to Egypt; one moment there was a molten lining to the light lying along the eastern horizon, and then the sun was up, volcanic. Almost at once the wind became a furnace blast.

Lucien Vernet was early to the treasure tent. He had waited for more than half an hour to receive the supplies, but finally had been signalled that British ships were in sight. The landing was postponed. Murat's dire prediction still troubled him. The general's temper was something to be feared and he took inordinate pride in the loot gathered there. Having nothing to do for another half hour, he had gone to inspect the treasure tent in the hope of quelling his apprehensions. Now he stared in disbelief at the guard he had just rolled over, afraid to open his mouth for fear he would vomit. Vernet saw that his hands were covered with the marine's blood, which was the same color as the gendarme officer's scarlet cuffs. It bothered him that he couldn't tell if his cuffs were stained. Standing up, the shocked officer backed a few steps away from the body and shuddered. He reminded himself he was a gendarme and inured to the sight of death.

In the first, long shadows of morning, this same marine private that had been guarding the tent during the day before now lay on his side in the cover of the treasure tent, his arms tightly bound, his uniform torn open, his shoulders and face horribly bruised; his throat had been so viciously slashed that the white of his spine showed in the wound. The detective in Vernet noted that the sword or knife must have been incredibly sharp. The man's musket was leaning against the tent, still charged as ordered. A leather cup, any water it once held long absorbed by the dry ground, lay on its side near the musket. A few dark spots almost a pace away from where the body lay indicated to Vernet's trained eye that the guard had been standing when the blade had cut his throat. The rough ground was too filled with footprints to give any clues.

A soft and distant sound of crockery being stacked brought Vernet back to himself. He took a long, uneven breath and then shouted loudly. "Captain of the guard! Soldiers! Guard!" Then he stood beside the corpse, waiting for others to come. Carefully he washed his hands in the sand and straightened his uniform. Vernet was frightened and dared not show it.

The camp commander's tent was the closest, and so General Desaix was the first to arrive, his dark hair disordered, his tunic unfastened. "What do you mean, shouting like—" He stopped as he saw the figure on the sand. "God have mercy," the commander whispered nervously, and surprisingly, crossed himself. The church and its forms were normally considered antirevolutionary by the Directoire.

He went down on one knee to check the dead man.

"Yes. Liberty and Equality! Yes, he's dead; they killed him, you can see," said Vernet, and forced himself to stop babbling. "I . . . I have just now found him." He made himself lean down to feel the forehead of the dead man. "He isn't completely cold."

"Not dead very long, then," said Desaix, straightening up.

"Probably not," Vernet agreed, swallowing hard to end the tightness in his throat. He had steeled himself against the sight of men wounded and killed in battle, but this one marine, trussed up like an Easter goose, struck him to the core. Professionally he tested the body's limbs for the hardening that followed death in such a predictable pattern. "Two hours, no more, since he was killed," the gendarme officer concluded aloud.

Desaix examined the body as half a dozen more men in various states of undress arrived. "Two hours, with so much blood gone." He dusted his hands against his thighs. He looked toward the treasure tent. "What is missing?"

"I . . ." Vernet felt a sudden rush of guilt. "I haven't looked yet." It was a confession, and said quietly.

Desaix gave Vernet a quick, hard glance. "And you raised the alarm?"

Before Vernet could answer, Berthier himself arrived, his clothes in disarray and his sword and scabbard in his hand. "What is the meaning of this? Futter the saints, there had better be a good reason—"

"The meaning of what?" asked Desaix, his face showing disapproval for the obscenity Berthier used. "Have more respect for the dead." He moved so that Berthier could have a clear view of the marine private.

"Jesus and Mary!" Berthier gasped, and earned himself another look of distaste from Desaix. "How did this happen? When?" He stared suddenly at the treasure tent and the booty under the tarpaulin inside. "The general's treasure. Is anything missing?"

"Who knows?" said Desaix. "No one's looked yet, according to Vernet." He motioned more of the soldiers who came running up to keep back, then addressed Vernet once more. "You said you hadn't looked, didn't you?"

In spite of the beginning heat of the day, Vernet went cold. "Yes," he said, and was astonished at how calm he sounded. "I thought my first duty was to alert the camp." In the growing light all three men could see a slash in the fabric of the tent. It was at the exact spot Vernet had lifted to show the scepter the evening before. The marine officer had arrived, and barely paid attention to his lost comrade. He strode over to the slash and raised the flap it created. As suspected, the scepter was missing.

Berthier's eyes narrowed and he looked more dyspeptic than ever as he gazed once more at the corpse at their feet. "And when d-did you ... f-find him?" The general's aide's slight hesitation in speech warned Vernet just how upset the man was.

"Possibly three, four minutes ago," said Vernet, not at all certain he ought to answer so readily. "I'd been out to sign for the supplies, but after a while we had a signal saying that there are too many British ships about to put out boats. They'll land them later, when it's safe again."

Berthier turned and stood as Joachim Murat strode up; he had been riding with the perimeter patrol for two hours and was brushing sand off his uniform. "What news?" he asked, not seeing the body.

Murat swung one hand in the air to catch nothing. "I don't know why we bother with these night patrols. The whole world's dark as the River Styx. We wear out the horses to no purpose." He saw the dead marine private. "What the Devil—"

"You have the right of it there," said Desaix. "This is truly the Devil's work." He indicated the body. "What are we to do?"

"Don't tell Napoleon," said Murat promptly, taking in the sodden corpse and slashed tent. "Not yet." He bent over the dead man. "It's not easy to cut a throat." He tried to get his fingers under the ropes, but there was no slack in them and the knots held. "Whoever did this ..."

"Whoever did it, they did it not so very long ago," said Vernet in a steady voice. "He isn't fully cold or stiff."

"No, he isn't," said Murat after testing the marine's cheek and bound arms. "An hour, then. Two at most."

"An Egyptian, do you think?" suggested Desaix.

"Not necessarily," Murat declared. "We've been watching for Egyptians on patrol. We didn't encounter any large, strong men; the killer would have to be large to overpower this man, and strong to make those knots. Also, the guard raised no alarm. He may have thought he recognized whomever approached, unless he was sneaked up upon. It is easy to do that to *one* man. There are English spies. And some of our own soldiers might not ..." His palm smacked into his dusty tunic. "No. I make no accusations."

"But what do you suspect?" asked Berthier, then made a motion for silence. "Not now. Too many will overhear us. We must reach a ... certain understanding." He pointed to the tent. "I want a complete inventory made at once. If anything else is missing, if it is only a button or a leather cup, I want to know about it."

"I'll attend to it," Vernet offered, eager to do something to expiate his failure.

"No," Berthier said, with so much feeling that Vernet was shocked. "Let someone else ... d-do that." He turned on his heel and signalled to one of his aides-de-camp. "I want you to arrange for the inventory. Use only men on my staff, and have three present at all times." He rounded on Vernet. "You will report to my quarters at once. You're to be available on call until I am able to determine what happened here." He shook his frizzy head emphatically and nibbled on his left thumbnail. "Someone bring a knife, and cut those ropes off him. And cover him decently. It isn't fitting for a Republican marine to lie there trussed up like a pig going to market."

"Not here in Egypt," said Murat. "They don't eat pigs here. It offends their sensibilities." He gave a wolfish smile to Vernet and a solemn glance at Berthier. "The best of luck, Inspector. I fear you are going to need it."

Vernet had no idea how to respond. He chose the safest course and saluted.

Berthier read the inventory over, as if on rereading he would find the scepter listed with the other plunder. It had been a very long and frustrating day and his soul felt worn. One thing held his thoughts, one thing that he could not accept and could not deny—the flail scepter, that ancient symbol of pharaonic power and the rulership of the kingdom of the Nile that his master had promised to send to Paris, was gone.

"Eugene," he called in a voice so rough he did not recognize it as his own, "bring your writing supplies and come here."

His secretary, a gawky stick of a man who looked out of place in his uniform, came through the tent flap, a portable desk slung around his neck by a wide leather strap. The man's uniform was meant to be that of a member of the general's staff. Actually the young man had forgotten to pin half the gold and white epaulets and only one white cuff was in place. This was typical of the corporal. Eugene Caronne had come over as the assistant to one of the savants who had accompanied the army. He had been ill when they landed, and left behind. When Berthier had learned of the man's clean handwriting and ability to copy maps accurately, he had quickly drafted him onto his own staff. He was probably the first man ever to be drafted into the armies of the Republic in Egypt, a distinction it was unlikely the former professor's assistant took any pleasure in. The scribe bowed slightly and took his seat on a leather-covered camp stool; he opened the portable desk and drew out pens and a standish of ink. Satisfied that the nib was properly trimmed, he selected two sheets of paper, closed the desk, and prepared to write.

"I want you to make a copy of this inventory," said Berthier, handing the paper to Eugene. "Then be so good as to speak with Madame Vernet; I want to call upon her at her earliest convenience." He placed his broad hands together, fingers fanned out. "I must get to the bottom of this at once, Eugene. I have my duty."

"Yes, sir," said Eugene, his attention on copying the inventory of loot. "Pardon me, sir, but what's this word, if you will?" He pointed to one line that had been smeared when the list was sanded.

"Tooled leather," Berthier said after peering at it. "Two tooled leather saddles, made in the Egyptian design with gems embedded. They took them off one of the Mameluke commanders after the battle. One was scarred by cannister."

"Thank you," said Eugene, and continued to write.

"I want you to leave paper and ink for me when you

finish, Eugene. I ... m-must write to Napoleon myself. He ought to be notified, at once." Napoleon's chief aide hated everything he was saying. He still didn't know how to soften the news. "This is a terrible turn of events."

"Yes, sir," said Eugene, not really listening. His pen scratched away at the paper.

Berthier sighed, then got up, staring out into the brilliant morning. He hated Egypt, with its flies and dust and jabbering natives and tainted water. But it was what Napoleon sought; for Berthier nothing else mattered. For some reason he remembered one of the remarks Vernet had made a few hours earlier. "What if there are British ships out there?"

Victoire Vernet received Berthier twenty minutes later, five minutes after his note was delivered. It was just after sunset and there was a hint of a cool breeze off the nearby bay. There was little she could do to make the tent presentable, but she busied herself creating a stricter look of order to the cramped quarters. By the time Berthier arrived she was dressed in the lightest muslin she could wear with propriety, her hair had been done up in a knot that was more practical than fashionable, and instead of slippers she wore sensible paddock boots on her slender feet. She curtsied to Berthier as she gave him the choice of two camp stools. "It is an honor to welcome you, Monsieur Berthier. It will distress Vernet that he was not here to greet you himself, but I am afraid that my husband has not yet returned from his duties."

"No, he has not," said Berthier, his tone so brusque that Victoire turned to look at him.

"Is something the matter?" she asked, her bluntness almost equally his own. "Have you brought me bad news?" Victoire felt her pulse race; had something happened to her husband?

Berthier shook his head. "Not the kind you mean," he said quickly. "I saw your husband ten minutes since and he was in good health." His smile went sour. "I hope you will clear up a mystery for me."

"Certainly," she said, curious. "What mystery is this?"

"One that has a stringent need for the utmost discretion. I must rely on you to keep everything we say confidential. Have I your word on that?"

"If it is necessary, then of course you have my word." She said it without fanfare. "I will not reveal what you say to me."

"Very good. I depend on you to hold by that. First, answer a few questions for me. I do not ask them capriciously. What time did your husband leave this morning?" Berthier's tone was as clipped as his occasional stammer would allow.

She regarded Berthier with a level gaze. "He said it was four-thirty when he left."

"And you are satisfied it was?" Berthier asked.

Victoire studied him, then answered, "I suppose so. My own watch is in my jewel box. It runs poorly; the sand has got into the works. I rose shortly after he left and it was then lacking fifteen minutes of five, according to my watch; there may be five minutes' difference either way." When Berthier said nothing more, she decided to ask a question. "Why do you want to know this?"

Berthier hesitated before answering. "There was a man found killed, one of the marines. We were hoping ... s-someone might have seen or heard something."

This puzzled her. "If you want to know about that, why not speak to my husband? His job is protecting the camp."

"We already have," said Berthier, and his tone was very chilly now. "But he hasn't been much help to us. He spent most of the day in Rosetta, hunting Englishmen, no doubt. Now he is inquiring as to why the watering parties have been recalled to the ships."

"I fear I shan't be, either," Victoire said, and although she spoke politely there was an edge in her manner that Berthier recognized at once.

"Madame Vernet, if you seek to help your husband, refusing to assist me is not wise. I do not ask these things because I think that there is reason to believe that your husband has done ... s-something criminal. I want to establish that he has not done this deed."

Now Victoire's manner was wooden. All the camp was talking about the murder and speculating on what had been stolen. "When he left, he said he would be meeting seamen who were bringing supplies. He expected to return by five-thirty or six. He has done this before, as you must surely know. You must be aware that we have need of more powder and more bandages, as well as better food." She tilted her chin up. "Supplies are usually landed at dawn, aren't they, when there's less chance of British naval patrols discovering our sailors?"

"Yes," said Berthier quietly. "But no supplies have been landed today."

From some distance away there was the sound of cannon fire.

"Perhaps," said Victoire, inadvertently turning her head toward the sound, "it was not safe to land supplies?"

"Perhaps," Berthier conceded.

Three cannon shots echoed a second time through the camp. Berthier looked lost for a moment, then concerned.

"Something's wrong. That's the d-danger signal." He then rose and hurried from the tent without a further word.

Victoire sat unmoving, wondering over the direction the aide's questions had been taking. She also discovered that she was mildly annoyed at his abrupt departure, with not so much as a by-your-leave. A third set of three blasts was followed by the sound of horses being ridden toward the shore. Vernet would have to return along the beach from Rosetta. If there was a problem, he would be in the middle of it. Concerned, the fair-haired Frenchwoman hurried from her tent and joined the stream of uniformed men heading for the harbor.

# 2

HER EYES STUNG with wind and dust from the first acrid gunsmoke that drifted onto the land from the triple signal guns each French warship had fired to recall its shore parties. This could only mean their captains felt a battle was imminent. Twelve years ago some men wounded in a sea battle had been put up in her father's house. All of them had been hideously wounded, mostly by splinters. The stench of their infected wounds had been intolerable. Victoire thought of the good men, loyal Frenchmen and impressed English peasants, who would soon be dying less than a mile away, and she felt tears well and slide down her cheeks.

She had climbed to the top of a small dune just behind the bench itself. This placed her high enough to see past the anchored French ships and observe the whole of Aboukir Bay. Ahead and to her left were a small island and one French ship, the *Conquerant*. Curving away to her right were anchored almost a dozen more of the massive ships of the line. Just visible on her right and closer to the beach were four frigates, staying safely behind the larger ships. It was just after dark, though the nearly full moon lit the bay and the warships anchored there with harsh clarity. The sails of the approaching British squadron were surprisingly bright against the dark waters of the sea beyond. The empty masts of the anchored French line stood in dark contrast to the moonlight and star-filled sky.

Exhausted as she was from the tension of the day and concern for her still-missing husband, Victoire still found

## NAPOLEON MUST DIE    17

herself wide awake and her pulse pounding as the British ships approached their fleet. She had heard rumors that Nelson, one of the most dreaded sea dogs, commanded the English ships. So fascinated by the unfurling drama, Victoire didn't notice a number of officers from the camp approach. She jumped slightly when Berthier spoke to another man a few feet behind her.

"The fleet is anchored so that each attacking British ship will have to face the full force of all their guns."

"If they sail directly at their center," a voice Victoire didn't recognize answered.

Turning, she saw that it was the marine officer that had been in charge of the guard detail on the tent.

"Shouldn't you be on board the *L'Orient?*" she asked, while gesturing toward the French ships. The *L'Orient* was the largest warship in the French navy, boasting one hundred twenty guns in her broadsides. She was easily half again larger than the ships anchored to either side of her.

"Too late, madame," came the reply in a slightly annoyed tone. "Too risky to take a boat out with them so close."

"Won't they be trapped on the far side?" Victoire asked, genuinely curious. She had never seen a naval battle, though her father had recounted a few to her during her childhood.

"That's Nelson," the marine confirmed, as if that answered her question.

"Come now," Desaix broke in after a moment's awkward silence. "Look how one flank is rested on the side of the harbor and the other near that island."

"And I see movement on the island," a red-haired aide named McCaffrey added. Victoire guessed he was part of the Brigade Irlandais, the Wild Geese of the Irish battalion. A few were serving with the artillery.

"Yes, sound flanks and a firm line. That is the key to victory," another voice added from the edge of the growing group of officers.

Victoire recognized the speaker as Jean Lannes, the commander of the division that had taken the brunt of the

Mameluke's charge at the Battle of the Nile. They had not only broken the charge of twice their number of heavy cavalry, but had eventually broken their squares to pursue the survivors. No one chose to disagree with the pronouncement of the hero of their most recent victory.

The English ships approached in silence. They were still beyond gun range for the French, and were unable to fire forward since nearly all the guns on their ships were aligned in rows along the sides of their hulls. The gun ports of the approaching ships were painted black, making them stand out in contrast to the thick yellow stripes painted along their sides. The water glistened as they cut through it, entering the bay toward the near edge of the immobile line of French ships.

The English formation broke apart. Each ship was more concerned with closing for battle than maintaining any formation. Victoire could hear an intake of breath as the entire English fleet tacked and made for the left end of the French line of battle. Suddenly it seemed that the white-sailed behemoths were coming straight for the beach. The nearest French ships began to fire.

"Damn, curse them and their spawn," a voice muttered as the first British ship began to slip around the stern of the last ship on the French left.

The broadsides from both sides were coming regularly now, making talking even on the beach a chancy thing. Pale smoke was once more rolling toward them and already Victoire's cheeks stung where a tiny piece of unburnt powder had drifted against it. To her eyes, the fire from the island that was supposed to stop the English from passing on that side seemed very feeble.

"He's only put six pounders there," Desaix moaned. "Those field guns don't have enough punch to hurt those oaken hulls."

He was right, the British men-of-war seemed to be ignoring the frantic efforts of the battery on the island to harm them.

Another rumble of broadsides came as the first of the English warships turned and brought its broadside to bear on the *Conquerant*. This made talking impossible. Victoire noticed that a second ship had approached and was firing at this same French warship on its far side. For several minutes the roar of battle rose and fell. To everyone on the shore it was soon apparent that the English gunners were firing almost twice as quickly as the defending Frenchmen, and doing twice as much damage as a result. Already one of the towering masts from the *Conquerant* had fallen, taking a second with it. She could see that more British ships were approaching the defending line at several points.

Victoire heard Vernet call her name during a rare lull in the three-hour-long naval battle. Gratefully she looked away from the battle. "Here, Vernet!" she cried out, her voice rough.

He came to her side, his face marred by drifting smuts. He put a consoling hand on her shoulder. "It's going badly."

"Yes, I fear it is," she said. Another pounding of cannon demanded her attention.

More British ships were breaking through the French line. Those that had passed around the left side of the defenders were sailing along their rear, firing rapidly. Only an occasional isolated cannon fired at these ships. Two of the French men-of-war, so majestic just a few hours earlier, had lost their masts, and a third was visibly listing and seemed likely to turn turtle. The first English ship, having run along the bulk of the French line, was still fighting. This time she was easily besting two frigates in an unequal battle that could only have a disastrous end for the frigates.

One ship, the fourth to pass behind the now sinking hulk that had been the *Conquerant*, was now crossing in front of those gathered on the dune. Even as she fired a broadside away from them, one man on the deck waved cheerfully at the shore.

"I shall organize men to fire upon them," Desaix announced, outraged. He then turned to make good on his oath.

"Not unless you want us all killed," Berthier corrected, grabbing the taller general's arm. His voice was sad, but firm. "Those ships each carry more guns than we have with the entire army, and each throws a shot weighing twenty-four pounds or more. Remember what piff-puffs our battery on the island were?"

Desaix was still undecided. Victoire sympathized. It was frustrating to stand and watch their comrades-in-arms slaughtered by the English. More so as they had been so confident of victory just a few hours earlier.

"Besides, they are out of musket range," a voice from a clump of officers and men watching nearby added. Then the roar made further argument impossible.

For a long time everyone watched in silence, each hoping some miracle would deliver retribution on Nelson's fleet, or at least on the ship containing the officer who had been so cheerful even while doling out death and ruin. As they watched, yet another ship struck. It had been four hours since the battle started. Smoke was now rising from the *L'Orient*. Her valiant crew was attempting to fight the guns on both sides at once. A cheer rang out when one British man-of-war, obviously foundering, withdrew from her duel with the French flagship, but it was quickly stifled by the appearance of another, fresh English warship to take her place.

A stray ball, no one could be sure who had fired it, cut a furrow in the sand a few hundred paces to the right of where they all stood. Several soldiers rushed to examine it. Victoire noted that it was so large that even half-buried, it came up to some of the men's knees. The battle had moved farther down the line of anchored ships, but now seemed to be coming closer again.

"It might not be safe to remain here," Vernet said as he watched the latest casualty wallowing toward them along the shore. The frigate was sinking fast, and the sailors were striving to get free of her before she went down.

"I'm not afraid," said Victoire, containing herself so that

she did not tremble. "There may be those who need our help."

"The fleet needs our help," said Vernet darkly.

"Admiral Bruey was caught napping, overconfident," Berthier added in tones that placed all the blame for the debacle on the naval commander's shoulders. "I'm just glad we moved most of the supply ships into Alexandria harbor or the fool would have cost us the campaign."

"Who could expect this?" Vernet protested. "We should have been prepared."

"It's the way of the British," Victoire agreed in a lower voice that only Vernet could hear. "Why should we admire their skill when they are doing this?"

"Who has said we should admire their skill? Still, they should have placed some heavy guns on that island," Vernet insisted.

Victoire shook her head, unwilling to reveal that it was her father who had expressed admiration for the British navy, ten years ago. She hated the smell of burning that filled the air. "Foolish people say it, those who do not have to fight them."

Vernet glared, his eyes reddened with smoke and wrath. "They have held sway on the ocean too long. They exploit every other nation. Their rule must end."

"Yes, yes—and how I regret it will not be today," said Victoire, raising her hand to her face to brush away her tears, leaving a smear across her cheek. She put her hand into Vernet's and took solace in his fingers tightening. A body had washed up to the shore. A French sailor, one arm missing and the other flapping as the waves washed past. No one moved off the dune to pull him further ashore. For a very long time they all watched as the rest of their fleet was pounded into ruin.

Most of their attention was being taken by the *L'Orient*. Even while black smoke poured from her sides, the flagship continued to fire with visible effect on her English tormentors. When a mast toppled off the gallant ship, Victoire buried her head briefly on Vernet's shoulder. She remembered a dinner in Alexandria, one held to celebrate their almost bloodless capture of the city. The *L'Orient*'s captain had sat at their table and asked her to dance. He had been a very good dancer, graceful in the same way as her dance instructor had been years ago. It was hard to picture a man with that captain's gentle touch amid all the horror.

Long after midnight, only the *L'Orient* still fought back with any vigor. Victoire suspected the crews of both sides were near exhaustion, or beyond. They had been fighting for over five hours. A few of the officers that had stood vigil with them had already drifted back to their tents. Most waited, hoping for something miraculous that could snatch victory from such utter defeat. Had not Napoleon led the army to many surprise victories in Italy?

The explosion, even over a mile distant, was strong enough to drive the tired spectators back a few steps. One moment the *L'Orient* was fighting on, her broadsides ragged but persistent. In an instant the proud, graceful flagship burst apart in a thunderous crash. Every ship in the harbor was racked back by the explosion. Victoire noticed that a frigate that had been listing badly could no longer be seen. Debris from the explosion rose skyward and began to shower over the entire bay. Small scraps of wood and metal rained down on the dune, none larger than a fraction of an inch across. The rumble of the explosion echoed back off the distant hills and city, rolling endlessly across the black waters of Aboukir Bay and the hundreds of men struggling to survive by clinging amid the flotsam. Where the *L'Orient* had sat, not even flotsam remained.

"Mary and Joseph," whispered Vernet, his oath lost in the thunder of *L'Orient*'s end. He held Victoire's hand more tightly.

Around them several people were weeping openly, and one cavalry captain swore loudly and continuously. Smoke rolled over the water toward them, hot and stinking. Many of the watchers had retreated, and now, as burning embers began to fall around them, most of those on the shore fell back, getting away from the presence of battle and defeat.

Vernet pulled Victoire after him, and together they

reached a line of makeshift stalls at the edge of the camp that provided some protection. Inside, horses milled and whinnied, fretting at the smell of burning.

"I ought to arrange to send you home," said Vernet seriously, looking down at his wife with genuine concern. "This is no place for you."

"What do you mean?" Victoire inquired, looking for some opportunity to vent her frustration and dismay.

"I mean I should never have let you come here. You're not a typical army wife, raised to follow the drum and live from camp to camp." He lowered his head. "It was my mistake. We have been married such a short time, I was selfish to want you with me, even against the general's wishes. You should be somewhere you can live as you deserve to live, not here where you—"

"This is exactly the place for me," Victoire corrected him with some heat. "I am your wife, Lucien Vernet. What sort of creature do you think I am? I am not a rich man's pampered darling, I'm from merchant stock. My mother knew what it was to unload shipping bales and to carry cargo from dusk until midnight, and so did her mother before her. Even when my father was elected to office, my mother continued to supervise our enterprise." She folded her arms. "What would I do in Paris, or Rouen, with you gone? Your salary would not go far, not with you here and me in France, and my competence would not support you and me as well. Would you like to see me as a governess in a high-born household, catering to the demands of half a dozen ill-informed brats? It could come to that. Do you think my cousin would welcome me into his household? Or were you intending that I should find a little cottage in the countryside where I could throw corn to chickens while you fight the British? My inheritance would cover those expenses well enough."

He had no answer for her, and so took refuge in bluster. "You make it sound as if I have no use for you and am looking for an excuse to be rid of you. That's far from the truth."

"Is it?" She put her hands on her hips in unconscious

imitation of her dead mother. "How can you suggest that I leave and then tell me you don't wish to be rid of me?" She stared at him. "Well?"

"You're overwrought," he mumbled.

"Nothing of the sort," she countered, but recognized there was some truth in his accusation. "I am worried. That's a very different matter."

"About the British," he said, glancing over his shoulder toward the smoke and chaos on the Nile.

She was just angry enough not to guard her tongue. "About Berthier," she said, and immediately fell silent.

"What about Berthier?" asked Vernet, very much on the alert.

Now that she had begun, she knew she had to finish. "Yes. He's spoken with me. He suspects you of killing the marine private."

"He told you this?" Vernet demanded, his face darkening.

"He didn't have to," she answered, making an effort to speak sensibly. "His investigation reveals it. When he questioned me, I could see he was already half-convinced that you had done the murder. He told me to keep his remarks in confidence, but I cannot conceal what he said from you. You are my husband. It may be that he expects me to tell you."

Vernet took a step back from her. "How could he think such a thing of me?" he asked the air.

"He has been trying to account for the time of all the officers who had some part in guarding the treasure, to discover who might have been able to kill the private without attracting attention," said Victoire, making herself speak clearly. "From the things he asked me, it was apparent that you are one he has not been able to account for. That has led him to suppose you might have been the killer. He must be under a lot of pressure."

"Grace and mercy," said Vernet, turning white. "But I have nothing to do with it."

"He is not convinced of that." She realized how distressed he was and did her best to offer him some reassurance. "I informed him that you would not do such a thing, but I doubt he believed me."

Vernet nodded several times. "He ought never to have talked with you. It's inexcusable to ask a man's wife to speak against him."

"So I told him, and assured him I would not be turned from you by his insinuations." She put her hand on his arm. "Vernet, it's a very dangerous game Berthier is playing. It seems to me that there is more at stake here than one dead marine private." As he gave her a startled glance, she explained, "This is a war, and marine privates die. Therefore the death of this one marine private must have special significance, or Berthier would not trouble himself over the matter."

"No, he wouldn't," said Vernet, his worry changing to perplexity. "What is his intention?"

"To fix blame on you, I fear, and so avoid any blame himself," said Victoire. She stood straighter. "And I will not permit that."

The lamplight cast tremendous shadows on the walls of the tent where Berthier sat, Eugene taking down the last of his day's dictation.

"One last thing," said Berthier to his secretary. "Then you may have supper and retire for the night. It is the matter of Inspector General Lucien Vernet." He scowled at the lamp as if it were Vernet himself. "I want to advise Napoleon to confine the man until he can be tried. Deliver this recommendation to Napoleon before you have your supper. It troubles me that Vernet is walking around where he can do more damage. I wish last night's battle had not so disrupted everything."

"And the scepter?" asked Eugene as he wrote.

"The scepter could be anywhere. I've ordered the Vernet tent searched, but it cannot be done until tomorrow, and if Vernet is half the man I suspect he is, the scepter will be gone before we can find it." Berthier leaned back and peered at the roof of the tent. "It's only to be expected. Men on campaign have many temptations. Some pursue women, some pursue treasure. There is nothing that can stop soldiers from—" He broke off as the flap of his tent was raised.

Napoleon Buonaparte came quickly through the space, Murat and Jean Baptiste Bessieres behind him. He stopped in front of Berthier's writing table. Though standing still, he had a motion about him, a pent-up energy that caught the attention of everyone who met him. "What's this about a missing scepter?" he asked without ceremony.

"You've read my report?" Berthier asked, making a signal to Eugene to stop writing.

"Yes, of course. And I've spoken with Murat and Desaix already. The guard was found dead. The scepter was missing." Napoleon regarded Berthier attentively, waiting.

"Yes. The scepter has not been found," said Berthier heavily. He rubbed his stubbled chin. "I was dictating a recommendation a moment since."

"In what regard?" Napoleon motioned Murat and Bessieres to move closer. "Keep your voices down. I don't want the details all over camp by morning."

"Of course," said Berthier. He faltered, then said, "I have reason to t-think that the man responsible for the death of the marine private and the theft of the flail scepter is the gendarme officer, Inspector Lucien Vernet. He has no one to account for his whereabouts except his wife, before the murder was discovered, and he was present when the guard over the treasure was set. It was his responsibility, in any case." He put his hands, palms down, on the writing table. "He is not a rich man, and he has a young wife that he dotes upon. He must make his fortune in the army."

"What's his reputation?" asked Napoleon of Bessieres. "Do you know anything to his discredit?"

"Nothing worth mentioning," said Bessieres. "His wife did come here against your wish that all wives stay home. He is considered a good man, logical, if a little unimaginative."

"Not a bad quality in an Inspector-General," said Napoleon. He swung around to face Berthier once more. "Find Desaix. I'll want him here in ten minutes. I want to discuss this with you after I talk to him." Saying that, he turned on his heel and strode to the tent door. "I will be back shortly. I expect you to be here."

As soon as he was gone, Murat shook his head in admiration. "He is always two jumps ahead of the rest of us." He chose one of the canvas chairs and sat down. "We might as well be ready when he returns."

Berthier was not so sanguine. "How am I to find Desaix?"

"Let Eugene do it," suggested Bessieres, one of Napoleon's most respected division commanders. "What else are secretaries for?" His long, lean frame was ill-suited to perching on canvas chairs, but he made the best of it, locking his hands around his knees.

"Eugene," said Berthier to his secretary.

"Yes. I will attend to it at once," said Eugene, setting his writing supplies aside and rising. "I will return shortly."

"With Desaix," Napoleon's aide added as he chewed the nail of his little finger. "This is a very bad thing, gentlemen. We must take care to keep the story from getting out."

"Why?" asked Bessieres. "Who will care what has become of a single marine private? Anyone who saw the battle this morning has more deaths to consider than one man's."

"But the scepter. The private was guarding the treasure and the scepter is gone. It is likely that whoever stole the scepter killed the private as well," said Berthier.

Murat slapped his hands on his knees. "It's the scepter that unquestionably matters the most. Those Egyptians want it returned to their control, more than they want most of the treasure. Not that there are a dozen men in Alexandria that would hesitate to steal us to perdition. It's more than a stick of gold to them. It's a symbol. Like our regimental flags. They would rally to it. There are men who benefitted from Mameluke rule. They'll pay well and ask no questions to have it returned. Surely there are desperate men who know this."

"That's what concerns me," said Berthier. "Who is to say that the thief was not acting at the behest of the Pasha? If a French officer is so compromised . . ."

"It won't be the first time an officer looked to improve himself with foreign gold," said Bessieres laconically. "Dismiss the man, and make an example of him. If there are others in it with him, hang one of them. That should put a stop to the thefts. A hanging and one or two officers released in disgrace would put the rest on notice that Napoleon will not tolerate any mischief."

"My thought exactly," said Berthier, cocking his head toward Murat.

"If he is the man," said Murat. "You say you are certain, but how can you be? Have you found the knife that slit the private's throat? The scepter is missing. The worst you have reported about Vernet is that he cannot account for half an hour at a time that many officers could not account for their movements. I was in camp, lost in Morpheus's grip." He shrugged. "Is that sufficient?"

"If it is not Vernet, then it must be you or Desaix. Or me," Berthier added conscientiously. "No one else was aware of the arrangements. Or that exact location for the scepter. The tent was cut directly where it lay."

"That we are all incontrovertibly aware of," added Murat. "But in a camp like this, there are bound to be spies, and what they overhear cannot be assessed."

Berthier scowled. "Why do you protect this man?"

"I don't," said Murat. "But I don't judge him, either, not yet." He looked toward Bessieres. "What do you think?"

"I don't know the fellow," said Bessieres. "But I think perhaps it would be better if we had more against him. So far from France, we must uphold our justice, for example. If we decide he is guilty and it turns out he is not, then it will look badly for the general."

This was the one argument that could shake Berthier. He swallowed hard and rose from his chair. "It wouldn't come to that," he said as if trying to convince himself.

"We must show swift punishment for crimes, or half the army will be more devoted to finding treasure than to advancing Napoleon's cause."

Bessieres's smile was cynical. "What makes you believe that isn't true already?"

Whatever Berthier might have answered, his indignation was silenced as Napoleon came back into the tent. "All right. Let us consider this." He broke off. "Where is Desaix?"

"He will be here in a moment," said Berthier, trusting it was so. He indicated his own chair, the only one in the tent that was not canvas.

Napoleon accepted it, but did not actually sit down. He took up his position behind the writing table and drew a packet of dispatches out of his tunic. "The private was killed with a knife, it says."

"Or a sabre; something with a heavy blade. That's right," said Murat. "He was very securely bound. Whoever made those knots did not intend him to escape."

"He showed signs of being beaten," Napoleon went on, consulting the sheets he opened. "One presumes that was before he was killed. He had a deep cut across the throat."

"The wound penetrated all the way to the spine," said Murat. "The killer knew what he was about. He was determined, too. You don't make a wound like that if you're craven. Though you might if you feared discovery. The private would make no sound dying and could not live more than a few minutes with such a wound."

"True enough," said Napoleon, looking up as Eugene escorted Desaix into the tent.

"I am sorry to be late," said Desaix in his quiet voice as he entered the tent. "I was attending to one of my men—he has an infection in his arm."

"Send him to Larrey," Napoleon recommended. "This is more pressing business." He motioned Desaix to one of the camp chairs. "Berthier wants to be rid of Major Lucien Vernet."

"Detention at the least," said Berthier.

"You mean prison?" asked Desaix politely. "What reason have we for that?"

"Plenty of reason, if he is guilty," said Berthier, his color heightening.

"If," echoed Desaix. "And if he is not?"

Napoleon cut into what was turning into a stalemate. "Guilty or not, I can't go throwing good officers into prison. I need this man. I knew him when I was only a captain. He has done his work well, from what I can see."

"But he might have killed the private and taken the scepter," said Bessieres, being reasonable.

"That isn't certain, it is merely possible," said Murat. "And if he's imprisoned, we most certainly will never know what became of the scepter, I'll put ten sous on that," he declared.

"All the more reason to keep him working," said Bessieres, enjoying his speculation. "If he flees, then we pursue him."

Berthier was driven to exclaim, "I don't understand you! This Vernet is very likely a killer! He has stolen treasure from Napoleon himself. How can we let him roam free? We must confine him. If you will not convene a court-martial, then at least put him in chains."

"But why should we do that?" asked Desaix. "He will not tell us where the scepter is from a cell." His youthful features showed sympathy. "He isn't a monster, is he?"

"A killer," Berthier insisted.

"Well, you have no proof of this and so are many of my officers," Napoleon said. "That isn't reason enough to put him in prison." He folded his arms and regarded his officers. "There are other places that stand between us and the Orient. We need that man in the field. For the time being, I am willing to extend to him the benefit of the doubt. What of the rest of you?"

Bessieres smiled wryly. "We're not about to debate that with you."

Murat cracked a laugh. "No, that we're not," he said, and added, "I don't think we can affix any blame on Vernet, not yet. I think we need more time to search for the scepter. If we find the scepter, then it may be that we will find out what happened to the private. After what happened last night, no one expects us to send anything back to Paris, not for a long time."

This was aggravating to Berthier, who bit the nail of his index finger off to the quick and sucked it to keep it from bleeding. "I'll do whatever you wish, General," he said sullenly. "But I must reiterate that I am certain this Lucien Vernet has stolen the scepter and murdered the marine guard. Who else was capable of the act? If you dismiss Vernet, then the rest of you"—he indicated all the men in the tent except the general—"come under suspicion. I think it is foolish to let him run free."

"Point taken," said Napoleon, staring down at the writing table as if there were hidden messages there. "Suppose I send him away from here? He will still be working for our cause, but he will not be able to interfere with the investigation to find the scepter."

"Where were you planning on sending him?" asked Desaix.

Napoleon thought about it. "What of Jaffa? We need more intelligence on that area before we act. We also need to establish a depot there. Let him do his best for us there." He looked at his officers. "What do you think?"

"I think it is the best of a bad situation," said Berthier heavily.

"It serves our purposes with a duality of good," said Murat. "He continues to advance our cause and our gendarme officer is kept away from any venture where he might cause mischief."

"I don't see any reason to object," Bessieres remarked. "If he sends regular reports, we will be able to keep track of him and gain needed intelligence at the same time."

Desaix nodded. "In the meantime, what do we do about the scepter?"

"I will decide what course to follow before the day after tomorrow," Napoleon informed them. "Make yourselves available that evening, if you will." It was as great a courtesy as Napoleon ever extended to his officers, and they accepted his brusqueness out of habit.

Berthier sighed. "When will you order him to leave for Jaffa?"

"Tomorrow afternoon, I think. That will be time enough," answered Napoleon. "If we send him away today, he might bolt for it."

"And his wife?" asked Berthier.

"His wife is with him," said Napoleon, his memory jogged. "Yes."

"Does she go with him?" Berthier prompted.

Napoleon pulled at his lower lip, bouncing once on the balls of his feet. "No," he decided. "She'll remain here, with most of the other wives. She can make herself useful with the wounded. That will give Vernet a reason to return, and something to bargain with, should it become necessary." He looked at Berthier. "So. Orders to Vernet for Jaffa. I want them delivered for my signature before dawn. Specify that Madame Vernet is to remain here, and provide some allowance for her, so that Vernet will not assume that she is being punished for our doubts about him. Recompense for assisting Larrey."

"If you think that's best," said Berthier, looking down at his feet.

"It appears so to me," said Napoleon in a way that brooked no argument.

Desaix watched Napoleon. "Is the missing scepter to be kept secret?"

"For now," said Napoleon. "Perhaps later we'll inform a few other officers. Until I decide otherwise, it must remain between us."

"As you say," Bessieres said, getting up from where he sat. "If there's nothing more, I have wounded to visit."

"Tend to them," said Napoleon, dismissing him. "The rest of you, be about your duties. Berthier, let me know what transportation we can provide acting Inspector-General Vernet. I will speak with you all shortly." He took his dispatches, shoved them back into his tunic, and headed for the tent door. "This meeting is over."

Murat stood for Napoleon as he departed, then looked back toward Berthier. "Tread carefully, Louis. My officers will remain loyal only so long as I am loyal to them as well. If you are mistaken about Vernet it could go badly for you."

Berthier glowered. "I'll keep that in mind."

"But how long will you be gone?" Victoire stared at her husband, one hand at her throat. The heat of their tent seemed suddenly chill.

"I don't know," said Vernet, holding out the orders. "These simply require me to go to Jaffa. I'm to prepare an advanced base, possibly in command."

"And I am to remain here," said Victoire, her blue eyes as bright and hard as jewels. "He is very astute."

"Napoleon?" said Vernet, not following his wife's thoughts.

"No; Berthier. He has found a way to hold you captive without visible chains. How clever of him." She rose from her cot, where she'd been mending a tear in one of Vernet's tunics.

"Why do you single out Berthier?" asked Vernet, letting his attention be diverted from the unwelcome orders he held.

"Who else is behind this? Not Napoleon—if he suspected you, then you would be confined at the moment. The others haven't the time or the authority to send you to Jaffa. So it must be Berthier; he is the one who has pursued you since the marine private was discovered. And now he is making sure that you will not be able to clear your name." She made fists of her slender hands. "He would sacrifice you to avoid any unpleasant moment with the general. I will not permit it."

"You?" In spite of his disappointments, Vernet felt a rush of affection for Victoire. "How can you stop it, if you are correct?"

"I'll find a way," said Victoire with purpose. "You may rest assured, Vernet, that I will show you had nothing to do with the death of that private, and that you had no part in that theft they are being so secretive about."

Vernet paled. "What do you know of a theft?" he whispered, as if saying the words made the crime worse.

"Only what I have been able to piece together. No one has said anything directly, but I know something of the world. This is my surmise: the marine guard was watching Napoleon's treasure. Why should he be killed, but to reach some of the treasure itself? And why should there be so much care taken, unless there has been theft as well as murder?" Her smile was without humor. "And if it were only murder, you would probably be accused by now. So they are looking for whatever was stolen."

"I hope that others are not as acute as you, my dear," said Vernet, his attempt at laughter failing.

"Others are not as motivated as I am," said Victoire. "I'm determined. I will see to it that your name is cleared, Vernet."

"You fill me with pride, Victoire," said Vernet, not knowing what else to say to her. "It succors my heart, your faith in me." He reached over and stroked the side of her face gently.

"This is not a matter of faith, husband," said Victoire with asperity. "This is a matter of your career and your future. It won't do to have suspicions remain. Therefore something must be done, and it appears that I am the only one willing to do it." She took a turn about the confines of the tent. "I'm going to somehow discover who killed that unfortunate marine, and when I've done that, I will recover whatever has been stolen. You may be sure of it. And Berthier can choke on the booty."

Vernet stopped her, holding her by her shoulders. "Have care, Victoire. You could expose yourself to great danger, and I would not like to think you were at risk for my sake."

She shook herself free of his hands. "You're absurd, Vernet. I'd be worth very little if I permitted my husband to suffer when it was within my power to alleviate it."

"Your concern is great solace," said Vernet, his arms going around her. "You're as fierce as a Cossack."

"My assistance is more to the point," she declared. She took the orders out of his hand and read them. "Jaffa. Where you can do nothing to prevent Berthier from implicating you more deeply than he has already. Well, he reckons without me."

Vernet was able to smile genuinely this time. "What a determined creature you are, Madame Vernet."

She considered this and accepted his compliment. "You are very good to me, Lucien." She looked into his face as she spoke his name. "Be sure that while you are in Jaffa, I will be busy here. Berthier will not be able to hoodwink me. You will not have to bear this stigma one instant longer than necessary."

"I believe that," said Vernet, then added more encouragement, "and if someone like Berthier has had a part in this, his days are surely numbered."

Victoire stared at him. "You may jest if you like, Vernet, but as you yourself have said, I'm determined."

"Yes, you are. You're a very determined woman." He bent and kissed her lightly. "I am going to miss you, little love. Being away from you will be a greater hardship than all the rest."

Her face softened. "Then we must hurry. You will need to get your fill of me, and I of you."

"I will never get my fill of you," Vernet said with utter conviction.

"Nor I of you," she said. "But that doesn't mean we can't try."

He tightened his arms around her. "No, it doesn't," he said softly, loosening the laces on the back of her gown. Soon his fingers danced down her graceful, arching back. Victoire pulled him closer, her hips swaying gently against him as she raised her lips to meet his.

# 3

❧

JEAN DOMINIQUE LARREY wore a blood-spattered smock and carried a basin in his left hand when he admitted Victoire Vernet to his quarters. The tent was full of medical instruments, books, and a skeleton hung from one tent pole. Victoire wasn't sure if the skeleton had come with the army's chief surgeon or from inside the wrappings of one of the local mummies. As always, even before noon the air in the tent was stifling. "You're not a very substantial woman," he observed when he had finished looking her over. "There's nothing much on your bones."

"I'm strong enough," she told him, taking no offense. "I am like a cavalry officer, all sinew."

From the physician's expression, he had his doubts. "You're not the sort who faints, are you?"

"No, I'm not. That is no bravura. I have seen wounds before, and I am no stranger to hospitals. My husband is Major-Inspector Vernet, and I have accompanied him at other times." She did not admit that they had only been married sixteen months and that the most travel she had undertaken with Vernet until they come to Egypt was a short, rugged holiday in the Alps. It had been two days since Vernet left and she had been unable to relax a moment of the time. This morning she had risen with the resolve to take an active role in defending her husband and assist Larrey with the wounded now arriving from battles from both the east and south. She stood a little straighter. "I do sometimes feel ill from heat, but not from anything you might require I look at."

"This morning," said Larrey bluntly, "I had to amputate the arm of a soldier. My greatest fear is that it will become infected. This place breeds infection. It is in the very air and water. Great care must be taken, more than you would in France. In this climate, laudable pus quickly turns pernicious unless an effort is made. Are you prepared to cleanse the wounds and change the dressings for this soldier, or would you rather bandage fingers?"

"Of course I would rather bandage fingers," said Victoire, and earned herself the first sign of approval from Larrey. "It is better to save fingers, but that is not mine to decide. If I am required to change the dressings or treat laudable pus, then I will do it."

Larrey nodded. "You may do, but if you do not know the difference between laudable and pernicious pus, then you will endanger lives," he declared after a brief moment of thought.

"I am aware of that," said Victoire, trying not to weep with anger at Larrey's suspicions. "If I have any doubts, I will ask you to inspect the wound."

"A reasonable precaution," said Larrey. "I understand your husband has been sent to Jaffa."

"Yes." Victoire volunteered no more.

"How long will he be there?' Larrey inquired.

"I have not been told," said Victoire truthfully, and once again was favored with approval.

"Just as well. Things never go as anticipated in war." He drew up a chair and sat down. "Since it appears that you will be helping us, let me inform you what some of your duties will be."

Victoire dropped him a slight curtsy before sitting down opposite him. She pulled a small notebook from her reticule and took out a pencil. "I will write them down, if you don't mind."

"Not in the least," said Larrey, this time openly approving. "I must emphasize again the need to guard against flies. These are not like the flies we see in France—oh, no. These are very difficult creatures. First, you must take care of flies. A swarm here is more dense than a storm cloud.

They are everywhere in this accursed country, and they are dangerous. Where there are flies there is infection. We have seen that again and again. You'll have to be most attentive that there are no flies around the wounded men, not merely on their wounds, but elsewhere, especially their eyes."

As she wrote, Victoire said, "I have some oil of citron. If it would be of help, I will use it on the wounded. Not near the eyes, of course, but there are other ways to use it, such as applying it to a poultice or spreading it in the hair."

Larrey was startled at this offer. "What possessed you to bring oil of citron with you?"

"I was told that it would prevent mosquito bites," she said. "I assume it will also discourage flies."

"Very true," said Larrey, growing more cordial. "Yes, oil of citron is most useful. We are not well supplied here, but I am promised more carbolic and bandages in the next few days, as soon as the ships in Alexandria harbor are able to land supplies in some safety. Their captains still fear Nelson will return." He cleared his throat. "You will have to be careful of the water. The Nile may do for the crops, but there are leeches and unhealthy animalcules in the water that lead to flux. If you wish water, then treat it with lemon or boil it to kill the animalcules. It is safer then, but never wholly safe. If you bathe in Nile water, treat it with iodine for the same reason. And do not drink it unless it has been boiled, to kill the animalcules. You will avoid more than flux that way, or the flukes that corrupt the liver. There are many creatures that live in the water."

Victoire wrote quickly. "This must be true of the wounded as well," she said. "They ought to be kept away from Nile water."

"More for them than the rest of us. They are already weakened and for that reason the animalcules may well flourish in their blood." He had set the basin aside. "Many of the wounded suffer from the flux. They must be tended almost constantly, and the work is unpleasant."

"I am prepared for that," said Victoire, doing her best to sound unflustered.

"This place has much fever as well as flux, and you will have to watch men with open wounds for any sign of fever. In this heat, fever is especially dangerous, and pernicious fevers are more common than in France."

"Pernicious fevers," repeated Victoire, making what she hoped were proper notes. "Flies are not to be tolerated. Nile water is to be treated with iodine. Other than this, I must care for fevers. Is that right thus far?" She held out her notebook.

"There is the question of serpents," said Larrey at his most daunting.

"Asps, I have been told," said Victoire, maintaining her composure. "They are deadly."

"Yes, they are," said Larrey. "And so are the scorpions. Both the asps and the scorpions like hidden places. You are not to put your hand into any place you cannot see. We had a young corporal killed last week for putting his hand on an asp under his bed. I don't want anything of that sort from those helping me. Is that clear?"

"It is clear," said Victoire. "You can want this no more than I do."

Larrey glared. "I suppose it is a beginning."

"No doubt you will think of other strictures in time." Her eyes wrinkled at the corners. "You have only to offer your assignment to me, Larrey, and I'll undertake to do my poor best on your behalf."

"My behalf, it is? It is Napoleon's behalf, not anyone else's." He lifted the flap that opened onto another length of tent. "Do you have any estimates prepared regarding our casualties?" It was a casual challenge, one intended to put her into her place.

"A few," said Victoire, "based upon a few of the most recent conflicts. There have been five moderately severely wounded to each one dead or hopeless, but that reckoned without cannon. Therefore it is my assumption that the recent engagement will show an increase of fatalities. Desaix says that a siege would be worse yet."

"There's good sense in what you tell me," agreed Larrey, his attention arrested at last. "You appreciate the military realities. A remarkable feat, Madame. I offer you my felicitations. Which I will extend to your husband as soon as possible. I wish there was a way to guess how many casualties there will be. We know one thing, the further the battles are from here, the less wounded will make it back." Victoire couldn't tell if the surgeon was being scientific, or really didn't feel the implications of what he was saying. Larrey studied the long rows of cots. "We try to keep these tents on the eastern side of the larger tents, and thereby reduce some of the heat." There was a helpless tone in the doctor's voice. The air in the tent was even hotter than the midday heat and there was a distinct smell of putrefaction.

"A sensible decision," said Victoire, unaware that she was saying anything offensive.

The Pasha's visitation to the French camp secured the attention of all the men who were not actively busy elsewhere. Even Victoire decided to devote several pages to it in her usual letter to Vernet.

> This is the Pasha who agreed to surrender. He is a fat man with many chins and he rides in a sort of carriage. He came with an escort of ten Mamelukes. They looked nervous, and most likely fought against us in that battle by the Pyramids. The guards were followed by treasure carriers, who brought a chest of silver and some elaborately carved chairs inlaid with gold trim.
>
> Behind this lot were the ladies of his hareem, heavily veiled and covered in clothing that must have been stifling in the heat. They were guarded by some striking men in loose shirts and tight trousers. Larrey said these were eunuchs, a most disgusting concept. I cannot see any Frenchman subjecting himself to such treatment. Since no men were allowed near them, I was asked to bring these ladies water and cloths to cool themselves. One spoke some Greek and we were able to converse.

She translated for the others. Many were quite intelligent, even witty. Their stories of being kept in isolated rooms, *purdah,* it is called, were most awful. They only get out on such state occasions as this. I think their master (I cannot think of that man as being a husband to them all) hoped to impress us with the size of his hareem.

What appears to be the main function of this procession, after all the display and compliments, was a gift offered to Napoleon by the Pasha himself. The gift was a Mameluke soldier. You may speculate on the reservations about Roustam-Raza, who has sworn to the Muslim gods to protect and preserve the life of Napoleon Buonaparte for as long as Napoleon stands against his enemies. He is said to be faithful unto death. Only when Napoleon has no enemies or when all his enemies are vanquished is Roustam-Raza released from his vow.

You may imagine, my husband, how Napoleon has been in a quandary about this soldier. To ignore the gift would offend the Pasha mightily, which is contrary to his interests at this time. At the same time, he is reluctant to set the Egyptian to tasks that could be of crucial importance to this campaign. He has stated that he will make his decision about the Mameluke known before the end of the day after tomorrow, and that in the meantime, the Mameluke is to hold himself in readiness, awaiting his orders.

She read over the words and decided that there could be no objection to what she had written since the whole of the camp buzzed with speculation about the Mameluke soldier. If her letter were read, no one could take exception to what she told Vernet, for surely he would have the same news from others. She signed it with great affection and scrawled her name.

When she had sealed the letter and addressed it, she went in search of the courier who would take letters to Jaffa. Messengers left regularly for Jaffa to deliver Napoleon's most recent instructions, and to keep him abreast of the developments there. She brought a few extra coins to ensure her letter's safe delivery.

"Seems a shame, leaving a pretty little wife like you alone while your husband camps outside the walls of Jaffa," said the courier when Victoire handed him the letter and the money. He was a hussar, the white fur in the lining of his pelisse tan from desert sand and dust. Like all hussars he wore his jacket hanging from one shoulder and sported a large moustache. "What with you coming all this way to be alone and there being so few other women here, er, for you talk with."

"He has trust in me as I have trust in him," said Victoire in a tone that left no doubt as to her meaning. "If that is what my husband's duty demands of me, I'll do my utmost to serve as best I can." She glared at the courier, then turned and walked off, her face set.

Napoleon glared at Berthier, the lamplight striking one side of his face only, leaving the other in deep shadow. "What am I to do with this gift of the Pasha? I cannot return him—that would be an intolerable insult and we'd be fighting again. But he's a Mameluke. Who knows what this oath to Allah means?" He slapped Berthier's desk. "I'd like your recommendation, Berthier."

"If you are truly interested in what I would do with him, it will be my pleasure to tell you." Berthier sighed and shoved himself to his feet. "If it were for me to decide, I would assign the Mameluke some duty that would occupy him in such a way that we could determine if he is as honorable as the Pasha claims he is."

"Do you have such a duty in mind?" demanded Napoleon. He spun on his heel at the sound of a horse approaching the tent. "Who are we expecting?"

"I don't know," said Berthier warily.

The horse went by the tent and a few seconds later there was a greeting shouted by one of the guards.

"A messenger from Desaix," said Berthier as the rider shouted out his name.

"What is this about?" Napoleon asked of the canvas. "I

have been demanding regular reports for over a week, and they still arrive at these hours. It had better be current news and urgent."

"Desaix would inform you himself if there were serious trouble brewing," said Berthier as he ran his hand through his curly hair. "And I would insist on presenting it to you, whatever the hour."

"For that, you have my gratitude," said Napoleon, his manner distracted. "This land is robbing many of our soldiers of their purpose. The heat draws away their strength and they are mesmerized by this place. They suppose that riches are hidden in the sand and they do not attend to their duties. We need to take action. Only when they are in the field again will these soldiers remember they're Frenchmen and not brigands."

"You are thinking of the scepter," said Berthier heavily.

"What progress have you made?" Napoleon asked, making no attempt to deny his interest. "I do not want to believe that your staff cannot do the work you assign."

Berthier moved a few of the papers on his desk. "What troubles me is that there has been no effort to move the scepter."

"You are assuming that Vernet has it?" Napoleon inquired. "Are you still as certain as you were before?"

"Who else am I to suspect? Your officers knew of the treasure and only a few of them were party to—" Berthier bit his thumbnail. "I don't want to speak against anyone, but the circumstances show that if any of them are likely, Vernet is the most likely."

"I won't dispute that," said Napoleon. "That's why he's in Jaffa. The thought of him betraying my trust is disturbing." He folded his arms. "You are not supposing that he has taken the scepter with him, are you?"

"No," Berthier said reluctantly. "That doesn't seem possible."

"There we agree," Napoleon declared. "So you continue to suspect that his wife has the scepter, that she is hiding it at her husband's orders. Is that a fair assumption."

"Yes," said Berthier. He glanced toward the door of the

tent as shouts rang in the distance. "They are learning to be away from home."

"You mean that they are learning to be on campaign," Napoleon corrected. "We have to season these troops quickly. I don't want to be distracted with trouble like Vernet. Nor can I have my officers stop trusting each other. Find some way to guard his wife without being too obvious."

"She's working with Larrey. He tells me she is very good with the wounded. She's also been tending to some of the women, the ones who are suffering from the heat." He fiddled with his papers again.

"It's good to know she isn't one of those who wilt," said Napoleon. "There are too many languishing wives with us. It is why I forbade them on the convoy." He put his hands on his side of Berthier's desk. "Now listen to me. I want this matter solved and I want no fuss about it."

Berthier nodded. "And the Mameluke?"

"Put him to work, something that will occupy him but will not give him access to anything too important. I don't want him running back to the Pasha with our plans in his powder horn." He paced in the confined tent, which only seemed to add to his tautness. "But I'm not satisfied. If this fellow is not truly my man, I have to know it. We must test him without disgracing him. I leave it to you to find the way to do that."

"I'll do everything I can," said Berthier with feeling.

"He speaks French, so I've been told," said Napoleon as an afterthought. "Do not be too open in your conversation with him. It would not be the first time a man spied with just his ears."

"I will be careful," said Berthier.

"I know you will," said Napoleon with a persuasive smile. "That is why I trust you with this task." He looked over the papers Berthier had spread out. "Not that you haven't enough to do."

Berthier paused before he responded. "You have only to give me work, General, and I will do it to the best of my ability. I believe in your greatness."

"And in the greatness of France," added Napoleon at once.

"Of course," said Berthier hastily, and stared down at the papers once more.

Everything about Roustam-Raza was foreign—the way he dressed, the way he moved, his accent, his attitude, his smell. He had braced his feet apart as if expecting to repel invaders as he stood where Napoleon had stood the night before. "I am told to follow your orders," he said, watching Berthier with hot eyes. It was mid-afternoon and he had just risen from his midday nap.

"So I was informed," said Berthier, acutely uncomfortable in the Mameluke's presence. The man refused to sit and towered over the aide-de-camp. "I've been told to find necessary work for you. And after much thought I have decided on what you are to do." He swabbed his handkerchief across his brow and told himself it was only the heat in his tent that made him sweat.

"I am ready," said Roustam-Raza, thumping his hand to his chest. The bright red material of his loosely worn shirt was left moist where it had been pressed against his chest. "I have been told by Napoleon to obey your orders as if they were his own."

Berthier coughed and then nibbled at the cuticle of his middle finger. "As his aide-de-camp I am obliged to act in his best interests. This is an instance when he and I are in accord." He made himself sit straighter. "There is a person you are to watch. I will introduce you to her shortly, and I expect—"

"A woman?" burst out Roustam-Raza before Berthier finished. "You wish me to guard a woman?"

"Yes," said Berthier stonily.

"This is Napoleon's woman," said Roustam-Raza hopefully, doing his best to salvage some honor from this unthinkable disgrace.

"No," said Berthier, dashing Roustam-Raza's hopes. "She is the wife of one of his officers."

Roustam-Raza drew himself up and spat. "I am not a eunuch in the hareem, that I must watch an errant wife."

Berthier realized he had made an error with the Mameluke and looked for some method to repair any damage he may have done. "It is very necessary that she be watched. It is possible that her husband has stolen"—he broke off before speaking of the scepter—"something of great value from Napoleon."

"I will watch the husband," stated Roustam-Raza.

"The husband is far away, where he can do no harm. His wife remains here. We suspect that her husband put the ... the valuable thing into her hands. We must discover what has become of it." Berthier wanted to sound stern but was afraid that he lacked the authority Roustam-Raza required.

"I will hunt for the valuable thing," he decided aloud. "I will bring it to Napoleon to show my devotion."

"You'll show your devotion better by watching this woman." He raised his hands in warning. "She's not to suspect you."

"Women are not clever enough to suspect me, or any man," Roustam-Raza said, dismissing the possibility. Finally the Mameluke chose to sit in the chair he had been offered earlier. Even sitting he seemed alert and ominous to Berthier, who was relieved he had found a reason to keep the warrior away from the general.

Berthier shook his head. "This is a clever woman, more like a promising boy than a woman. She has learning and wit. You're not to underestimate her."

"No woman is clever," Roustam-Raza informed Berthier. "But her husband may be, and if she is obedient, she will be hard to defeat." He fondled the hilt of the long dagger in his belt. "If she is stubborn, I will do what must be done to persuade her."

"No," said Berthier emphatically. "There's to be nothing of that sort. You are to watch her, to see what action she undertakes and to stop her from moving the valuable thing beyond our reach."

"I will consider what you tell me," said Roustam-Raza, his tone not very promising. "Who is this clever woman?"

"She is the wife of Gendarme Major, Inspector Lucien Vernet." He studied the back of his hand, frowning at the nails. "He is acting Inspector-General."

"Gendarme officer," said Roustam-Raza with the manner of someone given a plate of rotten meat. "Such men should not betray."

"Yes. Precisely." Berthier sighed. "His wife, Madame Vernet, must be watched. She is not to be permitted to assist her husband."

"It is fitting for a woman to assist her husband," said Roustam-Raza with sudden stubbornness. "There are a few things women must do; they must be mothers and they must obey the will of their fathers and husbands. Anything else is unnatural."

"Very true," said Berthier, and for an instant thought only of his own fruitless love of a married aristocratic woman whose name he dared not speak aloud for fear of compromising her. "But women are such ... whimsical creatures."

"Exactly why it is necessary they obey men," said Roustam-Raza, satisfied that he and Berthier understood one another. "I will not do anything that will lead a woman away from her tasks. I will do nothing to incite her to set aside the will of her husband. But anything short of that I will do." He regarded Berthier ferociously. "I will permit no danger to Napoleon. I have sworn this."

"So you have, so you have." He rose. "She is coming here when she is through tending the wounded. She ought to be here shortly."

"Tending the wounded is worthy," said Roustam-Raza, "so long as she is not in blood herself. A woman in blood will cause men to bleed as well."

Berthier colored. "I know nothing about that," he said stiffly.

"It would be wise to learn." Roustam-Raza touched the weapons he carried, a wickedly curved sword and two well-oiled pistols of English make, and nodded. "What will her husband say when he learns of this?"

"He won't learn of it. And even if he does, he'll say nothing," said Berthier with certainty. "He is in enough trouble as it is."

"A wise man does not behave in any way that will cause others to question his character," Roustam-Raza declared. "How is it that this man can be under suspicion and have advanced so far, and with a silly wife?"

"She isn't silly; I've warned you about that. He cannot account for his time when the . . . object was taken. We all stood there together and only we knew of it. The others have someone to vouch for them. Other than just a wife." Berthier fingered the back of his chair. "And of all of them, he has the least money and the poorest expectations. His father-in-law left his daughter an independence but it is not enough to support a military officer."

"So he is nothing more than a thief," said Roustam-Raza contemptuously. "He is not deserving of his advancement."

"If he is the thief, you are correct," said Berthier. "But until I am certain that he took the object, I will not act against him, nor encourage anyone else to." He gave Roustam-Raza a long, hard stare. "If you alert them, you will share the burden of their guilt."

"Of course," said Roustam-Raza. "That is correct." He sank down onto the floor of the tent, his legs crossing as he made himself comfortable.

Berthier did his best to contain his misgivings. "You must treat her with respect. Frenchwomen expect it."

"You French are very foolish about women. It is not necessary that you respect them, only that you turn them to good purpose. But it is the teaching of your faith that softens you." He made a gesture to show that he did not object to the weakness of French Christians. "The Prophet defended his mother. Is this Madame Vernet a mother of sons?"

"No," said Berthier awkwardly. He saw disapproval in

Roustam-Raza's eyes and did his best to explain. "They haven't been married long."

"If she has many sons, she will be a rose among women," said Roustam-Raza with approval. "Her husband will be fortunate."

"Yes, I suppose he will, but not on his army pay," said Berthier, smiling a little at his own feeble witticism.

Light steps approached the tent and Berthier heard Eugene call out from his desk just outside the tent, "Who is coming?"

"Madame Vernet," said Victoire. "I believe Berthier is expecting me. He sent me a note—"

"Yes," said Eugene, and came at once to the entrance of Berthier's tent. "Madame Vernet is—"

"Send her in, Eugene," he told his secretary, adding to Roustam-Raza, "It is polite to stand when she is present."

"A foolish thing to do," said Roustam-Raza, staying where he was.

Victoire entered the tent in a direct way, all but marching up to Berthier. "You wished to speak with me?" she asked without any of the courtesies Berthier might have expected of her. There was a smear of blood on her muslin skirt and the sleeve of her light pelisse was torn in two places; her pale hair was disordered.

"Yes, Madame Vernet, I did." He glanced at Roustam-Raza, who reclined on the rough rugs that made up the floor of the tent. "It seems I must . . . ask a favor of you."

"Of me?" repeated Victoire incredulously.

"Yes," said Berthier, coloring a little. "I have need of your . . . assistance." He indicated the Mameluke. "You know of the Pasha's gift to Napoleon?"

"I saw the ceremony," said Victoire carefully. She could not imagine what Berthier was up to this time.

"Roustam-Raza is not . . . familiar with the customs and conduct in our camp, or the lives of Frenchman. I need someone to instruct him so that he will not disgrace Napoleon. Every officer is much too busy, nor have many been to a school to learn such things. You are said to be the best educated of the officers' wives, and so I have come to you." He gave a diplomatic cough. "If you would be willing?"

"To teach this man?" she inquired, looking down at Roustam-Raza. "Why do you want him taught? And what do you want him taught?"

"There are many things he must learn," said Berthier ambiguously. "I don't know what is most urgent. If you will make a point of observing him, you will decide for yourself what the man must know." His smile was wide and insincere.

Victoire was not fooled. "In other words, you expect to get two services for the price of one." She saw the startled look in Berthier's eyes. "You will have me under guard and the guard will benefit." She put her hands on her hips. "I suppose it is useless to protest."

"It isn't wise," said Berthier. "But you must do as you think best."

"Of course," said Victoire sarcastically. "And if I do not choose what you wish me to do, it will go badly for me and for my husband. Is that a fair assessment, would you say?"

"Fair," Berthier allowed.

Victoire looked at Roustam-Raza again. "Do you speak any French?" she asked him, speaking very slowly and carefully.

"I have been taught French," Roustam-Raza answered at once. His accent was rough but he clearly was comfortable with the language.

"That's an advantage." She considered him, saying to him in passable Greek, "And do you understand this?"

"Moderately well," answered Roustam-Raza in Greek. This was not surprising, as most of the trade brought to Egypt from other countries came on Greek transport.

She pursed her lips, thinking swiftly. "You are going to have someone watching me no matter what I say, aren't you?" she asked Berthier.

"Yes," he said bluntly.

"So it isn't a question of if I am watched, but who watches me," she said. "Have I understood?"

"Well enough, Madame," said Berthier. "What is it to be?"

Victoire sighed. "I suppose it must be the obvious one," she answered, knowing that it was the wiser course. "I will do what I can to instruct this ... gift in French ways. And he will watch me for you." She shook her head. "It is a very poor bargain for both of us, Berthier."

"But one you will accept," he said.

"If the Mameluke will accept it, who am I to dispute you?" She said it cordially enough but there was ire in her blue eyes. She turned away from Berthier and addressed Roustam-Raza directly. "Since we are being thrown together, we might as well begin at once."

Roustam-Raza remained where he was on the floor. "It isn't correct for a woman to tell a man what to do."

"It had better be, if you are to learn anything from me," said Victoire, undaunted. "I wish you would stand up."

"Do as she says, for Napoleon," added Berthier quietly.

Roustam-Raza got to his feet at once. "I am sworn to serve him until all his enemies are dead, or he is."

"Very commendable, I'm certain," said Victoire. An idea had just occurred to her—with an Egyptian to advise her, she might be able to learn more about the missing scepter, for the Mameluke could go places and speak to those Victoire was unable to reach. "Let's strive to make the best of this very unsatisfactory situation," she suggested to Roustam-Raza, offering him her hand to kiss.

Roustam-Raza refused to touch her. "You are a married woman."

"And devoted to my husband," said Victoire. "But among the French, it is correct to kiss the hands of married women. Berthier," she went on, her hand extended, "will you be good enough to show this soldier how it's done?"

As Berthier bent over her hand and brushed her knuckles with his lips he had the oddest sensation that he had forfeited this round to Madame Vernet.

# 4

VICTOIRE WROTE TO Lucien three nights later.

> So you are not to worry, my dear husband. I am determined to make the best of this lamentable coil. If Berthier seeks to check me by setting the Mameluke to guard me, why, I will not resist him. I know it is what he expects me to do, but I am not such a fool that I will fall prey to that ploy.
> He has been told by several of the officers' wives that it is not correct for him to assign an Egyptian soldier to guard a Frenchwoman, but he is not willing to listen to their objections. His defense is that we are at war and unusual measures are called for.

She turned the paper to the other side and continued, crossing her original lines with care. Her handwriting was very precise and she had trimmed the nib of her pen as fine as she could. She had little need to blot the page as she wrote, for the air was so dry that the ink often clogged the pen.

> I have it in mind to attempt to bring the Mameluke to my side as an ally instead of a guard. He is loath to speak with women, but as I am supposed to instruct him in our ways, he has little choice. I confess that he frightened me at first, but now I am persuaded that he and I will deal extremely well together once we grow more accustomed to each other. But you have no reason to

fear for me; this Roustam-Raza does not admire fair women. Only this morning he said I looked too much like the dead. He prefers his women dark and dusky, with large bodies soft as pillows. Not that he has said anything of the sort to me, but I have watched his eyes when the Egyptian women come to the camp and I know what I see.

She looked over the page and nodded her satisfaction. Her closing paragraph was much more personal; she felt herself flush as she put the words on the page. As she signed it, she decided to seal the letter properly, with wax instead of a wafer, so that if it were read, Vernet would know.

At the door of her tent she found Roustam-Raza waiting, sitting on a mat on the sand. He watched her, unspeaking.

"Don't you ever sleep?" she inquired, no longer troubled by his ferocious scowl.

"I have been ordered to keep watch on you," he answered.

"It is after nine, and half the camp is sleeping," she said, holding her letter tightly.

"You are not," said Roustam-Raza.

"True, but I will be shortly, as soon as I return from handing this to the Jaffa courier," she said.

The Mameluke got to his feet. "I will come with you."

"It's not necessary," said Victoire, her eyes bright with annoyance. "It's only a short distance."

"Nevertheless, I will come," said Roustam-Raza.

She shrugged. "As you wish." It was useless to argue with him, she knew from experience. But she was determined not to speak with him, a silence which she maintained until they passed Berthier's tent, where she saw that the general's aide was just mounting his horse, a cloak wrapped around him. "Another one of his mysterious missions to Cairo," she said to Roustam-Raza. "I wish I knew what they were for."

Roustam-Raza pursed his lips. "There are women. And boys."

Victoire did not quite laugh; she shook her head in dismissal. "He claims to be in love with a married woman. He does not speak her name for fear of dishonoring her."

"It is wrong to love a married woman," said Roustam-Raza. "Women are not made for such loving. Men are made so that they can have more than one woman."

"Not in France, they're not," said Victoire with asperity. "Not that there are not times it might be best," she added in a more thoughtful way as they continued to the tent where the couriers were dispatched.

Behind them Berthier headed off into the darkness.

"You see!" approved Roustam-Raza. "Not all French ways are for the best every time." He slapped his wide, hard hand against his thigh. "Men should have women of their own, to give them sons of their own."

"Berthier isn't married," said Victoire. "He hasn't the time. I believe he fears the obligations of a family would compromise his duty to Napoleon."

"He is right to worry. But he is wrong not to marry," said Roustam-Raza, settling the matter.

As they came up to the dispatch tent, Victoire looked about with some anxiety. "The courier is supposed to leave before first light. I don't want my husband to have to wait too long to have word from me."

"You are a sensible woman," said Roustam-Raza, and offered no further explanation.

"I strive to be," she said, and made a sign to the corporal sitting in front of the tent. She handed him her letter and two coins. "In gratitude for a swift delivery," she told him.

"Very good," said the corporal, and tucked the letter into a crested saddlebag. He gave Roustam-Raza a swift, comprehensive glance, then made a notation on his roster. "Good evening, Madame Vernet."

Victoire recognized the dismissal for what it was. "And to you, corporal." She motioned to Roustam-Raza, and they started back toward her tent. As she walked, an idea burgeoned in her mind. Choosing her words very carefully, she said to the Mameluke, "I am troubled in my mind."

"Women are often afflicted," said Roustam-Raza.

"No, not that way," she countered. "I am troubled by what Berthier is doing. I have heard him leave for Cairo on four different nights, and this causes me apprehension."

"Why should it concern you?" asked Roustam-Raza, deeply puzzled.

"Because he has accused my husband of a crime. I know that my husband is innocent, and so I wish to discover who has done the crime. Since Berthier accuses him, I do not trust his motives. And now he rides to Cairo in secret. I cannot like it, Roustam-Raza." She made herself speak very calmly, for any show of emotion would turn the Mameluke against her.

"Why should his movements have any bearing on your husband's crime?" he asked, his interest piqued.

"Why should they not?" When he did not answer, she went on. "I have nowhere to begin, except with the man who accuses Vernet. He also knew of the object. And his own time is unaccounted for. If I can exonerate Berthier, then perhaps I can persuade him to investigate further. But if he is the one who has committed the crime, then he will do nothing to turn his accusation from my husband, and my husband will bear the burden of guilt that belongs to another." She could not see well enough to read Roustam-Raza's face, but she sensed a lessening in his disapproval. "If only I knew what he did in Cairo."

"You tell me he has gone there often." His tone was speculative, and his attitude no longer challenged her.

"Four times that I know of since Vernet left. Tonight is the fifth." She wanted to say more but prudence dictated that she hold her tongue.

"Five times he has gone at night to Cairo," mused Roustam-Raza. "And in so short a time. He has always gone alone?"

"As far as I know," answered Victoire.

"And other officers? Do they go to Cairo in secret?"

Victoire smiled inwardly. "Not that I'm aware of. Occasionally three or four of them will go together, but I have not heard of anyone going there alone as Berthier does."

They were nearing her tent and she paused, looking up at him. "It troubles me." She expected another Muslim aphorism about the minds of women and therefore was pleased when Roustam-Raza bit his lower lip in thought.

At last he said, "I think it troubles me, as well."

It took her the better part of a week to persuade Roustam-Raza to take her to Cairo the next time Berthier went there.

"You would be in great danger there. Frenchwomen are not welcome in Cairo unless they are with their men," he argued the first time she brought her project up.

"But how am I to find out what he is doing if I don't follow him? You will not leave me unguarded to see where he goes, so it must be my task to watch him. And you will watch me." She favored him with a small nod of approval, as if he could not fault her logic.

"A woman alone might be kidnapped. It occurs there. If you were kidnapped, you would probably be sold. Once that happened, there would be nothing I or any of the French could do to save you. The Pasha himself could not demand your return." His black eyes showed a shine of concern, which heartened her.

"That is why you will be with me. Who would dare to kidnap me if I am with a Mameluke?" It was her final point and she saw that she had his attention.

He scowled. "It would be very dangerous."

"Roustam-Raza, my husband is accused of a serious crime. The crime would disgrace him if he's found guilty. I cannot sit idly by and do nothing. If there's danger for me, think how much greater the danger is for him." She raised her chin stubbornly, daring him to refuse her.

"I will consider it," he informed her.

The second time she discussed it with him, she found him more tractable.

"It would not be wise to go at night." He folded his arms, intending to make her reconsider.

"He does not usually return until noon of the following day. We will leave here before dawn and be in Cairo before he leaves, but after first light." She cocked her head to the side. "Would that suit you?"

"There is a great risk," he insisted.

"We've been through this, Roustam-Raza. If you have no other argument, then let us return to how you must conduct yourself during treaty or peace negotiations." She reached for the notebook she carried, but allowed him to stop her.

"I do not want to be the one who must report your abduction. You are asking that of me." His face was lined and worried. "It would disgrace me."

"Then I'll do my best not to be abducted," Victoire said. "And I will depend on you to guard me well."

Roustam-Raza flung his hands into the air. "Perhaps. Perhaps."

Before Berthier made his next bolt to Cairo, Victoire had persuaded Roustam-Raza.

The desert ended abruptly perhaps three miles outside Cairo. Victoire was surprised at what a relief it was to see green, healthy plants again. There were none near the camp near Alexandria. Cairo itself was less appealing. Sprawling along the Nile, the city's odor, a mixture of open sewers and spices, rivaled even the notorious smell of Paris after a thaw. All along the Nile they had passed small villages, the homes barely large enough to hold more than a few people at one time. Most were made of a gray or brown concrete or plaster that was comprised mostly of the abundant sand and shared its color. Many of the poorer homes, Victoire was astonished to notice, had no roofs. As they approached Cairo itself, the houses became larger, with elaborate decorations painted or carved into their walls.

The city itself had no walls, nor any real boundary. The buildings, now a mixture of homes, shops, and granaries, simply became more densely packed. Occasionally they would cross through a small courtyard, though none of the markets they sometimes housed were occurring. At Roustam-Raza's request, Victoire was almost completely covered with robes borrowed from one of the camp followers who were beginning to appear even in this exotic land. With her in disguise, the Mameluke attracted much more attention, almost dread, and Victoire began to wonder just what their reign had been like.

They left their horses with the city garrison, entrusted to a Bernaise sergeant whose face was almost as long and soulful as the horses he tended. Cairo was a jumble of narrow streets, some almost too small for them to walk side by side. Only occasionally did they travel along a wide roadway, paved with large stone blocks. Several times they passed buildings whose age or design made them stand out from the others. A few of the savants that had accompanied the army were scurrying over one, measuring it and making sketches. Victoire almost stopped to chat with another Frenchman, but Roustam-Raza signalled they should keep moving.

While the streets were incredibly crowded, the crowd seemed to part for the Mameluke. The Frenchwoman also noted that even when there was almost no space for them to pass, the Egyptian peasants were careful to avoid even brushing against her. Their trek ended in a massive market that bordered the Nile. Occasionally a cool breeze off the water tempered the dry heat that made the air shimmer inside the merchant's stalls. The clamor of bargaining, braying camels, and clanging pottery rose to a din that made talking difficult.

"You cannot expect to find Berthier in this crowd," Roustam-Raza said to Victoire as they made their way through the booths of brass sellers. "You do not know where he is in the city." He clapped his hands in aggravation. "You should never have come here. I was a fool to listen to you. There is no worth in the plans of women."

"Do be quiet," said Victoire as she tugged on his sleeve. "You're attracting attention."

"I am not. You are attracting attention. That yellow silk over your face fools no one. Your skin is white and your clothes can be seen whenever the breeze stirs the cloth.

Everyone knows that you are French." His accent was rougher, as if his frustration worked on his tongue.

"And you are making them certain of it, if they were in doubt," she reminded him. She paused to stare at three enormous platters of hammered brass. At another time she would have been tempted to bargain with the vendor for such beautiful work. "Ask this man if he has seen Berthier."

"No," said Roustam-Raza. "He will not know one Frenchman from another, and he would lie, in any case."

"I don't know enough to ask him myself," said Victoire with false innocence.

Roustam-Raza turned on her. "You will not do such a thing. He will not speak with a Frenchwoman, no matter what words she uses." He made a sweeping gesture to take in the bazaar. "Why would Berthier be purchasing brass, in any case?"

"I don't know. I don't know why he is in Cairo," she reminded him. "What is in the next street? Is there another market?" She did her best to sound optimistic but inwardly she had begun to doubt the wisdom of their action.

"There are sellers of incense two streets away," said Roustam-Raza, his manner suddenly acquiescent, which roused her suspicions.

"Should we go there?" she asked in some surprise.

"We should go somewhere; we are being followed." He hitched his shoulder to indicate an area behind him.

Victoire glanced in that direction but could make out no one who appeared to be after them. "Are you certain?"

"Of course I am certain," said Roustam-Raza.

"Then let us proceed to the street of the incense sellers. We might be able to find out who they are and why they are following us," she said, pleased that the fear that had taken hold of her had not reached her voice.

"I do not want to know why. I want them to stop," said Roustam-Raza darkly as he moved her ahead of him and drew his dagger from his sheath. "If they come for us, stay behind me."

It took her a moment to answer. "They're not going to come for us, Roustam-Raza."

"If it is the will of Allah," he answered doubtfully.

They slipped through an alley and down a narrow street where the buildings leaned together, throwing everything beneath into perpetual twilight.

"This is not a good place," said Roustam-Raza. "Hurry. Through that passage." He shoved her ahead of him, all the while glancing back over his shoulder. "They will try to rush us here."

Victoire did not argue. She could sense the Mameluke's concern and knew that it was more than his Muslim apprehension of women that prompted his urgency. "Have you seen anyone?"

"They are coming," he answered, volunteering nothing more.

"Can you see them?" she persisted, making her way past a drooping mule laden with bales of flax.

"They are coming," he repeated. "Hurry."

"Yes, all right," she said, stumbling ahead while trying to keep her face covered with the length of yellow silk he had insisted she wear.

The street of the incense merchants was lined with canvas booths, much the way the brass sellers' had been. But here there were the heady scents of spices and flowers and rare oils, and the merchants were graver, as suited those purveying incense.

Roustam-Raza came up behind Victoire. "Be careful. Stay very close to me. They are going to try to separate us."

"I will," she said, and looked down the curving street as far as she could see. "Is it always this crowded?"

"Oh, yes. Sometimes it is much worse," he said. "These merchants are busy every day but holy days." He kept her moving. "I don't like this. I don't like to be chased."

"Neither do I," said Victoire. "But at present there is little we can do about it." She looked around, wondering what it was that alerted Roustam-Raza to their danger—if they were truly in danger. As her eyes lingered on a cavernous doorway, she spotted a familiar figure. "Roustam-Raza!" she cried urgently. "There! Berthier!"

The Mameluke glanced where she was pointing and he straightened.

"Indeed," he said, as he recognized the general's aide. "What would he want here?"

"We must find out," said Victoire, her determination renewed. She was prepared to push through the crowd but Roustam-Raza held her back.

"No. It would not be proper. And it would bring more attention to you. It isn't wise, Madame Vernet." He still held his dagger at the ready. "Stay with me, a step behind. I will try to reach the door."

"We don't want him seeing us," she reminded the Mameluke.

His gesture was resigned. "Then we will wait until he is gone." He glanced around again. "If we are permitted to."

"Have the followers found us?" she asked, still not wholly convinced they existed anywhere but in Roustam-Raza's imagination.

"I have seen only one." He shocked them both by taking hold of her elbow. "Come. We must distract them or they will be able to surround us, and then we will have no recourse but to fight, and that would be . . . foolish."

She wondered what he was going to say instead of foolish, but she kept the speculation to herself. "What do you plan to do?"

"Cause an upset," he answered, and made his way through the merchants and patrons toward a little square at the end of the street where bundles were stacked in large pyramids almost as tall as a grown man. "Those are their supplies, the material for making incense," he explained as he pointed at the stacks.

"What are you going to do?" asked Victoire, more curious than frightened.

"Stay back and you'll see," said Roustam-Raza as he moved quickly, his shoulder slamming into the most top-heavy of the pyramids. He grunted as the stack wavered, toppled, and gave way, crashing into the pyramid beside it and breaking it apart as well.

A loud wail of protest went up throughout the market and men lurched and stumbled out of their booths to save their precious materials.

"There they are," said Roustam-Raza, moving backward to Victoire's side. He pointed to the far side of the little square; four men were emerging from the narrow side street, all of them armed with cutlasses and two pistols in leather belts. "They aren't Egyptians."

"I can see that," said Victoire, astonished at the methodical way the men started to make their way through the newly erupting chaos to where she and the Mameluke were.

"We'd better leave," said Roustam-Raza, pointing to an opening in the crowd. "Go to the right and then we will be able to return to the district of cloth merchants. We'll get away."

"So will Berthier," said Victoire heavily. "We've come so close."

"As have the men following us," Roustam-Raza said with urgency. "Move. Hurry."

"But Berthier—" she protested, then did as he required of her.

They reckoned without the incense merchants, for the shouting and confusion was spreading, and what had been a disruption was fast becoming a riot.

The men behind them began to push harder through the crowd. As they did, an elderly man whom they thrust aside fell against another pyramid of baskets. It rumbled to the beaten dust of the street; one basket broke open and spilled a red powder onto the ground. At that several merchants yelled in despair and rushed toward the chaos. Another, fearing the clamor was a thief's intended distraction or lucky opportunity, raised a cry which Victoire later learned merchants used to warn each other that there was a thief in their midst. Blocked by the crowd, one of the men fired a pistol into the air. Rather than clearing a path, this stirred the natives to greater excitement. Knives began to appear and the Mameluke kept his hand on his scimitar.

The four Europeans had just cleared the fallen baskets when a young man in a yellow robe broke out of a knot of milling men and charged their pursuers. As he ran he drew a wicked-looking knife from his belt. He rose to strike, but fell away when another of the four men shot him in the chest. Suddenly the small square was filled with cries of outrage. Several more men began running toward the four Europeans, while calmer men tried to restrain them.

Victoire did not object when Roustam-Raza shielded her body with his own and started a very slow progress along the wall. He had drawn his scimitar now that the fighting had grown so fierce.

The four men had ceased trying to push after Victoire and the Mameluke had begun a hurried retreat. Even as they did so, a shot fired from a nearby rooftop echoed between the buildings. To her left Victoire saw a stall filled with shelves of jars and pots collapse under the pressure of the mob. Someone to her left grabbed the Frenchwoman's arm and stared with wild eyes at her fair skin and blonde hair. His outraged scream was cut short by the sudden impact of Roustam-Raza's elbow on his neck. His eyes glazed almost instantly and he collapsed at her feet.

Then there was another sound at the far end of the street—the shrill, echoing blare of a trumpet.

The four men were now standing with their cutlasses drawn and their backs against the wall. A ring of local men stood threateningly a few steps away, most brandishing clubs or knives. Several smaller fights had broken out all over the square. Victoire saw one man, his dagger red with blood, shove his way into a side street. In the square the combatants faltered, then began again.

A second, louder bray of the trumpet came, and with it the clatter of many hooves. A few moments later a squadron of French cavalry pressed its way into the little square, stopping the last of the fray at once. Instantly the mob began to disperse, but the hussars spurred at them, swords drawn. The horsemen began to drive the Egyptians back to their houses and stalls using the flat sides of their swords.

The men who had been following Victoire and Roustam-Raza disappeared with the bulk of the crowd and the injured.

Roustam-Raza stepped toward the leader of the cavalry as the dark-haired and devilishly handsome young officer in splendid uniform swung off his glossy ermine dun. He bowed in the Egyptian manner and said, "You are a very welcome sight." Victoire noticed that he had reinjured his arm.

The officer blinked, then understanding came into his eyes. "Oh, yes. You're that Egyptian the Pasha gave to Napoleon, aren't you?"

"I am," said Roustam-Raza, standing more straight with pride. "Your appearance was fortunate. We had been followed by foreign brigands. In all this . . . activity, I feared they might do us harm."

"Us," said the officer. "And who is us?"

Roustam-Raza stood aside and permitted Victoire to come forward. She made a point of thanking the Mameluke before giving her attention to the cavalry officer, a man she recognized as one of the many eager young officers around Napoleon. This one had been at the beach when they watched that horrible disaster. "I am most grateful for your arrival," she said, holding out her hand. "I am Madame Vernet. My husband is Gendarme Major Lucien Vernet, currently posted to Jaffa, as Inspector-General."

A quick look of puzzlement and sympathy passed over the officer's face, then he bowed in form and gave her a dazzling smile. "I am General Joachim Murat, very much at your service, madame." He touched the back of her hand with his lips. "And the next time I see your husband, I will tell him what a lucky man he is."

All the way back to the French camp the troopers moved slowly to keep the horses from growing too tired or thirsty in the heat. It was a long ride, taking several hours, and seemed longer in the afternoon heat. As they went, Murat engaged Victoire in light and affable conversation, spicing it with just enough gossip to make it interesting for them both. The day began to fade toward a blazing sunset. Only when their tents were in sight did he become more serious. "I don't want to cause you any alarm, madame, but your Egyptian guard was right when he told you it wasn't safe to go to Cairo. In future I recommend you listen to him and take his advice."

"Are you telling me I can't count on you to appear at the crucial moment next time?" she asked, striving to keep the light and gallant tone he had used before.

"Alas, no. Those were most likely Turks, or Greeks. If they had caught you—and I am assuming that the Mameluke is correct and you were being stalked, it has happened before to European women—there would have been no way to rescue you. Women here are less than cattle, Madame Vernet; once taken as a man's property there's no power in the country to release you, unless you are sold."

"If they wanted to hold me for ransom," she said, choosing deliberately to misunderstand him, "they chose the wrong woman. My family is not rich, I have no influential relatives, and my husband is in similar circumstances." She looked down at the reins she held. "General Murat, I do take your warning to heart. But you say you know how things stand for my husband. You must also see that I cannot sit idly by while he is accused falsely."

As they spoke, the squadron passed inside the pickets that surrounded the base camp. Murat pulled his horse to a halt and motioned for his company to do the same. He rose in his stirrups and turned to the men. "You're dismissed. I'll escort Madame Vernet to her quarters." His gesture sent the rest of the troopers trotting off toward the makeshift stalls where the horses were stabled. When the men were out of hearing range, he looked from Victoire to Roustam-Raza. "How much do you know of this?" he asked the Egyptian.

"Not very much," said Roustam-Raza.

"Then perhaps you will permit me to speak privately

with Madame Vernet? You may watch from a short distance, if you think it necessary," said Murat, and fell silent while the Mameluke rode off a short way, turning his horse so that he could watch Victoire and Murat.

Victoire looked directly at Murat. "What is troubling you, sir?"

"Why, you are, Madame Vernet," he said, his manner now grave instead of playful. "You have put yourself at hazard. I applaud your courage, but I cannot condone your lack of prudence." He paused. "Are you certain you saw Berthier in Cairo?"

"In the street where you found us, where the incense makers have their market," she said. "He was in his Hessian-blue coat with the striped revers; you've seen it. And his hair is unmistakable."

"Incense." Murat shook his head. "It must be that shrine of his. More fool he," Murat added softly. As they spoke, they walked their horses through the camp toward Victoire's tent.

"Shrine?" asked Victoire. "Is he a religious man?"

This time Murat laughed a little. "Very; devoutly, but not the way you mean. He loves a married woman, Madame Vernet."

"That's no secret," said Victoire. She chafed at her arms; between the sun and the sand her skin was parched and sore.

"No, I suppose not," said Murat. "He maintains a triptych to Giovanna"—he was pleased at the quick gasp Victoire gave at the mention of the woman's name—"with her portrait and a lock of her hair. He burns candles before it. And incense. Near sacrilegious."

"Gracious," whispered Victoire, remembering vaguely that General Murat had once studied in a seminary.

"So there is the finale of that mystery, madame; Berthier is not a sinister criminal, only a love-besotted lunatic," he said with a hint of regret, and added with his mercurial smile, "Still, it is lamentable that it isn't safe to go adventuring in Egypt: I believe it would be a rare pleasure to go adventuring with you." He lifted the reins and offered her a proper salute before wheeling his dun and cantering off in the direction his men had gone.

Roustam-Raza waited unmoving as Victoire rode up to him. "In Egypt married women do not speak with men except their husbands and their sons."

"Well, Frenchwomen are not so constrained," said Victoire automatically. She paid no heed to his disapproval. "Murat tells me that Berthier had private reasons for being in Cairo. But I am not convinced, not completely."

"Then we're to watch him still?" asked Roustam-Raza.

She did not give a direct answer. "Let's ride by his tent before we dismount. I want to see if he has actually returned." There was a set to her jaw that Roustam-Raza was coming to know well.

"As you wish," he acceded, and legged his horse down the aisle toward Berthier's quarters.

As they neared Berthier's tent, Victoire was startled to see that Berthier's horse, still saddled, waited in front of the tent. "He must have just returned," she said to Roustam-Raza.

"The horse is not sweating," the Mameluke observed. "That bucket beside him is empty, so he has been watered."

"But not unsaddled and groomed," said Victoire, her blue eyes bright with speculation. "How very odd."

Roustam-Raza gave her a resigned stare. "Are we to watch, Madame?"

She nodded and slipped out of her saddle, keeping hold of the reins as her gelding sidled. "I think it might be best."

"Very well." Roustam-Raza dismounted and took charge of both horses. "We had better get behind that tent," he added, gesturing toward the nearest of them. "We will not be observed."

They had just taken up their self-appointed post when they saw someone arrive at Berthier's tent.

"Who is that? Can you make out?" asked Victoire, not daring to peek around the tent another time.

"No; that cloak conceals everything," said Roustam-Raza, watching the stranger dismount. "All I am certain of is that the hair is light brown—fair, but not so light as yours."

Victoire frowned. "I wonder—"

The stranger entered Berthier's tent, and Roustam-Raza pulled at his moustache in disapproval. "Napoleon should know of this."

"Napoleon is climbing the Pyramids today; unless you're of a mind to chase him up them to tell him he will have to be informed later," said Victoire, and added, "and how busy Berthier is while Napoleon is occupied."

"To be sure," Roustam-Raza concurred, and held up a warning hand to quiet her. "They may have someone else with them."

"Yes," said Victoire, not liking that possibility at all. She was content to remain hidden, seeing only a slice of the door to Berthier's tent.

Within ten minutes the cloaked person hurried out of the tent once more, and was followed immediately by Berthier, who grabbed the reins of his horse and clambered into the saddle as the stranger mounted.

"I can see—long, fair hair," Victoire agreed, although by now the first molten glow of sunset turned even the tents to Roman gold; the stranger might have been white-haired or auburn for all she could tell.

Berthier said something to the stranger that neither Victoire nor Roustam-Raza could hear, and at the next instant both he and the stranger were trotting away from his tent.

"Where do you suppose they are going?" asked Victoire very quietly.

"Do you want to follow them?" asked Roustam-Raza, a bit reluctantly.

She shook her head. "Not now. It will be dark soon. It gets dark so quickly in the desert." She patted her horse's neck. "He needs a grooming and a handful of oats." With a shake of her head she put aside the idea of going after Berthier.

"It would be sensible, Madame," said Roustam-Raza, a trace of approval in his manner now.

"Yes." She started away from their hiding place, then stopped. "But we can keep watch tomorrow. Perhaps the cloaked figure will come again."

"And we will try to discover who it is," said Roustam-Raza in foreboding.

She smiled over her shoulder at him. "Why, certainly," she said.

# 5

⚜

"CONVALESCENT LEAVE OR no, I really don't know why I let you persuade me to watch with you, madame; Berthier hasn't done a thing in days," said Murat to Victoire was the two of them crouched in the lee of the tent nearest Berthier's.

She kept her voice low, motioning for him to do the same. "You said it wasn't proper for a woman to be about in the camp at night by herself, and with Roustam-Raza watching the other side of the tent, you—"

"I know what I said," he cut her off. "I must have been mad. That's the only explanation. Madness." He rocked back on his heels. "If this cloaked person ever comes back, it could well turn out to be someone who has every proper reason to be here. It might not be wise of us to know about his presence. We aren't Napoleon's spies," he reminded her.

"Yes, we are, if we catch a traitor," she declared in a crisp undervoice.

"You can't be sure it's treason. The fellow might be an Egyptian supplying necessary information to Berthier. Or possibly an Englishman, not adverse to earning a coin or two from our side." He was challenging her and both of them knew it.

"We've discussed the possibilities before, Murat," she said, not rising to the bait. She wrapped her shawl more closely around her shoulders, for the air was growing chilly now that night had settled over the desert.

Murat threw up his hands in mock despair. The gesture

caused the dozens of silver bangles adorning the finely made waistcoat he was wearing to jangle. "But how long are we to keep at this? It's been almost three weeks since we began. It may be that the man in the cloak will not come again." He yawned deliberately. "I miss my sleep, Madame. The trumpet sounds early for cavalry, and when I—"

This time she interrupted him. "You would not be asleep now, Murat; you would be gambling or drinking or wenching or something equally disreputable."

"I might be," he conceded. "But not every night." He rubbed his eyes. "Besides, Madame, I like gambling and drinking and wenching. I don't like standing about in the dark keeping watch on Berthier's tent. That's a task for sentries, not officers."

"I've said it isn't necessary for you to stay with me. You can leave whenever it suits your purpose," she said in her most reasonable tone, which only served to annoy him.

"You know my answer to that, Madame," he said, coming back to her side. "Very well. I'll keep our bargain. One more week, and then that's the end of it. Do you agree?"

She bit her lip to keep from pleading with him; Joachim Murat was not a man to be swayed by wifely supplication. "I will accept that. I told you when we began that the terms were—"

"You're splitting hairs again, Madame Vernet." He looked down at her, amusement making his features more handsome. "For such a little dab of a thing you have the courage of a tiger."

"And the tenacity of a mule," she added, taking the flirtation out of his compliment. "You've remarked on this before."

He recognized her tactics for what they were and chuckled. "By God, Madame, if you were not a married woman, I swear that I—"

"If I were not a married women, I wouldn't be here and you wouldn't be in this predicament," she said staunchly.

He shook his head, willing to be put off. "Shall we have a truce for the rest of this dismal watch?"

"I would certainly prefer it," she said.

He lifted his hands in acquiescence. "I pray I never have to meet you as an enemy, Madame, and that is the truth before God."

"That's a rare compliment," she approved. "I thank you sincerely." She peered around the flank of the tent. "Eugene has been gone for half an hour. Berthier ought to have dressed for bed by now. He has been so for the last two weeks."

"But he hasn't tonight," said Murat, taking up their task once more. "And his horse hasn't been stabled; Roustam-Raza said that it is on the far side of the tent, saddled." He waited several seconds. "You know, if we're caught doing this, we'll have a great deal of explaining to do."

"I suspect you will know how best to pull our boots out of the fire," she said calmly, continuing her surveillance.

At that he gave up. "Another hour, then, and if he is still not in bed, we will continue a while after if that's—"

She grabbed his wrist to warn him. "A horse," she whispered.

He was all attention. "A courier, perhaps."

"At this hour, and to Berthier's tent first?" she asked.

"It might be urgent," he said without conviction; they both knew that such messengers went directly to Napoleon himself.

"Look!" she hissed. "That horse."

The figure riding was concealed by a long cloak, and when the horse stopped near Berthier's tent flap, the rider dismounted quickly.

A moment later Berthier himself bustled out of his tent, his hands moving nervously over his coat. "Good evening, though it is late," he said to the figure. "I was afraid you would not be here."

Whatever the answer was neither Victoire nor Murat could hear.

"We'd better hurry. We're waited on," he said. "My horse is ready. I've only to bring him around." He started around the tent only to find his way blocked by Roustam-Raza. "What the devil—"

Victoire rushed from her hiding place with Murat on her heels. "We have you now!" she cried out, wishing she had a charged pistol with her.

Berthier backed up, his face darkening with anger. "By what right do you do this?" He spun around to face Victoire. "I might have known it would be you," he bellowed at her, and then dropped his voice. The aide's face was red with anger; only the pronounced dimple on his chin wasn't visibly darker even in the moonlight.

"She's not alone," said Murat, sauntering up behind her and favoring Berthier with a sketchy salute. "You have to excuse us, but we're curious about your friend. Do you think he would be kind enough to ... unwrap a trifle? Enough to show your face?"

Berthier at once became flustered. "It ... it w-would not be a ... very wise ..." He glanced at the cloaked stranger. "Truly, Murat, it would be best if you went your way and paid no attention to ... anything you might see here." He sniffed nervously. "And if you could c-convince Madame Vernet to ... to be discreet?"

"What is there to be discreet about?" demanded Victoire. "Or don't you want it known that you are receiving foreigners?" With that she reached out and tugged at the cloak, pulling it back from the unknown's face.

"Don't!" Berthier protested.

But it was too late. There was a squeal as the cloak fell, leaving Pauline Foures exposed. She was dressed in a fine rose silk ballgown and wearing a necklace of pearls. Her perfume was a heady combination of roses, jasmine, and violets.

There was a stunned silence, and then Murat laughed. "Good God," he said, going down on one knee to retrieve the cloak. "So that's the game." He held the cloak up to the lovely Madame Foures. "Best put it back on before anyone else sees."

She took the cloak and flung it around her shoulders with a swift, elegant gesture. Her expression had no trace of embarrassment. "Thank you, General Murat."

"Oh, the pleasure's mine," said Murat, his brown eyes alight with humor. He stepped back to Victoire's side.

"What is it?" she asked him.

"A tryst in the making," said Murat. "By the look of it."

Berthier had now had recovered enough from the shock of their discovery to work himself into a proper rage. "How dare you! Murat, I am offended! And you!" He rounded on Victoire. "What possessed you, Madame Vernet, to take it upon yourself to disgrace this woman?"

"This woman?" echoed Victoire, uncertain what she had interrupted. "I meant no harm to her. You are the one I watched."

"I?" He was aghast. "By what authority?"

"As a loyal wife," she began, determined not to be put off by Berthier again. "You want to discredit my husband, and I will not have it."

Murat came nearer to her side, touching her arm gently before closing his hand around her wrist. "Madame," he said, not quite laughing, "I think it would be best if we leave Berthier to tend to Madame Foures." He bowed to Pauline, and then to Berthier, all the while keeping a firm hold on Victoire. "Forgive the intrusion. And forgive our suspicions. It was merely a misunderstanding." Before Victoire could protest, he turned and muttered, "Not one word, Madame," as he made her step back into the shadows.

It took two good wrenches to break free of his grip and by then they were four tents away, Roustam-Raza trailing after them. "What is the meaning of this?" she asked indignantly. "You see a woman and you cannot contain yourself, is that it?"

"No, you foolish woman, that's most unfortunately not it," he said, motioning for her to keep her voice down.

"You didn't ask them any questions!" she burst out, unwilling to be silenced.

"Because I didn't have to," he said, and signalled Roustam-Raza to approach. "That woman is Pauline Foures."

"I know who she is," said Victoire. "What has that to

do with anything? You saw the way she came to Berthier's tent. Her husband is an important officer—"

"And that is the issue, her husband," said Murat with less merriment. "He's always at the front. He claims he likes to be there." He looked down at his feet then back at Victoire. "You have to give me your word that what I tell you now you will keep in utter confidence."

"Of course," she said, standing straighter. "Only my husband will be informed, if it's—"

"Not even your husband, Madame," Murat said sternly, and looked over at the Mameluke. "You have sworn loyalty to Napoleon. Therefore you must remain silent about what I tell you."

"If it is necessary, then I will," said Roustam-Raza purposefully.

Victoire was torn between impatience and a growing sense of dismay. "Why can't I tell Vernet?"

"Because it would be unwise. There is enough against your husband, madame, without adding this to his burden of demerits." Murat coughed delicately. "You see, we are very far from Paris. And the rumors about Josephine are quite specific, disturbingly consistent, and cruel. Madame Foures provides . . . needed companionship for Napoleon."

Victoire cocked her head to the side. "You mean she is his mistress?"

Her bluntness brought a single chuckle from Murat. "It is precisely what I am attempting to discreetly communicate," he said to her. "One of the reasons Foures is always at the front—where he has had the ill grace to survive—is for the convenience of his wife."

"You mean he knows of this?" Roustam-Raza demanded, thoroughly scandalized.

"Let us say that he does his best not to know of it. He does not want to show himself a cuckold; but the favor of Napoleon has its undoubted benefits." Murat's smile was cynical.

"Not if it keeps Foures at the front," said Victoire with asperity.

"How is it that Napoleon disgraces his officer in this

way? How can he bring such dishonor upon himself?" Roustam-Raza was more baffled than outraged now. "He's the leader. If he must have bodies, there are young men enough here who would gladly accept his favor."

Murat stared at Roustam-Raza. "Muslims," he said comprehensively. "It is not Napoleon's way to bed men, I fear. His taste is for women. Frenchwomen."

"Then find the houses where women are," said Roustam-Raza at his most reasonable. "They will accommodate him. Or find a village and rape the ones that please the eye." He drew up his shoulders. "But to take a married woman . . . The Prophet would not permit it."

"Napoleon is a married man," Murat reminded him. Then he threw back his head. "When I was in the seminary, I would probably have agreed with you. But the army has taught me pragmatism. Napoleon likes the bodies of women and prefers devotion in those he beds. Thus Pauline Foures. If her husband is not killed, they both will profit from the alliance. Napoleon is not shabby."

Victoire regarded him with new interest. "You were in the seminary?"

"I thought I had the vocation," he answered. "But I suppose what I wanted was the education. When it came to living a priest's life, I hadn't the aptitude."

"That appears obvious," said Victoire. Then she sighed. "We have been chasing a chimera."

"Not a chimera," said Murat gently, "but the wrong person, that's certain." He looked around the camp. "It's late. And unless I miss my guess we'll have an early summons from Berthier. He hasn't done with us yet." He glanced around the camp. "See her back to her quarters, Roustam-Raza, and keep watch over her. If she's right, and the thief is at large, he may wish to put an end to her meddling."

The hope that had been fading in Victoire's heart surged again. "You mean that you don't doubt me? In spite of this?"

"Well," Murat said, his eyes fixed intently in the middle distance, "I know that I did not take the scepter. I have been told that all the others can account for their time except your husband. And you say that he did not take the scepter. Assuming that you are correct and your husband is not the culprit, it follows that there is a desperate thief who has already killed one man in order to take his prize. I have no reason to think that he is not prepared to silence you."

This somber assessment silenced all three of them. Then Victoire squared her shoulders. "I'm fortunate to have good friends to guard me," she announced with more confidence than she felt.

"Yes, Madame, you are," said Murat. "For I fear that without us, you won't live to see France again."

# 6

BERTHIER'S FACE WAS pink and his frizzy hair in disarray, but the stern set of his mouth made his appearance sinister instead of ridiculous. For the last quarter hour he had catalogued Victoire's offenses to her and had at last run out of vitriol. He glowered at Victoire as he drummed his blunt fingers on his writing table. "I will say I expected a more convincing explanation than that, Madame Vernet. How can you claim that you are defending your husband by spying on me?"

She had not turned a hair while he upbraided her; now she did not quail at his accusation, nor wilt under his scathing gaze. "I've a duty to my husband, and to Napoleon. My husband is no thief, and Napoleon has lost a marine and part of his treasure. Since no one else seems to be taking steps to find the guilty man or to recover the scepter, I've taken it as my task."

"Women!" Berthier exclaimed. "Fine words, Madame Vernet. But you have shamed me and Madame Foures and you have dragged Murat into a fruitless venture. I will have no more of it."

Victoire met his eyes directly. "I will not keep watch for Madame Foures again. She is not . . . culpable."

"Generous of you to say so," Berthier responded with heavy sarcasm. The slight jowls that had begun to form on the officer shook as his jaw clenched between words. "Will you permit me to inform her that she need not fear you?"

"If you wish," said Victoire, pretending she was not insulted. "But you cannot ask me to keep from trying to exonerate my husband. I'd be a poor excuse for a wife if I did." She curtsied. "If that is all?"

"Not quite," said Berthier. "I have already spoken to Murat about you. He has given me his word that he will not be taken from his duties by your importunities again. Is that clear?"

"Yes," said Victoire quietly.

"And Roustam-Raza has orders to report to me about all your activities. If you attempt anything unauthorized, I will know about it before midnight and I will take whatever steps are necessary to stop you. Do you understand me?"

"I understand you very well." Her sapphire-blue eyes were dry and her fair skin was paler than usual. "Now may I go?"

Berthier shook his head. "All right," he said. "But remember what I've said, and for God's Nails, woman, use what little sense you've been given before you go off on another such start."

For once she quivered, stung. "If I had no good sense, General Berthier, I would never have questioned your persecution of my husband." She curtsied again, nothing more than a perfunctory bob, then she turned without any leave-taking. As she walked out of the tent, she heard Berthier swear.

The young lancer's arm had mortified and Larrey shook his head as he examined it. "There's nothing for it. We must have it off or the rot will spread and kill him." He frowned at Victoire as she prepared fresh bandages for the infected wound. "Mix brandy and opium for him. You know how to do it. Give it to him in an hour. I'll get two of my surgeons to assist me then." He rubbed his bloody smock. "It's the heat. The animalcules breed in the heat."

Victoire was appalled at the stench of the putrescent wound but managed to keep her voice level. "What's to prevent the infection from occurring again, where it cannot be stopped?"

Larrey looked at her and nodded slowly. "I can't answer that. You're right, the rot might come again, and if it does the lad will die." He pulled at his moustache. "But if we do not amputate, then he is dead already. If we take the arm, then the rest of the body has a chance." He bent over the cot again, touching the young lancer's face. "His fever is rising. If we don't act quickly, he will generate enough heat within himself to breed more animalcules."

"Poor boy," said Victoire, though the trooper was less than five years younger than she. As she finished tying the bandages, she said, "I'll see he gets his opium and brandy. Do you want me to notify you when he has drunk it?"

"Yes, if you will. I'll be with Madame Chargerres. She miscarried yesterday and she is ... heavily in blood. I don't know what I can do but give her a composer, but perhaps that will be sufficient." He frowned. "She tells me that this is the third time she has miscarried."

"How unfortunate," said Victoire with feeling.

"Captain Chargerres is very troubled. There are no heirs alive and they have been married eight years." Larrey started away from the cot. "Perhaps you will be good enough to speak to Madame Tounorrai. She has ability as a midwife, I'm told. She will know more how to deal with Madame Chargerres."

"If that's what you wish," said Victoire. "I'll attend to it as soon as I have given this soldier the medication you wish him to have." She was aware how much she wanted a distraction. She could not let herself dwell on the young trooper's fate and she was exhausted with worry for her husband. She made herself be more attentive. "Is there anything else?"

"Not at the moment. Undoubtedly later there will be," warned Larrey, wiping his brow. "This is a damned horrible place. I don't know why I came here." With that he went off, looking from one wounded soldier to another as he marched down the aisle of cots.

\* \* \*

By the time sunset came, Victoire was haggard. The screams and whimpers of the young lancer still rang in her ears, though he had sunk into deep sleep more than two hours ago. She wandered to the entrance of the medical tents where Roustam-Raza was waiting for her; as she approached him, she asked, "What is for supper tonight?" as she realized that she did not want anything at all.

"Roast goat with onions," said Roustam-Raza with obvious satisfaction. "You can smell it if—"

"No," said Victoire, waving him away. "Not after everything I've smelled today." She stared up at the sky, doing her best not to feel queasy. "Find me some cheese and bread. That will suffice me."

"If you insist." Roustam-Raza hesitated. "Would you prefer I have bread and cheese as well?"

"Oh, no, of course not; have anything you want," she said quickly, trying to steady her thoughts. "I'm not really hungry, but I ought to have something." She looked down at her hands. "And I need a bath. Arrange for that, will you?"

"I will," said Roustam-Raza with an Egyptian bow. There was a slight smile on the brightly dressed Mameluke's face. It had been weeks since he had taken any offense at assisting the Frenchwoman. "When I have eaten."

Victoire stretched. "When it's possible," she said, and fell into step beside the Mameluke. "I'll stay within sight while you eat, so Berthier won't have cause to be angry." This evening she was dispirited and downcast, and her mood was reflected in the way she moved and spoke.

"It's an unreasonable imposition," said Roustam-Raza as he watched her. "You have complied with his wishes."

"I've had no reason not to," she said wistfully. "If only I could discover something, anything, that would point me in the right direction."

"It is in the hands of Allah," said Roustam-Raza as they

reached the place where four goats turned on spits over fires. "We must resign ourselves."

"Perhaps you must," said Victoire, then shook her head. "If I had your faith ... but, alas—" She broke off as Roustam-Raza hurried toward the spits where cooks were starting to cut off strips of meat.

Waiting at the edge of the troopers' mess Victoire was surprised to see Gaspard Monge, the mathematician, deep in conversation with Napoleon's currently favorite artist, Dominique Denon. The two men did not mingle with the soldiers but kept to themselves, and there was something about their attitude that struck Victoire as being furtive.

Out of her habitual curiosity, Victoire moved a little closer, wondering what could demand such concentrated attention from two such distinguished men.

"—according to the report, it's worth a fortune to anyone who can pay the price the jeweler is asking," Denon was saying, his face alight with the ruddy sunset and fascination.

"But the thing is in Alexandria," Monge said. "And what you've reported is only a rumor. That's a long way to go for a rumor."

"But it's more than a rumor," said Denon with heat. "I had it from someone who is always abreast of the world's secrets. It's one of those things that is sold covertly. I know it'll be nowhere near the price it could command because of how it is being disposed." He slapped one hand into the other. "Think of it. For an investment of only a fraction of the worth of the piece, we could lay our hands on a real treasure."

"Perhaps. But what if the report is faulty, or the treasure is nothing more than gold-plated brass? Or worse—if it is something that could bring disgrace with it." Monge shook his head. "If that jeweler in Alexandria has something so important that it must be sold in this irregular way, then we had better find out before we do anything—" He broke off as he noticed that Victoire was standing nearby. He gestured for silence, moving away with Denon.

Victoire felt her pulse strengthen and purpose flow back into her veins. She looked around for Roustam-Raza, and saw that he was eating with a few of the lancer officers. At last she had stumbled upon a clue. Or, she admitted, a possible clue.

Someone had a valuable treasure to sell covertly. "The scepter," she whispered, adding dutifully to herself, "It's a possibility." For days she had languished, fearing that there would be nothing more she could do to save Vernet. Now she had information that hinted on—what? She would have to go to Alexandria to find out. Alexandria! The difficulties of such a journey could not turn her from her purpose. It was all she could do to remain where she stood. She wanted to hurry over to him and demand his full attention at once. There must be some way for her to find this item offered for sale. If it was the scepter, she could trace who supplied it, and surely Vernet would emerge vindicated ...

"Something troubling you, Madame Vernet?" asked a familiar voice from behind her.

She turned around. "General Murat!" she cried out. "How good it is to see you." She held out her hand as he approached, smiling as he bent to kiss her fingers. "And what good luck that you should come at the time I have need of your help. You are the very man I want most to—"

He stood up with alacrity. "Oh, no. You're up to something and you're going to try to drag me into it."

"Nothing of the sort," said Victoire roundly. "I want only to seek your advice."

"About what, Madame?" he inquired politely, and spoiled his gallantry by adding, "And don't seek to disguise your purpose from me."

"About Alexandria," said Victoire, holding back the urge to request more. "Tell me about Alexandria."

"Why?" asked Murat, watching her closely. "What about Alexandria has caught your attention?"

"Something I have heard very recently ... from a French source." She looked over to where Roustam-Raza was eating and saw that he was nearly finished. "I believe that there is information that would be beneficial to my husband's case in Alexandria."

"Beneficial? How beneficial?" He did not allow her time to answer. "And this information came from a French source, you say?" He stared at her. "I should not listen to you. But damn me! I don't know—" He rocked back on his heels. "It happens that I am going to Alexandria in a few days. Of course you did not know this. That would be ridiculous." He watched her with a skeptical eye. "Very well. If you'll tell me what you want, I'll endeavor to do what I can to find it or garner the information, or whatever else you might require of me."

She beamed at him. "How good you are!" Her face brightened. "I knew that you'd offer your assistance. And I'm certain you would do a superior job for me."

Murat was suddenly cautious. "I would do? What are your reservations, then? And don't tell me you don't have them."

"Not reservations," she said quickly, "no. Not that. But it would not be reasonable of me to demand you spend time on my behalf when you are doubtless going there on Napoleon's orders, as his officer."

He took a step back. "Oh, no. You don't catch me in that trap twice," he warned her. "I will not consent to any scheme of yours if you present your case this way."

"What way?" she asked, the image of innocence. "I'm only concerned on your behalf. I've already dragged you into embarrassment; I won't be so unthinking again. I do not want your work compromised by my claims upon you. Which, of course, I don't have in any case." She looked away, not trusting herself to watch Murat any longer.

"You are as ruthless as an Austrian dragoon, and that's the truth," said Murat with feeling. "What are you proposing? For you are proposing something, aren't you?"

She turned back to him. "I was about to suggest that you permit Roustam-Raza and me to accompany you to Alexandria. We could be about our business there and you would not have to interrupt your duty to Napoleon."

Her blue eyes were candid as a child's at First Communion.

"No," he said firmly. "Absolutely not."

She shook her head. "Then I will not impose upon you. You've already done so much for me."

He was more wary than ever. "You are giving in much too readily, Madame Vernet." He made no apology for the tone of his remark.

Victoire paid no heed. "I'd prefer to travel in your company, to have your protection, but I am sure that Roustam-Raza is a worthy companion, if I should require one." She motioned to the Mameluke as she saw him stand up.

"Meaning you will go to Alexandria no matter what I say," Murat declared.

"It's no concern of yours," responded Victoire with a curtsy. "I'm grateful to you for hearing me out." She started away toward Roustam-Raza, watching as he paused to get a small loaf of bread and a round of cheese from the larder clerk.

"Come back here," Murat ordered without raising his voice.

She paused and looked at him. "Thank you for your . . . good advice, General Murat."

"Madame Vernet!" he called after her.

This time she did not turn around.

The salt marshes near Alexandria were filled with all sorts of water birds, and Murat set his best marksmen to bagging some for their supper. As the troopers pitched tents for the night, he took Victoire aside. "Tomorrow we'll be in Alexandria," he said, indicating the road leading to the city. "Unless I can create a discourse that will grant you sense tonight."

"You've been very sensible all the way here," said Victoire. "If I'd had to rely on Roustam-Raza, I fear the journey would not have been nearly as pleasant."

"You mean it would not have been possible. Berthier may be distracted from time to time, but he has better sense than to allow a Frenchwoman to go careering about

Egypt with only a Mameluke for escort." He looked away from her to where the cook was starting his first fire.

Victoire smiled at him, not caring whether he saw her expression or not. "Then it was doubly kind of you to intervene with Berthier. I'm certain he would have refused to let me come if I had asked it. But since you made the request, he could not refuse you."

"I'll probably burn a few more years in hell for it, too," said Murat reflectively. "At least you're a good enough horsewoman to keep up with my hussars."

"I have had some experience of hard riding, Murat," she said, unwilling to admit that she was sore the length of her body. "Not all women confine their hours in the saddle to once around the park at a walk."

Murat laughed. "As you say, Madame Vernet." He gestured in the direction of Roustam-Raza. "I know how you snagged me into this, but how did you manage to get him in your coils, as well?"

She ignored the unflattering reference and answered directly, "I reminded him that he's been set to watch me in order to demonstrate his trustworthiness. Surely nothing could do that more effectively than an undertaking like this one."

"And he accepted that argument?" Murat asked in surprise.

"Not at first, but after a time he realized that my point was well taken." She smiled at him. "As you have done."

"You mean you wore him down," said Murat. "Small wonder. You have a sinister aptitude for convincing others to take your point of view."

"That's very gracious." She watched as two campfires flared. "I am sure you will be more in charity with me when we don't have to sleep on the sand in tents."

"Are you?" Murat asked her. The he brushed the ever-present dust off his scarlet jacket and teal trousers. "You may be right." He moved away from her, then came back to her side. "I haven't been avoiding you on our travels here, Madame Vernet."

She looked directly into his eyes. "No. You've been protecting my reputation. That was clear at the outset, and I am grateful for it. Those who are seeking to disgrace my husband would be pleased to claim that I am worse than he is."

"Something of the sort," he said. "Which is why we ought not to talk much longer. I will want you to keep close to me and my men once we are inside Alexandria."

"You and Roustam-Raza are obsessed with kidnappers," protested Victoire.

"Not obsessed, Madame, concerned. As we have every reason to be." He continued to walk back toward the campfires. "As long as you are with French soldiers you will be safe."

"Roustam-Raza is an excellent protector," protested Victoire.

"But there is only one of him," Murat reminded. "Where I have twenty soldiers. I like the odds better, Madame."

She inclined her head. "I will do as you suggest. Once we are established within the city, I will make what arrangements I can, with Roustam-Raza's help."

"Very well," said Murat, and began issuing orders to the soldiers setting up camp for the night.

"These pantaloons are very comfortable," said Victoire as she set out for Murat's headquarters beside Roustam-Raza; around them the streets of Alexandria teemed with seafaring men from all over the Mediterranean. Occasionally there would be someone from far beyond—a Portuguese slave-trader, an American whaler, an African coast-trading merchant plying the waters the length of the Dark Continent. Although they had not found the scepter, she was determined not to be disheartened.

"Keep your voice down!" ordered the Mameluke. "Do you want everyone to know that you are in disguise? There would be serious consequences if you are discovered."

"You've described them to me," she said just above a whisper.

"And speak Greek. You're supposed to be a Greek boy. It was your idea, if you recall." He had one hand closed around the hilt of his scimitar.

She went a short distance in silence, then said, "Do you think we ought to have purchased the piece? A pendant so ancient, surely someone would be pleased to have it."

"It was not what you are seeking," said Roustam-Raza, settling the matter.

She shrugged, but could not resist saying, "What a beautiful thing it was. A high priest or a Pharaoh must have worn it."

"All the more reason to let the jeweler deal with it. Honorable men do not trade in loot from tombs." He checked behind them once more.

"We're safe?" she asked.

"As far as I can determine," he said, gesturing to her to move faster. "I don't like this."

"That we aren't being followed?" she asked, puzzled by his attitude.

"That I can't be certain we're not being followed," Roustam-Raza corrected her. "Watch carefully. In such a crowd as this . . ." He substituted a gesture for the words he could not find.

She stifled her doubt and began to observe the passers-by more closely. It helped her set aside the keen disappointment she felt at discovering the jeweler was not selling the scepter. She had been so certain and her certainty had been dashed.

Then something caught her attention and she stared at a man approaching her. He looked very much like many of the Egyptians around them. His dress was the same white burnoose and turban that most of the men wore. His beard was black and carefully trimmed; his face was darkened with sun and weather, like so many of the other seafarers around them. What was it that held Victoire's attention? She was about to look away when she saw it again: at the neck opening of the burnoose she saw a flash of gold. This time she was able to see it clearly. And then she realized the rest. She had seen such a collar before.

The man was wearing a British naval uniform beneath his Egyptian garb.

# 7

"IT'S MOST INCONVENIENT having Murat gone on patrol," said Victoire to Roustam-Raza as they rode through the crowded streets of Alexandria. "I feel we are given this task for no reason but to keep us occupied while he is off with his troops." She had worn her fashionable woman's shako with the widest brim; her sunburn was peeling and she was grateful for once that Lucien Vernet was in Jaffa instead of being with her. Her riding habit was new, made for the desert of fine linen instead of wool, trimmed to her slender frame and ornamented with a standing hussar's collar and embroidered epaulets. She had even adopted shorter boots that reached no higher than the swell of her calf.

"*About all I could do to be cooler is ride in my shift and stockings,*" she had remarked to Vernet in her letter. "*This is the best I can do to relieve myself of the heat. I wish I had the fortitude of character that the Great Catherine of Russia had, and could bring myself to have breeches made so I might ride astride.*" She had assured him at once that she would not do so shocking a thing. "*Doubtless Napoleon would direct one of his scathing remarks at me, and all the wives who do not shun me now would be glad of the excuse to treat me as if I were invisible.*" She had decided that was too oppressive in tone, and so she added, "*Not that I seek to be always in the social whirl, for no one feels much like whirling in this godforsaken place.*" Gracious, she had thought as she read her letter, am I always going to complain to him? "*Your predicament gives me megrims from time to time. I beg you will pay them no heed. Not that I will not be glad to be back in France for all this country's fascinating mysteries.*

*"And speaking of mysteries and megrims,"* she had continued, *"I dare to hope that we may have made some progress on unraveling how you came to be in this coil. We—Roustam-Raza, Murat, and I—have found proof that there is a spy for the English who has been in the camp. If there is some way to link that spy to the missing scepter, then Berthier will have to direct his inquiries elsewhere, and you, my dearest husband, may return to me at last."*

Now, as she and Roustam-Raza rode toward the villa, she observed, "I believe that if we can produce this Englishman, we must consider my husband exonerated of the suspicion that has been put upon him."

Roustam-Raza was riding on her left so that she would not have to swivel about in the saddle in order to speak to him. "If we can produce the Englishman, if he will talk, and if what he says has anything to do with the stolen scepter. Then, perhaps you are right, and your husband will no longer be blamed for the theft." He shook his head in condemnation. "It was a bad act, taking that ancient scepter. No one who has honor will do it. There are men who steal from the dead—especially the long dead—but they are no worse than the ghouls who come into the graveyards at night to feed on the flesh of the newly buried."

"Roustam-Raza!" Victoire cried, revolted at the idea. "What on earth are you talking about?"

"The demons who defile corpses, who come to pull them out of their graves and devour them down to the bones." He took a wicked delight in dwelling on this horror. "No wise man goes near a graveyard once night has fallen, for the ghouls would turn upon him. Living flesh is more desirable than the dead." He smacked his lips, which Victoire found grotesque. "Every Muslim knows this."

Victoire suppressed a shudder. "There are other explanations for why the dead might be disturbed, and there is no need of supernatural agents to explain it. Doubtless there are stray dogs that dig up bodies." She swallowed hard and made herself go on unconcernedly. "From time to time such things happen in France, and only the ignorant attribute the events to the *loup-garou* or demons."

"The *loup-garou?*" asked Roustam-Raza. They had reached the old south gate now and were passing beyond the city.

"The man who is cursed to be a wolf, or so the legends tell," said Victoire, going on with feigned nonchalance. "There are many superstitious people who believe in those curses."

"They are not so superstitious," said Roustam-Raza. "We know of these, as well. But they are not wolves, they are leopards and hyenas and foxes."

As they started down the road, Victoire changed the subject. "We're coming to know the way quite well, aren't we?"

Roustam-Raza accepted this shift in direction. "Better every day. If we continue to watch another week, the horses will come of their own accord and we will not need our reins." He motioned her to the edge of the road so that farmers bound for market could maneuver their carts and their asses.

"Do you think anyone will return there? If they know we have discovered them, might they not find another meeting place?" She hated to hear her own voice speak such ominous words, but the questions had been building in her since she rose that morning.

"With Murat on patrol, I think it is possible they will come back. They will assume it is safe because Murat is not in Alexandria. Which is why it is best that we watch them." He touched the scimitar in his belt. "They will not expect us to be on guard."

"How do you mean?" Victoire asked. "Why is this better?"

"Because they are foolish men, I think, who believe that Mamelukes are children. They will learn otherwise." He chuckled. "The French have learned it already."

"Yes," said Victoire thoughtfully. They were about halfway to the isolated villa and the morning was growing steadily hotter. "Wherever they are, you may be certain they'll rest through the heat of the day, as any sensible person ought to."

"The English are not sensible," said Roustam-Raza. "Often they work while the sun is at its height. It is not a sensible thing to do. They turn red as Tyre dye." He laughed aloud.

"I've heard it said they collapse from the heat on occasion." She felt a sudden urge to defend the English.

"They don't bring salt-dried fish with them, and they become ill." He shook his head merrily. "They are very foolish."

"And if they attack at midday, what then?" Victoire watched him, her eyes bright. "Do you let them run over you, or do you mount up and fight?"

"It is very bad for the horses, but we fight," said Roustam-Raza. "Because they are foolish, we are made to suffer."

"That may be said of more than English soldiers," Victoire told him.

The Mameluke sighed. "The Infidel is everywhere."

Victoire had heard this complaint from Muslims before and she no longer rose to respond, knowing it was futile. Muslims did not see the world as Europeans did, and there was nothing she could do that would change them. Many times she was puzzled by what Roustam-Raza thought was obvious, but she had done her best to accept him on his terms. She directed her attention ahead on the road where the track turned off. "Look. Aren't those—" She pointed to the four deep, new ruts.

"A buggy; not large enough for a proper carriage." Roustam-Raza pulled in his horse and dismounted. "It passed this way not very long ago," he said as he knelt down beside the narrow way.

"That means it could still be here?" asked Victoire, feeling excited.

"If it has not left another way," said Roustam-Raza before he vaulted back into the saddle. "Let us be cautious, Madame."

"Yes," said Victoire with alacrity. She felt a ripple of excitement go through her, like wind passing over a field of grain. "This is a very good thing, finding someone at this villa," she said as she followed Roustam-Raza across the little bridge. If only she could convince herself of it.

As they came up to the villa, they could see an old four-wheeled tilbury standing in front of the garden gate, the aged gray horse contentedly chewing from his nosebag.

"Whoever is here, they're not afraid of being discovered," Victoire observed, trying not to be disappointed.

"No, but I will speak with them in any case," added Roustam-Raza as he swung out of the saddle. "You must remain out here." Before Victoire could sputter her objection, the Mameluke added, "So that you may lead away the horse and carriage, in case they attempt an escape."

Victoire regarded him skeptically. "I know when I'm being maneuvered, sir," she warned him.

"Since we do not know who is in there or how they may be armed it would be best for you to remain out here, where you can cut off their escape if things go ill with me." He drew his scimitar and started into the villa, moving with stealth.

As she watched him go, Victoire nudged her mount nearer the gray harnessed to the carriage. "Don't cut up, fellow," she said to the horse as she reached for the rein. "We're not going far."

The old horse chuffed a warning, but after an initial resistance allowed her to lead him some short distance from the villa. There was no shade to be had, and both Victoire's mount and the gray were sweating. Victoire took a handkerchief from her sleeve and wiped her brow. "I'll see you both have water shortly," she promised the horses.

It was almost ten minutes later that Roustam-Raza emerged from the garden gate and summoned Victoire with a lavish sweep of his arm. "All safe!" he shouted at her.

Victoire took hold of the carriage horse with her right hand and her mount's reins with her left. She got them moving with a cluck or two, letting them set their own slow pace.

"There is a caretaker," said Roustam-Raza as Victoire came up to him. "This is his tilbury and his horse." He held both animals while Victoire dismounted. "I have spoken with him. He is in the central room."

"May I talk to him?" asked Victoire.

"That is uncertain," said Roustam-Raza. "He is a very pious man and does not speak with Infidel, most especially Infidel women." He pursed his lips, spat, and pulled on his moustache. "I suppose if you will cover your face he might consent to speak with you."

Victoire rolled her eyes heavenward. "Do you think it is necessary to go so far?"

"It may not be, but I suspect he will not speak at all once he is offended." He rubbed his big hands together. "Do you have anything that will serve as a veil?"

"My handkerchief," she said, resigned. She pulled it out of her sleeve where she had tucked it once more. "It's edged in lace. Is that satisfactory to your pious caretaker?"

"It may be," said Roustam-Raza dubiously. "If he objects, we must find another way to present him with your questions."

"Have you asked him questions already?" Victoire inquired as she fussed with the handkerchief, trying to secure it to her lady's shako.

"Not very many. There are courtesies . . ."

"Of course," she said, struggling with knotting the fine lace. "It's going to be ruined," she muttered as she worked.

"There is coffee, but it would be wrong for him to serve you. I will see that coffee is prepared when we are once again in Alexandria. If you drink any while the caretaker is there, he will be—"

"Offended," Victoire finished with him. "Naturally."

"He is a simple man, and he is trying to do the bidding of the masters of this villa." Roustam-Raza looked at her closely, nodding his approval. "It will suffice. And your habit is modest, given what it is. He will be offended at the color, but that can't be helped."

Victoire shrugged, and permitted Roustam-Raza to lead the way into the garden. "The fountain ought to be cleaned," she said as they passed it. "Look at the algae and scum floating there."

"It is for the masters here to correct that," said Roustam-Raza. "You will say nothing of it."

"As you wish," she assured him as they entered the house itself.

In the main room, the caretaker sat, a cup of thick, sweet coffee in his hand. He was a small man, older than she expected and dressed all in white. The room was cooler than Victoire expected, with a slight breeze coming in through windows low on the wall. The high ceiling was painted in an elaborate, abstract pattern of reds, blues, and gold. His expression froze as Roustam-Raza led Victoire into the room, bowed in form, and burst into a long speech in Arabic. The caretaker listened, his face a study in disapproval.

"Bow to him, Madame, and do not look at him while we speak," Roustam-Raza instructed her, indicating a hassock across the room.

"If it's necessary," she said, and did as he instructed her. Once she was seated, she said to the Mameluke, "Find out from him where the men are who were here four nights ago."

Roustam-Raza went into another expostulation, speaking with great feeling and energy. When the caretaker had answered, Roustam-Raza said to Victoire, "He says that the men who were here are gone now."

"Is that all?" asked Victoire in surprise. "I thought he said a great deal more than that."

"There are ways this is done, Madame," he said firmly. "You must respect that."

"Very well," she said, keeping her face averted. "Find out if he knows where they have gone. And be as specific as you can."

"Of course, Madame," said Roustam-Raza, and launched once more into effusive Arabic. This time there was a bit of dialogue between the two men, as if they were clearing up a point. Finally Roustam-Raza turned to Victoire once more. "He says that the foreigners who had leased this place paid for two months beyond this time. He says that they were crazy men. Not entirely because they were foreigners, but because they were planning to go upriver without proper escort. He informs me that they were in haste. He claims he warned them of the dangers but they did not heed him."

"Upriver," said Victoire, winnowing out the one salient fact. "Did they say where upriver?"

There was another energetic exchange and Roustam-Raza said, "They wanted to go to the place called the Treasure-chest of Robbers."

"Do you know where that is?" asked Victoire, who had never heard of such a place.

"It is on the west bank of the Nile, some distance from here." He made an apologetic gesture. "I don't know more than that."

Victoire was growing frustrated at the clumsiness of their interview with the caretaker. She did her best to subdue it. "Find out how long ago they left."

After some involved discussion, Roustam-Raza said to Victoire, "I don't think he knows. He has said that it was no longer ago than a man might make a visit. For an Arab, such a visit is anything from two to six days."

"I see." Victoire caught her lower lip between her teeth and snagged a bit of her handkerchief along with it. She pulled it loose and inadvertently tore her handkerchief away from her hat, leaving part of her face exposed.

The caretaker rose abruptly and spat out several guttural phrases directed first at Victoire and then at Roustam-Raza. That done, he stormed out of the villa and was soon heard clattering away in his tilbury.

"What was that about?" asked Victoire when the man had gone.

Roustam-Raza shook his head several times. "You revealed your face. He was unprepared to have that happen. I told him you would not shame him, and now he is more angry at me than he is at you. He thinks that I ordered you to show him your face." His frown deepened. "He is not pleased at what we have done."

"I could tell that," said Victoire, taking the handkerchief off entirely. "A pity. We might have learned more from him."

"Pardon, Madame, but I do not think so." Roustam-Raza stared up at the ceiling. "I believe he truly does not know more than he told us. He is one who does not want to have much contact with foreigners. And Infidels."

"I thought as much," said Victoire. "Very well, we will not require him to. I think this might be the time to look elsewhere for our answers. If the men went up the river, they must have hired a boat. Therefore we must find out who has taken such a commission and learn where they were bound." She tapped her lips with her forefinger. "I suppose it would be best if we find Murat as soon as possible."

"He is on patrol, Madame," said Roustam-Raza. "It won't be easy to find him." He ventured a suggestion. "He will return shortly. A day or two more at most. Why not wait until then?"

"Why not?" Victoire echoed as if she had not heard him correctly. "Why should I jeopardize our chance of catching those . . . criminals waiting for Murat? He may be delayed, and then we would be farther behind than we are already." She tapped her foot impatiently. "He said that the men who were here have paid for the use of this place for at least another month, didn't he?"

"Yes, he did," said Roustam-Raza.

"That may well mean that they plan on coming back. In which case," she went on, expanding on the notion that had caught her attention, "therefore it is likely that they still have associates here. Why else would they pay for the use of this villa for so long a period?"

Roustam-Raza nodded, following her thoughts. "If there

are associates still in this area, they might well return here. Is that how you see it?"

"Yes," said Victoire eagerly. "That is precisely how I see it. Our task of watching this place hasn't ended, Roustam-Raza. We have much to do still. And we will send word to Murat at first light, when we should know more." She sighed. "I don't want to spend another night in the weeds. Little as I was dressed for it before, I'm less clothed for it now."

"Well, then we will pass the night in the stable," said Roustam-Raza. "There is room for our horses, and you can sleep in the hayloft. You will be protected there, by the horses as well as by the hay. I will sleep in the garden. That way no one can come here that we will not know of it."

Victoire nodded. "Yes. I like it." How good it felt to be doing something of value, something that could prove useful to Napoleon and deliver her husband from his ordeal at the same time! She wadded up her torn handkerchief. "Let's tend to the horses. We'll decide about the food afterward."

It was after midnight and Roustam-Raza was once again on his self-appointed rounds. He stopped where the horses were stalled and called very softly, "Madame Vernet?"

"I'm awake," she answered from the hayloft, doing her best not to take her ill-humor out on him. "I doubt I'll sleep an hour in this place. I keep thinking I hear rats."

"No doubt you do," said Roustam-Raza. "In a place like this, you must expect them."

Victoire wanted to issue a sharp rejoinder but managed to keep silent. The rats were not Roustam-Raza's fault, and as a soldier's wife she ought to be inured to such inconveniences, as she had accustomed herself to sand in her food. She tossed on the brittle hay and took a deep sigh. "I suppose now we're here we might as well remain. But I doubt anyone will come here so late at night."

"It would be strange," said Roustam-Raza carefully.

"Would you prefer to return to Alexandria and try again at first light?"

"Yes," she said, and then immediately, "No. If we could be there instantly and back here the same magical way, I would want to return to the bed that waits for me. But it is an hour into the city and an hour back. We would be very poor sentries if we behaved so." She stretched, hoping that she might find a position that was a little more comfortable than the one she currently occupied.

"I am sorry these precautions are unpleasant," said Roustam-Raza.

Victoire answered him in rallying tones. "I'm sure it is far more unpleasant to be wakened by someone holding a knife to your throat, which I fear could happen if we slept inside the house."

Roustam-Raza was truly shocked. "We could not both sleep inside, madame. It isn't possible. You must not think such a thing, or say it, even in jest."

She pulled herself to the edge of the loft to look down at him. "But surely in circumstances like these . . ."

"Madame Vernet," he said firmly, "I will not disgrace you and myself."

"I never thought you would," said Victoire, surprised at the heat of his tone. "But I can't see how—"

"I will make a place for you to sleep inside, if that is what you truly wish—although I must advise against it as unsafe—but I will not behave immorally." He coughed. "You cannot tell me that your husband would approve of my sharing this place with you, not without protection."

"He would prefer I avoid compromising situations, but if I am required to make the best of a difficult—" she began, only to be cut off.

"You do not want to shame him," said Roustam-Raza firmly.

"Of course not," said Victoire, realizing now that he was deeply affronted. "I didn't realize how strict your precepts are, Roustam-Raza. You'll have to forgive me."

"I will," said Roustam-Raza. He paused. "Do you want to sleep inside the villa?"

"Very much," she answered with feeling. "But I won't."

He started to laugh, and then he froze. A moment later he carefully motioned her to silence. Beside him, one of the horses whickered.

"What is it?" Victoire whispered when the tension grew too great for her.

"Someone is coming," said Roustam-Raza very softly. "The river animals are quiet, and the horse—"

"You're certain?" Victoire asked, her voice just loud enough to reach him. "I hear nothing."

"Yes. Because someone is coming." He came a little nearer the loft. "Remain here. And keep the knife you have ready. If you must, take the horses and go."

"But—" she protested.

Roustam-Raza moved away, more like a shadow than a man.

Then she heard a horse—just one horse—come to the villa, and in a short while, the steps of a man leading the horse around to the stalls. Victoire hunkered down in the loft, listening so intently that she heard the little sounds of her clothes scratched by the hay.

The newcomer was almost inside the stalls when he pulled back. "What the devil?" he exclaimed in English.

Victoire's mare whinnied, and the newly arrived horse whinnied in answer. The noise, in such close quarters, was deafening.

"Bloody sod," said the Englishman, slapping his horse with the rein or a crop. He came a few steps closer to Victoire's hiding place. "Whose are these?"

If he expected an answer, he was disappointed. He chose the remaining stall and put his horse in it, but did not remove the saddle or bridle.

He thinks he will have to escape, thought Victoire as she peered over the edge of the loft, a loose tangle of hay in front of her as camouflage.

The man was on the alert. He took a pistol from his belt and held it at the ready as he came to examine the two horses. "French gear," he muttered as he fingered the tack. "Well, well, well." The edge in his voice made this commonplace utterance frightening. He returned to his own mount and took something from the saddle. Then there was the sound of gentle pouring as his horse whuffled.

He must be giving him oats, thought Victoire, and heard the horse start to chew.

"Make the most of it," the Englishman advised the animal as he made his way out of the stall, his pistol raised.

In the next instant a tremendous shadow filled the door to the stalls: Roustam-Raza stood at his full height, his scimitar over his head as he rushed at the intruder.

The Englishman fired his pistol, the ball going wild.

Roustam-Raza ran directly at him, shouting so loudly that the horses fidgeted in their stalls. The Mameluke's opponent bent low, dodging under the sword, and met the charge. Roustam-Raza crashed into the Englishman, his scimitar leaping from his hand with the fury of their collision, and the two men went down together, thrashing on the floor.

At first Victoire was amazed at what she saw, and she gazed in repelled fascination as the two men kicked and jabbed and pounded and grunted. She had seen workmen brawl before, but never with this concentrated, deadly intent. Then she saw what she thought was the shine of a blade. That brought her into action at once. She clambered down from the loft and searched for a weapon in the dim light as the fight went on relentlessly.

There was a wooden pitchfork—not very dangerous, and possibly harmful if she handled it badly. After a first satisfaction, she changed her mind and abandoned it for something more practical.

The Englishman swore, his voice laden with fury. He struck out, smashing Roustam-Raza in the face. Blood trickled from the side of the Mameluke's mouth, who bellowed wordlessly and kicked as hard as he could. The Englishman dodged, but in jumping away he slammed into one of the thick pillars that lined the walls. The Mameluke followed him and drove a shoulder into his midsection, only to be thrown back when his opponent drove his knee into the darker man's face. Both stood a few steps apart, panting. Then Roustam-Raza charged and the two grappled.

Victoire could not concentrate on her search; she deliberately turned her back on the battle so that she could think clearly. She made herself keep her mind on what she had to do. She found a large, wooden bucket. Very carefully she lifted it, weighing it in her hands to judge if it was heavy enough.

Roustam-Raza hissed and uttered a guttural snarl as he clawed at the Englishman's ears. Both men slammed into the straw that covered the floor, each trying to gain a death grip on the other.

Turning, lifting the bucket high over her head, Victoire stood as near to the fray as she dared, waiting for her chance.

A hand struck her leg, and fingers closed around her ankle. She tried to pull away, fighting the urge to scream. Screaming would do no good. Her anger, her fear would help her.

And Victoire slammed the bucket down, hoping she would strike true.

There was a grunt and half a word; one of the men fell back, his head striking the stone flooring with a solid thud.

Roustam-Raza got to his feet and dusted himself quickly. "I didn't expect you to be ... You are brave, Madame," he said to Victoire when he had bent down once more and placed his hand on the Englishman's neck. "There is a pulse. It is well he isn't dead."

"Oh, yes," said Victoire with feeling. The thought of actually killing someone made her nauseated.

"He will not be unconscious long," said Roustam-Raza, watching the Englishman through narrowed eyes. "I will not have long to wait."

"For what?" asked Victoire, apprehension returning twofold. "Why does it matter?"

"There are any number of reasons," said Roustam-Raza. "But first of them is that I wish to ask this man questions." He looked away from her toward the open door. "It will probably be best if you conceal his horse. If he is planning to meet others, we do not want them to know he has been here."

"It is a precaution," she agreed tentatively. "But surely no one else will come so late at night."

"We cannot be certain of that," said Roustam-Raza remotely as he leaned down and seized one of the Englishman's arms and lugged him upward. "If you will take the horse some little way and secure it—" He broke off. "There is a tall stand of reeds a short distance from here, away from the road."

"I think I know what you mean," said Victoire, not sure she liked the sound of what he was telling her.

"If his horse is left there, at least until we are prepared to depart ourselves, it would not alert any others to his presence." He grunted as he swung the Englishman onto his shoulders. "Will you conceal his horse for me?"

She suspected that this was as much a ploy for getting her away from the villa as an attempt to hide the horse, but she did not protest. "If you're convinced it's necessary."

"Oh, yes." He started toward the door, made ungainly by his burden. "Return as soon as the horse is tethered. Or hobbled."

She shook her head, wanting to ask why he wanted her away from the villa but afraid of the answer she might receive. "As you wish," she said, reaching for the reins of the Englishman's horse.

"Remember where you leave him; we will want him later." He swung around once more and vanished around the corner of the villa, the Englishman slung over his shoulder like a huge sack of grain.

Victoire did not remove the nosebag as she started to lead the horse from the stall. She patted the animal's neck and made her way out into the night.

It was more than an hour later when she approached the villa once more. Walking on the ill-defined track in the dark had taken longer than she had anticipated, and her own fear had slowed her steps even more. Little as she wanted to admit it, she was afraid of discovery. And something else trouble her—what Roustam-Raza might do to the Englishman. Nothing she could tell herself quite convinced her that the Mameluke would not hurt their captive in order to gain needed information.

As she neared the villa, she stopped. A high, undulating cry rent the night. It was a sound she could not—would not—believe was human. "It must be one of the water birds," she said to herself, as if speaking aloud made her assertion more true. "They make very strange noises."

Ten minutes later she stood in the entrance to the garden, debating with herself if she ought to go inside. The last thing she wanted to do was offend Roustam-Raza's strict sense of propriety, but standing here she felt woefully exposed. She hesitated, then called out softly. "I've come back."

There was no sound to indicate anyone was inside, let alone that she had been heard. She fidgeted as she waited, thinking it might be prudent to take cover in the overgrown garden.

"Madame Vernet," said Roustam-Raza, seeming to materialize in front of her. "I am pleased you have returned." He bowed slightly to her, but kept a respectful distance.

"I've hobbled the horse," she said, watching as Roustam-Raza went to wash his hands in the brackish fountain. "I took his nosebag but left him food. There is water nearby."

"Sensible as always," said Roustam-Raza with genuine approval.

She could think of nothing else to say. Her questions stopped in her throat. She felt very tired now, as if all the activities of the day had at last caught up with her.

Roustam-Raza sensed this in her. "The Englishman said that his associates are gone. They are seeking a place called the Treasure-chest of Robbers." He turned toward her, shaking the water off of his hands. "I do not know where it is." The last admission embarrassed him, and he could not meet her eyes.

"The Treasure-chest of Robbers." Victoire hesitated. "The caretaker spoke of the place, didn't he."

"Yes," said Roustam-Raza. He still did not meet her eyes. "I know that there are legends of the place where the cliffs are filled with the tombs of kings. There are those who claim that they steal from them." He made a sign against the Evil Eye. "Tombs are unsafe for pious men."

"And you don't know where these cliffs are, in any case," said Victoire, feeling defeat.

"I know there are legends of them, but nothing more than that." At last he turned toward her. "Every Egyptian has heard stories about the dead kings of long ago who lie in winding sheets of gold with gems where their eyes have been."

"But you don't believe the stories," she said, making a reasonable guess.

"They may be true. I have seen mummies and golden scarabs. The rest—the kings and their treasure—may exist somewhere." His tone of voice contradicted his words.

Victoire came a few steps closer. "If you don't know where this place is, why not ask the Englishman? If his associates are going there, he must know where they are bound."

Roustam-Raza spat. "We cannot ask him."

She stared at him, wishing the night were not so dark so that she could read his face. "Why not?"

"He will not answer," Roustam-Raza said flatly. "Whatever he knew of their destination died with him."

How simply he said it, she thought as she winced at what he told her. Victoire felt a deep, sudden chill. "How do you . . ." Then words failed her and she lapsed into a silence that quieted her thoughts as well as her questions.

Roustam-Raza stared at her. "Madame Vernet? Are you well?"

She made herself answer him. "Why yes," she answered; this was not enough, and she added, "It is quite late. I'm . . . tired."

"And dawn comes quickly," said Roustam-Raza. "We

must be away from here within the hour." He started back into the villa, then looked in her direction again. "It would be best if you remain outside."

"Yes," she said. "It would be best."

## 8

KEMAL NUSAIR RECEIVED Murat and Madame Vernet with a show of courtesy and deference that would have shamed a bishop. The villa would have passed for a palace in France. It was two stories high, an unusual thing for the area, and covered with a pale yellow stucco. The gate of the courtyard was covered in delicate decorated brass, though Victoire noticed that the edge showed it to have a core of good, solid iron. Even more striking were the grass and flowering shrubs that filled the entranceway. In so dry a climate, they must have required immense efforts to cultivate. The merchant himself ushered them into the central room of his house and summoned the servants to serve coffee. If he was nonplused by the presence of a European woman, he did not reveal his feelings to her.

"You're very kind to receive us on such short notice," said Murat as he took one of the three European chairs in the room.

"Nonsense, nonsense," said the merchant, beaming with pleasure. "It is the least I can do." He regarded Victoire, and ventured an unexpected suggestion. "Perhaps you would feel more comfortable, Madame, if my first wife and daughter joined us."

Victoire did her best to respond with aplomb. "That would be most welcome if you're not inconvenienced, nor they." Murat had told her that Nusair was more European in his taste and conduct than were most of the Egyptians she might meet, but his very French manners still surprised her. "I understood such things are not done," she said.

"That is not wholly correct," said Nusair. "In this household, we do what we can to live in the world." He clapped his hands again, and when the household slave appeared, he said, "Bring my first wife and oldest daughter to meet my guests. And none of your sullen looks, or you'll be thrashed for it."

The slave bowed deeply and hurried away.

Kemal Nusair folded down onto one of the tremendous cushions. "Your note intrigued me, Murat," he said, his attitude very satisfied. "It is a pleasure to be of service to the men of Napoleon. Surely he is a very great man."

"Most surely," said Murat, and motioned to Victoire to be silent. "Which is why we rely on your discretion in this matter." He leaned forward, elbows on his knees. "We must find out where these Englishmen have gone, and we must do it without any undue attention falling upon us."

"I understand your predicament," said Nusair. "You would not serve Napoleon well if you made all the world privy to his actions."

"Exactly," said Murat.

Three servants came into the room carrying a large brass tray laden with fruit and sweetmeats. They put this down on the frame that waited at the center of the room, and then went to Murat with a ewer of rosewater and a basin.

As he held out his hands, he said to Victoire, "They will do this for you, too. Wash your hands and use the towel they provide."

"Very well," said Victoire, who had heard about this custom but had never seen it before. She glanced at Nusair. "I must thank you for including me in your entertainment. I realize that few women . . . visit as I have."

"It is a thing that may change in time," said Nusair with a philosophical gesture. "I have done my poor best to change the most limiting of our customs." He watched as she washed her hands in the stream of rosewater. "Permit me to say, Madame Vernet, that you have very fair skin."

She glanced at him, a bit startled by his observation. "In this climate, I would prefer to have darker. As you see, the heat and dryness exact a toll. Many European women have to deal with this; I am not the only one." As she finished wiping her hands, she held them out, revealing her chapped knuckles.

"Yes; the sun is very harsh here, and more so to those who are pale," he said, and looked around as the slave led two veiled women into the room. "There you are," he said to them, indicating the cushions. "We have guests, as you see."

The two women stared at Victoire over their veils with kohl-rimmed eyes. "It is a pleasure," said the slighter of the two.

"My daughter, Lirylah. This is Madame Vernet. Murat you already know. And my First Wife. She is old-fashioned; I hope you will not be offended if she doesn't speak to you." Nusair leaned back and made an extravagant gesture of approval. "Very cozy. Very European."

Neither Murat nor Victoire disabused him of the notion. Murat half-rose as the women sat down, compromising as best he could between proper Egyptian and French conduct. "Let me thank you for your hospitality of the other night," he said to the women.

"Very gracious," answered Lirylah. Her French was strongly accented and she spoke hesitantly, but there was no translation needed for the way she stared at Joachim Murat.

"I have had a most interesting note from Murat," said Nusair. "He tells me that he needs our assistance. It would be appropriate for us to hear him out. And Madame Vernet, as well." The afterthought of her name reminded Victoire how out of place she was in this setting.

Murat accepted the transfer of interest. "Yes," he said slowly, looking over toward Lirylah. "We have a . . . necessary errand we must perform, and for that we need information and . . . help."

"What nature of help?" asked Nusair for the benefit of his family.

"There is a place we have to find. Napoleon's enemies are bound for it now, and we must stop them." Murat looked over at Victoire. "Madame Vernet was the one who stumbled upon the plot, and she has been instrumental in our discoveries." He sat back in the chair. "The enemies of Napoleon are going to a place called the Treasure-chest of Robbers."

Nusair chuckled, and looked over at his daughter. "You see? I have said that it is sensible to teach women something other than the raising of children and the pleasuring of men." He regarded his guests. "I have been at pains to be certain that my daughter receives some degree of education. She has learned French, as you are aware, but she has also learned other things, including geography." He grinned. "I was told she was an apt pupil."

"Indeed?" said Victoire, looking at Lirylah with new interest. "Who was her tutor?"

"A very well-educated Italian, one who came here many years ago, to study the old monuments. When the river was in flood he was forced to remain here and earn his bread with his wits. He agreed to teach her in exchange for access to my ships. He was not interested in the places my agents go, but there were sites along the Nile he made the most of." Nusair clapped his hands together. "Recite for them, Lirylah. The one that has to do with the teacher in the dark wood. I like the sound of that one."

Obediently Lirylah began the first canto of the *Inferno,* her Italian more accented than her French. She had gone a dozen lines into the poem when she faltered, losing herself in a tangle of words.

Victoire took it up where Lirylah left off. " 'At the end of the precipitous and rough-faced valley/That until this moment had pierced my soul with dread,/I lifted my eyes, and saw the mountain-ridge shining ...' " She let the words trail off as she looked directly at Lirylah. "It is a very great poem."

"It offends many people," said Lirylah seriously.

"Good Muslims do not believe in the same Heaven and

Hell as we do," said Murat, encouraging Nusair's daughter to continue. "You recite it very well."

"My tutor was strict," said Lirylah, and volunteered nothing more.

Nusair was not put off. "This is a very canny girl," he said of his daughter with great pride. "She is not as other women. God has put a man's brain into her body."

Victoire, who had heard similar remarks made about herself most of her life, bristled in Lirylah's defense. "It is not God who provides the knowledge, but human study, sir. Your daughter is an apt pupil because she loves learning, not because she ought to be a son."

Murat's breath caught in his throat and he prepared to intervene in a pitched battle. "Madame Vernet has been very well educated, you see—" he began, only to be cut off by Nusair's amused laughter.

"What heat you reveal, Madame Vernet," he said, wiping his eyes with the hem of his sleeve. "I have heard that Frenchwomen have hot tempers, but you are more ferocious than half the soldiers of the Pasha." He shook his finger at his daughter. "You see what education can do to females. Be warned, my girl. I will not have contention in my house."

"No, treasured father," said Lirylah. She glanced swiftly at Victoire, then at Murat.

With a great show of patience, Murat nudged their conversation back in the direction he wished it to go. "About this place called the Treasure-chest of Robbers. If your tutor taught you geography, is it too much to hope that he let you know where this site is?"

"He told me of his explorations there," said Lirylah, abashed, as if admitting to such knowledge was tantamount to knowing state secrets.

"Ah," said Murat, trying not to sound too enthusiastic. "And do you think you could indicate the place to us on the map?"

"It is . . . possible," she said. "But every year the river changes a little, and I might not reveal the correct landmarks."

Murat sat very still, then turned toward Victoire. "What do you think?" he asked, his frown revealing more of his thoughts than he realized.

"I think that we need the information, however we must go about getting it," she responded softly. "If we're going after the English, that is."

"We must do that, unless we find the . . . object here in Alexandria, and that no longer seems likely," said Murat, grim purpose behind his easy smile. "If the English have the . . . object, or know where it is, we have to recover it." He looked directly at Nusair. "We're at your mercy, I fear."

"At my mercy?" repeated their host as he reached for one of the sweetmeats. "What an outlandish notion. Surely it is we Egyptians who are at the mercy of you French."

Murat stared at Nusair. "I am not here as a conqueror, sir. You forget we represent Liberté, Fraternité, Egalité."

"Of course you are not, but there are those among the French who are not made of the same stuff." He indicated a pastry dripping honey. "This is very good. You must have some."

Murat was not about to be put off with tidbits. "I am a French officer, Mister Nusair, and I am proud of my rank, but let me assure you that I am not here to cause any distress to you, your family, or your country. If you do not believe this, then excuse Madame Vernet and me for bothering you in this unseemly way."

Lirylah turned to her father, her eyes enormous with dismay. She spoke rapidly to her father, who was watching Murat dumbfounded. He answered her before he collected himself and addressed Murat. "I don't know what I have said that has offended you, but I hope you will disregard it, General Murat. My words were hasty, the talk of one unfamiliar with the language and prone to error." He signalled the servants for coffee. "Please. Have—"

There was another, softer outburst from Lirylah which evoked an astonished series of questions from her father. Victoire listened, using what little Arabic she had learned from Roustam-Raza, but recognized only a few words, not enough to make sense of what passed between them. She tried to appear that she could not understand anything, for she suspected that would be regarded as intolerably rude by Kemal Nusair.

At last Nusair slapped his hand down on the table—narrowly missing the sweetmeats—and after a burst of rapid Arabic, he regarded Murat. "This daughter of mine tells me that she knows where to find the place you seek. She was shown maps by her tutor." He shot her a fulminating glance, and returned his attention to Murat. "She is suggesting an unacceptable thing. I will not bring more shame on her by telling you what she says."

Victoire spoke before Murat did. "I think it would be helpful, sir, if you will let us know what your daughter is saying, for I have a suggestion to make that I know will be at least as upsetting to you as anything she has put forth to you thus far."

"What would that be?" asked Nusair, frowning portentously.

Victoire motioned to Murat, warning him not to interrupt her. "Mister Nusair, it is my intention to travel upriver with General of the Cavalry Murat. I have a task to perform on behalf of my husband, who is away in Jaffa and cannot act for himself. I will require another woman for the journey. I would like to arrange for your daughter to accompany me, so that we may all travel with propriety." She had said it in a rush, as if afraid that if she stopped she could not continue. "It is a great imposition, and ordinarily I would not dare to put forth such a suggestion. But this is a very important mission, one that'll have lasting consequences on Napoleon's campaign in Egypt. Those who render assistance in this may be certain of his gratitude at its conclusion."

Nusair was staring at her, too astonished to be affronted. He swallowed hard twice before he said, "You are proposing that my daughter travel with you? Away from this house? Out of the company of her mother?"

"I am proposing that she come with us so that she may aid us in finding the Treasure-chest of Robbers, as well as making it acceptable for me to go with General Murat. As a married woman, I must not travel with him alone. I would be compromised beyond recall." Victoire lowered her eyes modestly in order not to see the expression of approval and amusement in Murat's brown eyes.

Nusair exchanged several short sentences with his First Wife, then looked at Lirylah. "And you? What do you want in this?" He spoke in French so that his guests would hear the answer for themselves. "You have my word as a true son of the Prophet, with my hand on the Quran. It will be as you wish."

Lirylah stared directly at Murat. "I will come with you, if Allah wills."

"Lirylah!" her father burst out.

"You asked me, treasured father," she said, flinching at the tone of his voice but sticking to her words. "I will accompany Madame Vernet. Otherwise she will have to go with a woman she does not know and cannot trust. Upriver that can be a great risk, and well you know it." Her veil obscured her mouth but Victoire sensed she was pouting.

"But—" Nusair began.

"You said I might decide, treasured father," Lirylah reminded him softly. "And who else can we recommend to them who is appropriate? How many women do you know who speak any French?"

Nusair coughed. "It is folly to educate a daughter. Everyone warned me and I would not listen." He folded his arms and glared at her. "Very well. Since you will have it, go with Madame Vernet on her quest. But if any dishonor comes to you, I will not take you back into the house."

Victoire intervened. "What dishonor could happen? She will assure my honor and I will assure hers. I have no wish to see her compromised and she cannot want to have any disrepute come to me. Roustam-Raza will be with us, and he is a most upright and correct Muslim. He will not permit your daughter to be taken advantage of, either out of intent or ignorance. What could be safer?"

"Staying under her father's roof," said Nusair bluntly. "But she has expressed her wish and I have said it will be granted. Why I should have had such a daughter—" He gave a gesture of vexation. "Very well."

"There are gardens in Paradise for you, treasured father," said Lirylah.

"Where your behavior will speedily send me," he responded gloomily. "Well, we had best set about our plans, before you depart on this madness."

Victoire and Murat exchanged glances, and then he moved to where Nusair sat and began to soothe the merchant's nerves with the assurances of the favor he would certainly enjoy.

Murat stood in the aft of the dhow, watching the first light change the surface of the river from indigo to silver to blush, his heart lightened by the beauty of it. He was dressed like a prosperous Greek merchant, his dashing cavalry whiskers shaved off in favor of a short new beard, and his curly brown hair was clipped close.

"We'll reach Abydos this morning, they tell me," Victoire said as she came up to him. She, too, wore Greek clothing, hers appropriate to a weaver from Hydra.

"Excellent," he said after a long, distracted moment. "Are the horses ready?"

"Probably more than ready," said Victoire. "They've been standing in stalls for the better part of five days. Roustam-Raza will have to exercise them with you before they're fit to ride." She regarded him, finding his face unusually set. "What is it, Murat? What's troubling you? Are you worried we will not recover the scepter?"

He looked at her, faintly startled. "Well, yes. Yes. That, of course . . ." He did not continue.

Victoire closed her eyes; Murat confirmed what she had suspected in the four and a half days they had been aboard the dhow. "Does she know? That you love her."

Murat was still for a dozen heartbeats, then shook his head. "I hope not," he said.

"Then you plan to say nothing?" she asked him. When he did speak, she went on, "For she loves you, Murat. It's in her face every time she looks at you."

He turned away from her. "Madame Vernet, please. It is hard enough to bear within myself. If I speak of her to you, it could weaken my resolve."

"To say nothing?" she asked.

"I am a man of honor, Madame Vernet. How could I speak to her?" His eyes were bright with an emotion that was not quite anger or despair.

"Would speaking alone dishonor either of you?" She was as aware of the strictures that bound him as he was. She sought for some solution to his turmoil.

"An acknowledgment is not a declaration."

"In my case, I fear it would have to be," he said very softly. "How could I tell her ... anything? It would take advantage of her innocence." He stared out toward the hot line of the eastern horizon where the sun was emerging.

"But she loves you, Murat, with all her soul," Victoire said simply.

His sigh was not quite steady. "I know."

"Is that so terrible?" Victoire did not give him time to answer. "How did we end up in Egypt, in any case? Why did France seek this place?"

Murat was visibly relieved. "Politics, Madame," he said with an attempt at his usual jauntiness.

"Politics, of course. We are Frenchmen, so it has to be politics or love." The cavalry officer glanced toward where Lirylah slept. "There is much every citizen knows about the great battles that saved the Republic. Few outside Paris realize the true nature of the Directoire that now rules our land." Murat lost some of his normal exuberance here. His voice took on an almost conspiratorial tone. "I must ask you to repeat none of this. I find you an exceptional, er, person and so will speak on it. In some places to talk so plainly could bring you a visit to Dr. Guillotine's merciful invention."

"I am the wife of a Gendarme officer," Victoire assured Murat.

"Of course," the cavalryman smiled. "And we are all here with Napoleon. In fact, we are all here because of Napoleon.

"You see, the members of the Directoire hold the reins of power as tightly as they dare. Even so, their grip is feeble and France a powerful steed. They can never feel in control of the land they run, much less comfortable or secure. All of today's Directoire gained their jobs, sometimes literally, over the bodies of those who preceded them. I cannot recall any who have retired peacefully from such employment. These men are ambitious. Perhaps more ambitious than competent. They fear anyone who could someday challenge them.

"Napoleon was such a man. He was a hero after he put down the rebellion at Toulon and forced the English to flee the city. To be rid of him, the Directoire sent the general to Italy. There a despondent and poorly trained army had been many times defeated by the Austrians. All France loves a winner, but has no memory for those who lose. They must have hoped that Napoleon would slow the inevitable Austrian success, or at worst, fail completely and lose his popularity.

"Instead, in battles so brilliant that they rival those of Alexander, our general drove two Austrian armies, each larger than our own, from Italy. This made him an even greater hero. And an even greater threat. They tried to leave Napoleon to rot with the honors they were forced to bestow on him. Ours is not a leader to sit idly by. He began to agitate, through powerful supporters in the city, for another command. For an expedition against the British.

"The British Empire is the bank for all the monarchs. Without English money we could all live in peace. It is English gold that pays the Austrian grenadiers and Russian cuirassiers to fight us. Their navy is still too strong for us to cross the Channel and defeat them on their own island. Instead Napoleon argued that we must cut them off from the source of their wealth, the Orient. Hence he argued for an expedition against Egypt, and, he has hinted, perhaps to conquer many more lands, even all those that were Alexander's.

"The Directoire, seeing another chance for Napoleon to disgrace himself, found the idea appealing. Even more appealing, I suspect, was to have the general so far from Paris."

Victoire could see Murat more clearly now that the sun was rising on their left, and the long shadows reached away from them toward the riverbank. "What do they want, those men in Paris?"

Murat actually grinned as he thought how to answer the question. Finally he spoke, his arms gesturing widely to emphasize each point.

"It is not what they want, but what they have. The members of the Directoire control France. Those few men control all the wealth, all the legions of battalions, every ship in the most powerful nation of the world. For a man of ambition, it must be a heady drink.

"But also this must be a disappointment. For they have no further to go. This, I suspect, drives them as much as any desire to spread Liberté, Fraternité, Egalité to the rest of Europe. And even so, to keep this power they have made themselves greater dictators than most kings. It must be a terrible fate, to have so much of what you desire that your only goal is not to lose it. But the people are not all fools. There has been a price. They say the loss of liberty was necessary to save us from the kings, but their control has not meant peace. The roads between the cities are not safe, the administrators corrupt, and the laws change daily. The people are tired of all this and search for a strong leader. If the Directors all ever agree on anything, it is to make sure no one arises that will be this leader. We are here with one man they rightly see as one who could lead all France, perhaps all Europe, and gloriously."

The sun was higher now and more of the crew was on deck. One of the hands—almost certainly a slave—brought food to the horses in stalls on the foredeck, and a new helmsman took over the tiller.

"We're in the way," said Murat to Victoire, and gestured to a place halfway along the deck. "That's safe enough. We won't be in anyone's path."

It was possible to sit on bales of cargo at this place, and Victoire availed herself of the lowest of them. "You implied that there are those in Paris who want to compromise Napoleon."

"Because there are," said Murat, his frown quick but less tormented than the one he had worn when she had first spoken to him. "There is a whole country at stake. There are men who would undertake . . . anything for such a prize."

"When you say there are men, you have someone in mind, don't you?" said Victoire, hoping that Murat would tell her everything he knew.

"Let us say that I have reason to be wary of certain ones."

"And of these men, who do you trust the least?" asked Victoire acutely.

Murat laughed without humor. "Tallyrand. He's more dangerous than all the others rolled together and doubled. He is a survivor, something any soldier admires. But not in the way he does it.

"Charles Maurice Tallyrand-Perigord L'Eveque d'Autun, Prince de Bénévent, began life as one of the nobility. When he was but twenty-one, his father purchased for him the position as head of the largest *abbaye* in Rheims. He quickly became an important figure in the clergy and rose to become bishop of Autun. When the Revolution began, he was one of the chief delegates from the Second Estate to the Estates General. He is one of the few of that Estate to accept the civil constitution.

"When the troubles began, he abandoned even his family and had himself appointed ambassador to London and then the United States in the Americas. He proved himself so valuable that each new government found it expedient to use his services. To retain his position he resigned his bishopric, which meant little, as the state had seized all church properties. When the Directoire no longer felt they could trust him, even that far away, he took up residence in Holland and then some of the German states. He returned just two years ago, now that Madame Guillotine is less thirsty for noble blood.

"He is not even a member of the Directoire. Yet he is

said to control two of those who are. Perhaps he thinks it is safer that way. You could say that Tallyrand has spent his life in service to the state. Others contend the state is more in service to him. Still, recently he has spoken out in favor of Napoleon. His efforts were vital in gaining the materials needed for this expedition. No one is sure why, but he made every effort to see us well equipped."

"But what you describe is an admirable servant," said Victoire ironically. "Who serves without taking the highest offices."

"That's his pose, certainly, and the reason that he has not fallen before now. Men like Tallyrand are like cats, always landing on their feet. I trust him, but only to be untrustworthy." Murat was about to go on when Lirylah, in Greek clothing like Victoire's, stepped onto the deck, shaking out her lustrous hair. Murat devoured her with his eyes until she turned toward him; he caught his lower lip in his teeth, averting his gaze.

Victoire put her hand on his arm. "She knows, Murat."

"Then let that be enough," he said brusquely.

But Victoire shook her head. "Knowing isn't enough. Unless she hears you say it, she will always wonder."

Murat shook his arm free. "We'd better prepare to land at Abydos," he said, and strode away from her.

Abydos was two days behind them, and the guides they had hired were starting to hint about higher fees as they neared Hiw. Their camp that night was close to the Nile—close enough to make Roustam-Raza mutter about crocodiles and rats and for Victoire to remember all of Larrey's warnings about animalcules making the water dangerous to drink or wash in.

"I spoke to the merchants who passed us before sunset," said Roustam-Raza as he prepared their campfire. "They said that the English are ahead of us still, bound invariably upriver."

"And do they know where they're going?" asked Murat, his temper shorter than usual. "Be damned to them."

The Mameluke warrior studiously went about his task,

glancing toward the tent where Victoire and Lirylah were cutting the goat meat he had bought. When he was certain he could speak with respect he said, "If we press hard tomorrow, we can close the gap between us. If you wish, we will dispense with the guides."

"You don't trust them, do you?" said Murat, looking over the campsite for the dozenth time. "You think we should be rid of them."

"So do you," said Roustam-Raza.

"I . . ." Murat was watching Lirylah and it took him a short while to resume his thought. "I suppose it would be wise. We don't want to lose the English, and with those guides . . ."

"The English may turn at Hiw and go south," said Roustam-Raza. "One must cross the desert, but it saves many leagues. The guides will not cross the desert without much more money."

Reluctantly Murat nodded, then called out, "Madame Vernet, will you and Mademoiselle Nusair come here, please? It appears we need expert advice." He moved stiffly, keeping the fire between him and Lirylah.

"Yes?" said Victoire as if she were unaware of the tension. "What will we have to do?"

"I'm concerned about our progress. This insidious heat has slowed us down and we have not come as far as I might wish," said Murat, sounding more like a priest speaking to an obdurate sinner than a man seeking information. "Roustam-Raza informs me that the English may not follow the river. Is there another route leading to the south that we can follow?"

Lirylah answered breathlessly. "There is a short caravan route, from Hiw to Darb el-Bakirat, and from there to Medinet Habu, across the river from Thebes. There are temples there on the west bank, or so my tutor said."

"I see," said Murat in the same forbidding tone.

"We will have to travel fast and early, or the heat will slow us more, no matter how many leagues we save." Roustam-Raza blew the fire into greater brightness. "If the

English go that way, they will have to be careful. As we must, as well."

Murat made an impatient gesture. "If I had some idea where this Treasure-chest of Robbers is, we could decide if it is worth crossing the desert, no matter what the English do." He met Lirylah's eyes, and for once could not turn away.

She moistened her lips before she could speak. "My tutor said it was near Medinet Habu, a little to the north and east, I think." She paused. "I know he crossed the desert to get there."

Murat scowled. "And helped himself to the treasure, no doubt." He started to pace, more than zeal pent up in him. As suddenly as he had begun, he stopped. "It could be very difficult. We would have to ride like troopers, and you are not . . ."

Victoire answered for them. "We are not delicate, silly playthings, Murat. We are women bent on our task." She indicated the fire. "We will take care of putting the meal together and you and Roustam-Raza can make whatever provisions are necessary for us to cross the desert. He can also," she added as an afterthought, "pay off the guides and dismiss them. I do not think it would be sensible to keep them with us any longer."

"Ah," said Murat, his fascination with Lirylah broken for the moment. "You are very clever, Madame Vernet."

"I like to think I haven't wasted my wits completely," she answered with asperity. "And," she added pointedly, "I like to think the same of you."

Murat had no answer for her; he motioned to Roustam-Raza. "Let us attend to the guides."

Victoire watched the two men move away from the fire. "You know," she said to Lirylah, "for an intelligent fellow, Murat can be infuriatingly dense."

Lirylah frowned at this. "I don't understand what you say."

"I suspect you do," said Victoire, turning to her and smiling ruefully. "You are . . . you are put at a disadvantage."

"He will never speak," said Lirylah sadly.

Victoire was silent for a short while and then spoke her thoughts. "For his sake, if not yours, I hope you are wrong."

Through the heat of the day they sheltered in tents and watched the horses consume most of their water.

"We will have to reach Darb el-Bakirat by nightfall. We haven't enough water for tomorrow," said Victoire to Roustam-Raza.

"We will ride into the night," said the Mameluke.

Victoire looked at him uneasily. "Won't we risk getting lost?"

"Yes, but there are signs to read if one has the eyes. And the river is always on our left." His face was stoic, but Victoire was beginning to understand the fierce Mameluke and she knew he was worried.

"As soon as we can, we must ride." She hesitated. "I think that the dun mare is becoming sand-lame."

"Yes. I think so, too," said Roustam-Raza. "It is unfortunate."

"But what are we to do?" asked Victoire reasonably.

"Ride her until she drops," said Roustam-Raza. "We cannot have any horse carrying a double load any longer than absolutely necessary. If we are short of water when she dies, we will drink her blood."

Victoire did her best not to show any revulsion at this, but there was enough horror in her eyes for the Mameluke to know how much she was repelled by what he said. "I'm sorry," she made herself tell him. "My reason tells me you are correct but I have not encountered such ... hardship before, and I am distressed."

"As many others are," said Roustam-Raza. "It is not easy to stay alive in the desert."

"No, it's not," said Victoire. She looked where Lirylah lay asleep; not far beyond Murat sat near the horses, watching the Egyptian girl with such naked longing that Victoire turned away as if she had intruded on some great intimacy.

\* \* \*

At Darb el-Bakirat there were camels as well as horses, and Roustam-Raza purchased four of the ungainly beasts, insisting that they were the better choice for the remainder of their journey. Murat was intrigued with the camels, but Victoire regarded them askance.

"Guardian angels," she said as Roustam-Raza led the animals toward them. "They stink."

"And they spit, too," said Murat. "But they'll get us over the desert a deal more handily than the horses will."

Lirylah, who had been uncertain about horses, watched the camels with dismay. "I do not know how—"

"Roustam-Raza will teach us," said Murat before she could go on. "And you will ride beside me. I will watch after you."

Victoire was surprised to hear this, and at once apprehensive and relieved. She went at once to Roustam-Raza and said heartily, "Well, you might as well show me how to go about it. How do you get them to kneel?"

An hour later they were all mounted on their camels, following Roustam-Raza around the perimeter of Darb el-Bakirat.

"This is worse than a sloop in a storm," observed Murat, laughing in spite of his discomfort. "We leave tomorrow before dawn. If that will not interfere with your prayers, Roustam-Raza."

"I will pray as I have, pausing in our travels," warned Roustam-Raza in a steady tone. "You will not have to be concerned."

"We haven't been, so far," said Murat. "But we haven't had to contend with camels before." He flashed his smile at Lirylah, and for once did not look away when she returned it.

Somewhat later they dismounted from their practice and left the camels in Roustam-Raza's care while they set about making ready for their midday rest.

Murat found an excuse to take Victoire aside. "Perhaps you're right, Madame Vernet."

"About what?" she asked, already guessing the answer.

"I have no right to speak to her, but . . . but I may never again have the opportunity. I want to tell her. I want her to hear me say the words to her. You're right about that. And I want to hear her say the words to me." He spread his hands, palms down, and looked at them as if he had never seen them before. "If she is upset, will you tend to her? As a favor to me?"

"I would do it no matter what the case," agreed Victoire at once. "There is no favor, Murat."

He nodded, making it a bow. "I am maladroit, Madame. Forgive me."

She regarded him with concern. "There is nothing to forgive."

"I pray you are right," he said with a twitch of a smile.

"There," said Lirylah, hanging onto the saddle of her camel. She was exhausted and exultant. "That *wadi,* that is the one. It has the track my tutor described."

The trek from Darb el-Bakirat to Medinet Habu had gone much more quickly than their ride from Hiw to Darb el-Bakirat. The camels had moved steadily over the wastes, less hampered by the heat than the four persons riding them. They covered the distance in a single day, and by the middle of the next morning their searches had brought them past the half-buried monuments to this long, deep canyon leading back into the desert plateaus.

"You're certain?" asked Murat, who rode beside her. He was more at his ease now, and more energetic. "There are other ravines—"

"No, this is the one," she said, her accent growing much stronger with excitement. "He told me about the track and the two . . . those." She pointed. "What do you call them?"

"Outcroppings," said Victoire.

"Guardians," corrected Roustam-Raza.

Murat paid no heed. "You're certain?" he asked again.

"This is the *wadi.*" She tapped her camel and set the beast moving, the others coming after her.

Roustam-Raza fell to the rear, remarking to Victoire as he did, "I have seen your general speaking with the merchant's daughter. They paid little attention to anything else. We do not know where these English are. We don't want them coming upon us unaware."

"I'd say not," agreed Victoire.

He glanced once toward Murat and Lirylah. "This thing, it is dangerous."

"Our quest or their affections?" asked Victoire, who was in no mood to observe the convoluted social forms demanded.

Roustam-Raza made the sign to ward off the Evil Eye. "Both," he said as he loosened his scimitar in its scabbard.

Ahead of them Murat drew in his camel and pointed down. "Fresh tracks," he called to the others. "Unshod asses, I'd speculate. And a camel."

"The English?" asked Victoire, moving her camel closer to him.

Murat chuckled. "I hope so. It wouldn't do to surprise anyone else." With that, he gave himself to the task of following the tracks in the glaring dust.

# 9

Afternoon shadows cast much of the floor of the valley into darkness. It was becoming difficult to see the creases and irregularities in the face of the canyon walls.

"They can't be far ahead," Murat said to Victoire.

"Unless they are behind us," she suggested.

"No," Roustam-Raza declared. "I would have seen them. They are ahead of us still." He lowered his voice. "And therefore we must go softly. We do not want to alert them."

"A wise precaution," said Murat. "And while we're employing wisdom, I think it might be best if we find a place where you women can wait for us. And keep our mounts as well." He glanced at Lirylah. "The English may be armed, and I won't expose you to that danger." He tapped the pistol tucked into his belt. "I am prepared for a fight, but you are not."

"Four is better than two," said Victoire, feeling cheated of victory.

Murat gave her the courtesy of a candid response. "If any harm should come to either of you, I would find it intolerable. And if either of you were used as a shield, I would have to surrender all."

Victoire looked at Lirylah, who drooped in the saddle. "Perhaps you're right," she allowed. "We'll conceal ourselves behind those boulders—those three leaning together, can you make them out?—and wait for you. And we'll hold the animals if that's what you wish. We'll stay there all night, if we must. Or until we see the English depart, and then we will look for you."

Lirylah seconded this. "If you do not come to us, we will find you." This clearly was intended for Murat alone.

There were a few reservations that troubled Victoire but she did not voice them. Suppose, she thought, the English overpowered Murat and Roustam-Raza, then waited for her and Lirylah to come to them? Or worse, what if they were found first, and used by the English to force Murat to surrender? She knew it was sensible to keep these fears to herself.

"There will be no such trouble," said Murat firmly. "We have the advantage of surprise and we will be prudent."

Victoire held her tongue. Murat was noted for many things but prudence was not often numbered among them. She put her hand on Lirylah's shoulder. "We'll be careful. Do what you must do."

"You're sensible, as always, Madame Vernet," said Murat, and offered her the suggestion of a salute. He signalled to Roustam-Raza, and the two of them drew in and dismounted. "Keep them concealed as best you can."

As she took the lead in her hand, Victoire said, "I hope that all goes well for you, Murat."

"Jesu et Marie," said Murat, "so do I." He turned then to Lirylah. "I will be back, never fear. And I will not be gone long."

"Please, not long," said Lirylah.

"I will try," said Murat, and kissed her hand, much to the disgust of Roustam-Raza.

"We'd better hurry," warned the Mameluke. "Otherwise they will get too far ahead of us."

"Right you are," said Murat, and checked his weapons quickly. "Let us proceed."

Roustam-Raza said nothing; he faded away into the shadows, Murat at his heels.

"I am very frightened for him," said Lirylah as the sounds of their footfalls faded to nothing.

"As well you might be," said Victoire, her face set. "I

can see why. I am worried for him as well, and I am not in love with him."

Dark though it was here in the shadow, and although her skin was the color of polished new oak, it was plain that she blushed. "It is my admiration," she said stiffly.

"In part, most surely," said Victoire. She regarded Lirylah seriously. "And he loves you as well. It must be very difficult for both of you."

Lirylah looked away from Victoire. "I've said nothing," she whispered.

"In words, perhaps, but your eyes are eloquent," said Victoire. "As are his." She looked about them. "I dislike wild places like this in the dark. Once night falls, I fear I will not be very sensible about it. It's foolish of me, but . . ."

"The dead are all around us here, hidden in the face of the cliffs, or so my tutor said," Lirylah said, doing her best to conceal her fright. "They say that grave robbers can find wealth beyond imagining, if they are not killed by rock slides or the curse of the dead kings." She shuddered, then made herself stop.

"Dead kings. A strange place to bury dead kings," said Victoire. "Merchants, perhaps, but kings?" She spoke in a rallying tone. "Don't be downcast, Lirylah. They'll be back shortly and we will—"

"But they might not escape!" Lirylah cried out, then once again silenced herself. "What then, if they do not?"

"I don't know," said Victoire candidly. "What did you fear would happen?"

"The curse of the ancient kings," she said very somberly. "Many have died of it. Perhaps even my old tutor." She looked around nervously. "The English might hurt them, too."

"Now that's a danger I can readily accept," said Victoire with energy. "And I think we must take action before dusk. Most of the valley is in shadow already. Only the rim shows light. If we don't act now we will not be able to act until morning." She had been searching for an excuse to do just that, and suddenly she felt she had sufficient reason. She started forward, then swung around to look at Lirylah. "It could be risky."

"It would be riskier without Murat, wouldn't it?" asked the Egyptian girl.

"Yes, it certainly would," answered Victoire with feeling. "You are right about that." She reached up for the reins of their mounts and went about securing them to a single, long line. "Help me with this," she said to Lirylah as she knotted one end around an outcropping of rock.

"There could be scorpions," said Lirylah uncertainly as she took the other end of the rope.

"So there could, but this way we'll have something to ride when we're ready to leave. Otherwise, the animals will wander off, and what will become of us then?" She finished securing one end, and, with an exasperated sigh, took the other end from Lirylah and searched out a similar boulder to tie it to. "We know which way they went, don't we?"

"Yes, we do," said Lirylah softly, as if ashamed of her hesitation.

"Then we must follow them, and quickly." She gathered up her skirts, wishing for the hundredth time that she could wear britches like men did. But the Egyptians were offended already at the immodest dress of European women. If she were to scandalize them even more by adopting men's riding apparel, Berthier would no doubt order her back to Paris. That is, if a ship were ever able to sneak into Alexandria and then slip past Nelson's ships to get back to the capital. When they had left, rumor had said they were cut off from all contact with France. She strode over the rough ground, Lirylah struggling to keep up with her. Victoire slowed to allow her to catch up, then said in an undervoice as they continued on their way, "Pick up rocks and keep them in your skirt. None too large, but not so small that they are nothing more than pebbles. You want to be able to throw them."

"Throw rocks?" repeated Lirylah.

"Why not? There is nothing else we can throw, is there? And neither of us carries a pistol, worse luck." She increased their pace a little, stopping from time to time as she came upon fist-sized rocks to toss into her skirt, which she now held basket-style in front of her.

Dutifully Lirylah did the same thing, though her eyes were distressed and she frowned at the rutted track. It was growing darker now, and it was increasingly difficult to pick out the way. "I have never thrown rocks," she said a little later.

"This is a good time to begin," Victoire stated.

They went on a short way in silence. Then a figure loomed out of the dark. "What?" whispered Victoire.

"I said you would not be content to wait," replied Roustam-Raza. "At least you left the camels behind." He indicated a place off the track. "We have been watching them. They will leave shortly."

"How can you be sure?" asked Victoire as she followed after the Mameluke, Lirylah trailing behind.

"Their guides will not remain when the sun is gone. They are afraid of spirits of the dead and of robbers who are alive." Roustam-Raza laughed very softly. "They are not very brave men."

"Apparently not," said Victoire, and found herself facing Murat.

"You're a handful, Madame Vernet," he said, but with approval in his brown eyes. "And you're probably right to come. I've been thinking that I did not want either one of you becoming hostages."

"I should think not," said Victoire.

He stared at Lirylah, his gaze eloquent, then shook himself. "We've found a very good position to watch from," he told them. "You'll see." He indicated a narrow footpath up the side of the cliff. "It doesn't go very far, but it overlooks the cave where they are busy." He had dropped his voice to little more than a murmur.

"Can you see what they are doing?" asked Victoire urgently, speaking quickly and softly.

"They are widening the entrance to a cave," said Murat, and motioned her to be quiet and follow him.

It was difficult to climb the steep, narrow trail, and

Victoire was more than once tempted to swear aloud when her foot slipped or her hold on an outcropping of rock slipped. Yet somehow she made it to the narrow shelf that overlooked the place where the English and their Egyptian guides worked.

"You understand them," Murat whispered in her ear.

"A little. Not very much," she warned him, and gave herself to the task of listening to what they said.

Below them the activity centered around three lanterns and a number of picks. The work was done hurriedly and stealthily, convincing Victoire more than ever that the men were up to no good. She caught a few words, but not enough of them to be able to guess what the purpose of this hasty digging might be.

"There!" whispered Murat, pointing to a canvas satchel containing a long, heavy object. "That's what they're—"

Roustam-Raza, looming behind him, reached out and put his hand across Murat's mouth, glowering at the men beneath them.

Victoire tried listening again, and learned just enough to realize that the main purpose of this activity was to embarrass the French and make it possible for the English to claim a remarkable discovery at a later, more fortuitous time. Most likely a time when the scepter would act as a rallying point for the Egyptians to revolt against French rule. That made very little sense to her, but she continued to listen, although she learned nothing more.

It was almost completely dark now, and the Egyptian guides were restless, anxious to be away from the place.

"We're almost done," said one of the English, the one who had been in charge of the party. His Egyptian accent was heavily distorted. His manner betrayed his military background. "We will be gone in an hour."

"The path is almost wide enough," said the other Englishman, a bearded man with a patch over one eye and the bearing of a scoundrel. "If you will work with us, we'll complete this later."

"How much later?" demanded one of the guides, making the sign to ward off the Evil Eye. "There are many spirits of the dead in these places."

"If they're dead, they'll be pleased at what we're doing," said the first Englishman. "We're returning what's rightfully theirs."

"It is a bad place to be," insisted the guide.

"Then with your help we will be out of it the sooner," said the second Englishman with asperity. "Lend your back to it, man."

Victoire translated this for Murat, speaking so softly that only with an effort could he understand her.

The men continued to work for ten more minutes, and then one of them gave a grunt of satisfaction. "There."

"You're through?" asked the first Englishman.

"So it appears," said the second, standing up and putting his hands against the small of his back. "First asses and now this. You have much to answer for."

The first Englishman paid no attention. He took the canvas satchel and opened it quickly, drawing out the treasure inside.

In the lantern light the fine gold of the royal flail seemed to be doubly alive. The guides stepped back in awe, and one of them reached for an amulet hung on a cord around his neck.

"I know where we could dispose of that and make ourselves rich as a nabob," said the second Englishman.

"That would cost too dearly: you would never live to spend your fortune," said the first.

"There are places the British lion does not hold power," said the second with a sneer. "Who is to say we could not learn to like the Americas? Or the islands in the Pacific Ocean?"

"Where the cannibals are?" the first challenged. "No, thank you. The captain said that all was arranged. If I am to enjoy the fruits of this night's work, I must be patient, and so must you, Gregson."

Gregson shrugged. "Who else might come here, and find this? There is a good reason this valley is called the Treasure-chest of Robbers." He nodded toward their guides. "They have relatives, and those relatives have relatives. This scepter will not be a secret for long, Hazlett. And I doubt it will be here when you come back for it." He folded his arms and favored his compatriot with a long, hard stare.

"You're mistaken," said Hazlett. "Look at the guides. They will not bring anyone here. They're afraid of the curse."

Their argument became too swift for Victoire to be able to follow them. She looked to Murat and shook her head. "I'm sorry," she mouthed.

He indicated he did not hold her at fault.

Suddenly Gregson took a swing at Hazlett with his pick. Hazlett leaped back, shouting as his clothes tore.

The guides babbled and pointed and stayed well clear of the fight.

Hazlett was the larger man, but Gregson was the more experienced fighter. The two wrestled and bludgeoned one another with hands and feet, but neither gained a clear advantage.

The scepter lay in the dust at the edge of their fighting ground.

And then Gregson had a pistol in his hand. He crouched back, away from Hazlett, his left-handed aim sure. "Get up," he ordered, unaware of the guides moving away from him for using his cursed hand to fire a pistol.

Hazlett, winded, lay on his back, blinking as he watched Gregson. "You don't want to kill me."

"Why not?" asked Gregson, getting slowly to his feet, his aim unwavering.

"There are those who know our errand. They will question you if I don't return." He tried to sound calm and very nearly succeeded.

"And I will tell them that you took a fever in the desert, that your legs swelled up and nothing could be done to save you." He spat and prepared to shoot. "Get on your feet."

Hazlett did not move.

"I'll shoot you where you lie, if you won't get up," said Gregson, chuckling mirthlessly.

"We ought to stop this," whispered Victoire to Murat. "We need to catch those men. We must have them alive."

"I agree, but I don't want to get between them," he whispered back to her.

Gregson shrugged and took a step closer to Hazlett, toeing the scepter away from where they fought.

And Hazlett kicked out, catching Gregson on the shin just below the knee with the full force of his leg.

Screaming, Gregson doubled over, falling as he tried to pull his own foot up off the ground. As he struck the ground, his pistol went off. Gregson stiffened, then died, his contorted limbs twitching eerily.

The guides were nowhere to be seen.

Very slowly Hazlett got up, his face set. "Bad luck, old son," he said to Gregson's body and then proceeded with his own task, taking the scepter and carrying it to the new break in the wall of the canyon. He stumbled once, as if the many blows he had been struck were only now finding their targets on his body. He all but vanished into the face of the cliff, but emerged again shortly, his clothes covered in fine sand. He slapped at the front of his Egyptian robe and coughed as more sand roiled.

"We could take him now," said Victoire very quietly to Murat.

"It would not be wise," said Roustam-Raza behind them, so softly that the wind off the distant river was louder. "He will leave and then we will have the scepter."

"Do you suppose so?" asked Victoire, but knew better than to dispute with Roustam-Raza.

"If he wants to keep the thing hidden," said Murat, "he'll have to do something about the guides. We'll have the way clear as soon as he leaves, as leave he must."

"And what about the dead man?" asked Lirylah, speaking a little louder than the others. "Will he be left?"

"We'll do something with the body," Murat promised her, "if Hazlett doesn't."

She seemed satisfied with his assurance and lapsed into stillness while the other three watched closely.

Hazlett went to grab Gregson's hands, but could not bring himself to touch the corpse. He looked down at his former comrade and shook his head. "I haven't the time to do it right, Gregson." He bowed over his folded hands for a moment, then hurried away into the night.

"I will follow the guides," said Roustam-Raza, speaking quietly. "I will learn what I can."

Victoire was tempted to stop him, remembering what had happened at the villa, but she knew better than to question the Mameluke. She kept her attention on Hazlett as he picked up the lanterns. "I wish," she said very softly to Murat, "that he would leave one behind."

"So do I," said Murat. "But I have flint and steel and paper enough to kindle a torch. If we must enter the cave—"

"And we must," said Victoire, steeling herself for the task. If the truth were to be told, dark, enclosed places made her edgy and unhappy.

"Yes, if we are to recover the scepter," said Murat, backing away from his vantage point on the ledge as the light of the lanterns faded.

Victoire scrambled after him, cursing as she heard the hem of her skirt tear on the rocks.

Lirylah came after her, moving very cautiously, her unfamiliar Greek clothes proving cumbersome to her. She did her best to keep up with Victoire and Murat as they headed around the rock to the place where Hazlett had been.

As they went, Murat busied himself wrapping his short vest around a stout wooden staff, securing it with tight leather thongs. "The flint and steel are in my wallet," he said to Victoire. "And my notebook is there."

"If you are certain you want to sacrifice it," said Victoire uncertainly.

"Of course I don't want to sacrifice it," said Murat gruffly. "All the more reason for doing it quickly. I don't want to stumble about in the dark, either."

Victoire did as he instructed her, and sighed with relief as the first sparks took the three folded pages, and then began to burn the cloth. They had a torch, and the night no longer held them in its inky palm.

Gregson was still lying, curled around the pistol that had killed him. There was little blood to be seen, for most of it had soaked deep into the sand.

The picks were still lying on the ground, and Murat handed the torch to Victoire as he picked up the nearest. "The entry has to be right in this area," he said, moving toward the face of the cliff. "Bring the torch and hold it for me."

"Certainly," said Victoire, keeping pace with him.

After several minutes of searching, Murat uttered an exclamation of surprise and stepped closer to the cliff. "By Saint Louis!" He stretched out, and in the next moment disappeared into what had appeared to be nothing more than a narrow crevice.

"Murat!" cried Lirylah.

Victoire was startled, but she held the torch steady. She knew it would serve no purpose to upbraid Lirylah for her distress, and so she concentrated on keeping the light placed for Murat, to ease his return.

In little more than a minute or two, Murat stepped into the light once again. "There is a great stone door within that cave. It's covered with hieroglyphics and murals, and there are several skeletons on the floor there. And"—he held up the scepter—"this."

This time it was more difficult for Victoire to maintain her hold on the torch. She blinked back tears as she stared at the flail and then looked at Murat. "My good friend," she said with feeling. "You've saved him."

Murat was fascinated with the flail. "An ancient Egyptian king held this scepter. He wielded it to show his authority." He gave Victoire a quizzical look. "We've saved who?"

She was astonished. "Why, my husband, of course," she said, and even as she spoke the words, she wondered if it were true.

He lowered the scepter; being solid gold, it was very heavy and he was unused to its heft. "When we return this, you mean," he said, doubt coloring his words.

"I suppose so," said Victoire. And then she shook her head. "If we can show that this was not a ploy to return the scepter. Berthier might think I have possessed it all along—he has certainly implied that. I would not put it past him to accuse me of treachery for coming with you, and you my dupe instead of my friend."

"I would testify otherwise," said Murat.

"And Berthier would compromise our reputations," said Victoire with certainty. "Oh, gracious." She looked over at Lirylah. "I can't explain it all to you. I'll try to . . ."

Murat weighed the scepter in his hand. "You couldn't have carried something this heavy without my knowing about it, and without Roustam-Raza knowing," said Murat. He held out the scepter to Victoire. "Have a care," he warned her as her hand closed around the haft of it.

He was right: the scepter was heavy. Victoire took the weight and tightened her arm and shoulder. "Yes, you would both know if I had brought this with us." She looked down at Gregson. "No wonder he wanted to sell it. So much gold is very tempting."

"To you, Madame Vernet?" asked Lirylah, and she was upset when Murat answered the challenge.

"Not to Madame Vernet," Murat told her sharply. "She is loyal and steadfast, as a good wife must be, and she is protecting the welfare of her husband. It would take more than a gold scepter to turn her head." He moved a little closer to Lirylah. "And you must not say such things where Frenchmen can hear you, little dove, for rumors travel like grassfire through regiments, and she would be disgraced for no reason. Give me your word that you will not speak of this with anyone but Madame Vernet and me."

She was astonished, and her eyes widened. "I would never . . ." she began, then faltered. "She has nothing to fear from me."

"I knew she would not," said Murat, then gave Victoire

his attention again. "We must have a strategy before we get back. That's unquestionably sure."

"A strategy?" said Victoire, troubled at the canny light in Murat's brown eyes. "Why—" She interrupted herself before he could speak. "Berthier. It's always Berthier."

"And Napoleon," said Murat. He held out his hand for the scepter. "Come, Madame Vernet; this man can rest with all the others who have ventured against that dead Egyptian king." He placed the scepter in his belt as if it were a large dagger, then crossed himself before bending over to take Gregson's arms. "Give Lirylah the torch, and let's get to work. We can't leave him out here for the vultures."

Much as she disliked the notion of entering the cave that served as a tomb, Victoire did not complain. She blessed herself, then reached down for Gregson's feet, lifting him when Murat gave the count.

This small procession followed the same path that the Egyptian priests had taken when they had hidden their dead king away, more than three thousand years before.

And generations of robbers since had profaned their devotion.

Roustam-Raza found them the next morning shortly after the sun had risen. Murat, Victoire, and Lirylah had already ridden most of the way to the mouth of the canyon and were approaching the first of a string of little towns lying along this sinuous bend in the Nile.

"Did you learn anything?" asked Murat once he had given a partial account of their doings the previous night.

"Do you mean, did I find the ones who were guides to the Englishmen, yes I did. It was not difficult." He beamed at Murat and Victoire. "You would be most pleased to know what I have discovered."

"No doubt," said Victoire, who was still tired and a little testy.

"I asked how it was that the English could come this far without being stopped, for we are to fight against the English and support the French. I fear that the answer is going to displease you," said Roustam-Raza.

"And that was?" asked Murat, finding the weight of the scepter a burden in many ways. "What did they say?"

"They were given the right to come this way. They carried an official pass issued by the Pasha himself in Cairo." This announcement was made with great determination, and brought the kind of stares that Roustam-Raza hoped it would. "They were not here clandestinely."

"The Pasha gave them official passes," said Murat, his brow furrowing as he turned this over in his mind, each new thought more unpleasant than the last.

A man leading a dozen white asses yelled at them for blocking the roadway, and raised as much dust as possible as he went by.

Roustam-Raza answered him pithily, and with words that Victoire did not know. He then said to Murat, "They are an ill thing, these passes."

"Yes, they are," said Murat. He glanced at Victoire. "If what the guide says is veracious, this concerns more than your husband, Madame Vernet."

"Oh, it is true enough," said Roustam-Raza, his face bright with smiles. "I made him place his hand on the Quran. He will surely be tormented by Shaitan when he dies if he does not speak the truth when his hand is on the Quran." There was such quiet confidence in him that Victoire could not keep herself from speaking, although she dreaded that he might have treated the guides as he treated the man at the villa.

"How is it that you're convinced? What if the guides had already sworn on the Quran not to reveal the truth to you or anyone?"

Moral quandaries were not in Roustam-Raza's mental vocabulary. He cocked his head to the side, studying Victoire as he answered, "Because they knew I would cut their tongues out, and they did not wish their last words to be lies."

She had been prepared for a shock, but this bald admission left Victoire with the taste of bile at the back of her mouth. She no longer wondered if he were capable of such acts; she hoped she would not let her own repugnance color the burgeoning respect she felt for the Mameluke. Knowing she had to say something, she said, "Then you're satisfied that . . . that it's true."

"Before Allah Himself, Madame," said Roustam-Raza, smiling.

# 10

"WE'RE AT GREATER risk going down the Nile on a dhow," said Victoire at her most reasonable as she leaned on the rail at the prow and let the occasional bits of river spray cool her.

"Yes, we are," agreed Murat, "but it's faster than we can go on land. And you and Lirylah are exhausted." In his colorful Greek disguise he fit into his surroundings far better than the very fair Victoire did. "Don't deny it, Madame Vernet. I know what to look for."

Victoire gave him a resigned look. "Well, since you are convinced, I suppose I must be persuaded." She straighted up. "Still, I don't like landing at night. If the river is fast, traveling day and night, as we did coming upstream, would be best."

"Try to convince the captain of this craft, if you can. I have already. So has Roustam-Raza. But the fellow is a very strict Muslim and he will not have unmarried women sleeping on his boat at night." He rubbed at his neck. "I hope that we have not lost that Englishman. I want to catch him by the heels before he reaches the delta." He shook his head. "Here it is a few days to Christmas and this place is an oven."

"They say there is snow in the mountains," Victoire remarked. Her thoughts were as distracted as Murat's. "If we can catch this Hazlett, do you think that his testimony would be sufficient to stop Berthier from destroying my husband's career?"

"I don't know," said Murat bluntly. "I wish I did. But

we don't know what Hazlett will tell us, assuming we catch him and he ventures to tell us anything." He touched his belt, where the scepter hung concealed in a heavy, shapeless scabbard. "He won't like learning about this."

"No, he won't," said Victoire. She had been despondent for the last day, and nothing she could do would shake her out of it. Very deliberately she changed the subject. "Speaking of impossible decisions, have you worked out what you wish to do about Lirylah?"

"What I wish to do and what I shall probably have to do are two different things, Madame Vernet." He glanced back along the deck of the dhow to where Lirylah, completely swathed in Greek linen, sat in the shelter of two enormous barrels of water. "But Napoleon would not be pleased if one of his generals took an Egyptian wife. He doesn't mind the mistresses, but he won't tolerate such marriages." He lowered his eyes. "And I will not seduce a virtuous girl. I have my limits."

"Then you will return her to her father and thank them both politely?" she asked, not completely believing him.

"As you rely on my support before Berthier, so I rely on your support before Nusair. I will not compromise that woman. As harsh as we French are on those girls of good quality who stray, the Muslims are five times as severe. She deserves better than that from me." His expression softened. "She is ten times the treasure to me that this scepter is, and I will never be permitted to have her."

"I'm sorry, Murat," said Victoire softly.

"So am I." He coughed delicately. "This Hazlett. When we land this evening, Roustam-Raza and I will scour the markets and the coffeehouses to find if he has been here. A few bribes and some of Roustam-Raza's fiercest looks ought to tell us what we want to know. And that will leave a little time for you and Lirylah to refresh yourselves."

Victoire stretched. "God on the Cross, I need a bath," she said at once. "My clothes are going to be rags by the time we return to Cairo. Two good new muslin dresses, and already they are frayed and torn. And my skin—well, it doesn't bear thinking about."

"Fair women do poorly in the desert," said Murat.

"Yes, and all clothes," said Victoire, indicating the state of the big, loose Greek shirt Murat wore.

"True enough," said Murat, for once sounding philosophical.

"They'll last as far as Cairo, I suppose." Victoire made an uneasy wave of her hand. "Perhaps by then this whole puzzle will be solved and all we will have to contend with is Berthier."

Murat's face grew cynical. "Perhaps."

They were at the outskirts of the village Samalut on the west bank of the Nile, in a green, fertile swath of land of wheat fields and date palms. Murat's little company made camp in the area the village elders gave them permission to use, and then, while Victoire and Lirylah took advantage of the shallow well and the sheltered location to bathe, Murat and Roustam-Raza marched off to the village to gather what information they could concerning the present whereabouts of Hazlett.

"I have longed for this," said Lirylah as she modestly turned aside, pulling her Greek clothing open. "The sand is everywhere."

"Truly," said Victoire, examining the lamentable state of her corset as she got out of her riding habit; it had faded from a russet shade to an uneven ruddy yellow. Her other habit was even worse. She shook her head. "I won't be able to mend this; I'll have to throw it away as soon as we return to camp." She frowned, remembering that she had only two other corsets with her. It was time to send word to her cousin in France to procure more for her if she had to remain in Egypt much longer. If the merchant captains were risking the passage yet.

"What troubles you, Madame?" asked Lirylah as she reached for the picket of water set on the ground between them, next to the ancient, stone-paved well. They were screened from any prying eyes by hanging curtains of canvas. More private than elegant, their hidden bath was secluded enough that the women were not afraid to converse while they washed.

"Oh, too many things. I am out of sorts today, Lirylah. I see only obstacles around us, and I am chagrined." She touched her corset. "This is just another such example."

Lirylah was curious about the garment. "Why do you wear such a thing?" she asked.

"Why, indeed," said Victoire, sounding world-weary. "Because it is what women of quality do, Lirylah. It is the fashion, and it is what those of good tone must do to appear acceptable." She was bare to the waist now, and set to washing her arms and chest. "The corsets in my mother's day were much more formidable—longer and tighter. These are much more comfortable." She felt the water slide down her lifted arm with almost sinful pleasure.

"So you must wear this thing, though no one can see it." Lirylah stared at it.

"No one but my maid—if I had one—and my husband. And my dressmaker, of course." She worked on the other arm, and began to feel some of the pall of irritation begin to lift.

"Yet it is required you wear it," Lirylah persisted.

"Yes. My clothes wouldn't fit properly if I didn't." She worked her way out of her skirt and her stockings. She felt grit around her waist and shook her head.

"It is the ruling of your Imam?" asked Lirylah, who was now quite nude and glistening with water.

Victoire required a little time to think her question through. "No, we have no Imams to tell us how to dress. We have dressmakers who set the fashion, and they make clothes for the most dashing noblewomen in Paris. All the world follows where they lead."

"I see," said Lirylah, who clearly did not. "How strange, to entrust the virtue of women to a dressmaker."

"I don't think virtue is their concern—fashion is." Victoire laughed a little at her own humor, and was pleased when Lirylah joined in, willing to be amused without knowing why.

They were still laughing a bit when the widest canvas

wall came down, and the ruddy figure of Hazlett emerged from the shadows of the date palms.

Lirylah shrieked and reached for her clothes to cover her head; Victoire grabbed her drying sheet and drew it around her, tucking the corner in under her arm. In the warm afternoon she felt very cold.

"Good afternoon, ladies," said Hazlett in dreadful French. "Since you've been trying so hard to find me, I thought I'd spare you further inconvenience and present myself." His bow was robbed of any politeness by the pistol he carried. He signalled, and three Egyptian men came forward to join him.

"Let's put an end to this game, shall we?"

"I do not know to what game you refer," said Victoire, amazed that she could sound so very cool when she was so frightened.

"You've been following me." Hazlett was not going to dispute it. "There's no point in denying it. My men have seen you on the river since I started south."

Then he did not know about the Treasure-chest of Robbers, thought Victoire with the first stirrings of hope. "Why do you think this, Englishman?"

Lirylah was whimpering.

Hazlett ignored her, though one of the Egyptians grinned and nudged his neighbor. "You were asking for me at the inn, just before I went aboard the felucca. The innkeeper came to warn me that Greeks who were not Greeks had been searching for me. I had my men watch on the river, to see if your captain seemed to follow the craft I was on. I'm certain you know that it was."

"You are English, monsieur," said Victoire. "England and France are at war. You cannot blame us for trying to discover what an enemy of our country is doing here in Egypt."

"That's a laugh," said Hazlett, his broad face setting into harsh lines. "Enemy of the French, is it?"

"What else would it be?" asked Victoire, truly puzzled. She had expected denial or bravado, but not this bitter indignation.

"You're either very clever or very naive, Madame," said Hazlett. "Not that it matters. I need you and that chit to finish my mission here, and you're not going to stop me. Your masters wouldn't like it if you did."

"What do you mean?" Victoire demanded, feeling very uneasy. Everything was wrong here. This Hazlett was much too sure of himself.

"I'm not part of the British navy, Madame. Sir Sidney Smith saw to that—and may the Devil dine on his liver for it! That overstuffed admiral didn't know what discipline was. How was I to know the lad would crumble under a mere taste of the lash? Men of my crew had stood a hundred without a whimper. Then that damned ensign goes and takes extra grog and I have to make an example of him. How was I to know his uncle was a duke? The Royal Navy has gone to hell and I'm well rid of the lot. Since Smith cashiered me, I have found other employment." He folded his arms and regarded her with sardonic amusement. "The men paying me for this work, Madame, are French."

Hazlett's camp was more than hour away from the place where Murat had left Victoire and Lirylah, and nearer the banks of the Nile. There was an odor of half-rotted vegetation mixed with the overwhelming scent of heady, night-blooming flowers filling the darkness with rich perfume. At another time it might have been pleasant; now it was dreadful.

"I know I am being foolish," Victoire confided to Lirylah as they sat bound back-to-back in a low-slung tent where they had been tied some time before, "but I cannot stop the fear that the crocodiles will come, or rats. You can hear the river." They had been dressed in white *djellabas,* disguising their age and sex; the loose garments settled around them, swathing them in cotton.

"I am more worried about those men," said Lirylah. "They could do anything to us. As it is, my father will be disgraced."

"Impossible," said Victoire, wishing it were so. "You

were brought here under duress. You did not seek these men out, and they have done nothing to you."

"What does that matter? They have had me as their captive." She could not stop one sob, though the rest were choked back. "I have disgraced my family."

"You have done no such thing," said Victoire staunchly. "And if your father thinks you have, I will explain it to him."

"It won't make any difference," said Lirylah. "He will have to cast me out or keep me as a servant. Anything else would bring him into disfavor." She sighed once. "He was afraid this would happen. I didn't listen. I should have."

"Lirylah—" Victoire began, then stopped herself and pulled on her bonds to signal Lirylah to silence as well.

Outside Hazlett was speaking with one of his men, his Egyptian accent hard to make out. The two kept their voices fairly low, making understanding them even more difficult. Another of the men joined them, and their discussion became more of an argument, and in a short time all three men moved away, one of them beginning to shout about money.

"There was no mention of food," said Lirylah; they had not eaten in ten hours and both of them were hungry.

"No, nor of water," said Victoire, forcing herself to think more aggressively. "I don't know how we are going to get out of here," she admitted, "but I know that we must."

"Surely Murat will find us," said Lirylah, the way she spoke his name an act of adoration.

"I hope he will, but we cannot assume it." She tested their bonds again—as she had been testing them since they were tied—and found no more play in them than before. At last she leaned back and looked up at the tent pole to which they were tied. "I wonder . . ." she murmured.

"We can't fight those men, Madame. It is better that we do not try."

"Now there, Lirylah, you are wrong," said Victoire.

"It is forbidden for a woman to raise her hand against a man," Lirylah whispered in despair.

"Perhaps in Egypt, but not in France, and I am a Frenchwoman," said Victoire with a great deal more determination than she actually felt. She twisted her fingers around so that she could touch the tent pole. "It's stout, but I think together we can bring it down. Only, once we do," she said, hoping Lirylah would listen to her carefully, "we will have to move quickly. They will come after us."

Lirylah called on the mercy of Allah, then calmed herself. "What are you planning to do, Madame?" she whispered.

"I think," said Victoire quietly, "I think that if we are very careful, we can move this tent pole out of its seating, and then slide it along until there is enough give for us to be able to slip our bonds beneath it. We should then be able to loosen the knots and get free." It sounded very plausible when she described it; she hoped it would actually work.

"I will try to help," Lirylah promised her, panic just beneath the words.

"Good. It will make you feel less afraid," said Victoire; she needed to steady her nerves as well.

"How long will it take?" Lirylah asked, her voice rising.

"We'll find out," said Victoire, and set about twisting her hands around enough to take hold of the tent pole, at the same time feeling for the tin seating sunk into the ground for it.

"The ropes are cutting into my wrists," said Lirylah, her tone steady.

"And mine," said Victoire as she continued to struggle for a good hold.

"I can't turn my hands, Madame."

"Then help me lift when I tell you," said Victoire, all the while trying to listen for Hazlett and his men. This would be the worst time for them to notice their captives. "We'd best work in silence."

Half an hour later, Lirylah whimpered. "How much longer?"

"A little while," said Victoire, feeling sweat all over her body from her constant struggle with the tent pole. The tension of the canvas made it difficult for her to get sufficient purchase to lift the wood against the ridge of the tent. Her shoulders were beginning to ache and her hands trembled. They would have to get free very soon or not at all.

"My hands are numb," said Lirylah quietly. "I can't close them at all. I can't feel them."

"Wait a little longer," Victoire pleaded, making one last valiant effort to move the tent pole.

And this time, driven by her final effort, the pole did move, just far enough for Victoire to slip it out of the seating. She struggled to hold it steady as it wobbled.

"What happened?" whispered Lirylah.

"We've got it out," Victoire answered softly, wanting to shout it. "Now, if you will slide a little toward . . ." She inched toward the slightly descending slope that led eventually to the Nile.

Lirylah wriggled, doing all that she could to help Victoire move the tent pole far enough to get the thongs that bound them underneath it. "The clothes are . . ."

"Climbing?" suggested Victoire, panting with effort. She felt the *djellaba* slither up her legs as she worked. "We'll lower them when we get out hands free."

"If we are discovered—" whispered Lirylah.

"The least we will have to worry about is an exposure of thigh," said Victoire with asperity, her shoulders and elbows arching as she continued to try to hold the tent pole erect as she moved it aside.

"It could fall," said Lirylah a short while later.

"And that'd attract attention. We mustn't do that until we're able to get away from here." She was drenched in sweat now, but the tent pole was moving a little more easily. If they could get near the edge of it, slip their bonds, and get under the edge before the tent fell, they had a chance of getting away. To distract herself from the exhausting effort she was making, Victoire attempted to determine what time of night it had to be. She decided it could not be much later than eleven o'clock—late enough for someone who rose before dawn—which meant that there was still a chance that Murat was looking for them: he would not call off his search until midnight.

The tent pole jiggered, the crest flapping as the pole was finally eased of slack from the canvas roof.

"Now!" whispered Victoire, nudging Lirylah with her shoulder. "Toward the Nile."

They tugged and sawed with their bonds, and in a few minutes, they had pulled them under the tent pole, releasing the tension on the knots that held them.

"I can't do—" Lirylah said. "My hands—"

"I'll tend to it," said Victoire, her scraped and bloody fingers plucking at the knots, breaking the last one of her nails in the process. She swore and kept on.

Then they were free. Victoire got to her feet on shaking legs and reached for the tent pole to keep it from falling. She felt weak now that she was free, and it was almost more than she could do to keep from lying down to rest. She made herself hold the tent pole and move it back toward the seating.

Lirylah slowly stood, holding out her hands as if she were dizzy. "I still can't feel my hands," she muttered.

"We have to get away," said Victoire. "We'll tend to your hands once we're safe."

"I can't feel them," she said again, holding them out in front of her.

"Be grateful. When the numbness goes they will hurt," said Victoire, deliberately blunt. She tried to lift the tent pole back into the seating but could not quite raise it. After another try, she abandoned the attempt. She shoved the tent pole hard into the sand, then moved back from it. "I hope it will hold."

Lirylah touched her face, her fingers open and stiff. "I have nothing to cover my head."

"No one will see. It's late. By morning we will find a veil for you," She moved nearer the edge of the tent. "If we work together we can pull up the stakes."

"But my hands—" Lirylah protested.

"With our shoulders, not our hands," said Victoire quietly. "Two good pushes and we can be out. The tent will probably fall, but if we run toward the river, we may find help."

"All right," said Lirylah, sounding far from certain.

Victoire knelt down and tugged on Lirylah's sleeve, moving them both to the edge of the tent.

Lirylah followed her. "How long will this take?"

"Not too long," said Victoire, certain that they would either escape or be discovered within the next five minutes. She bent down until she felt the canvas bow and stretch across her back. "Get ready. When I tell you, try to stand up."

"I will," said Lirylah, great determination in her voice.

At Victoire's signal the two women shoved themselves upward against the tent. There was great resistance, and then one side came free, so quickly that Victoire nearly fell over. Lirylah stumbled through the flapping edge into the night.

"Down the hill. Toward the Nile," whispered Victoire urgently.

"Yes," whispered Lirylah, and started to run.

Behind them, the tent tottered and swayed, then fell as the tent pole lost the tension of the canvas.

The rocks and sand scored their feet, and suddenly Lirylah gave a short, high cry. Her foot had been badly cut by a sharp outcropping of stone that was hidden by the dim night shadows.

Behind them was the first alarm. One of the men shouted.

"I can't run," Lirylah protested as Victoire came up to her.

"With my help you can," said Victoire, putting her arm around Lirylah and supporting her, half-hopping, half-running.

There were more yells behind them, and then the report of a pistol.

"Keep running," said Victoire, making her voice quiet so that Hazlett would not be able to aim at the sound of it.

"I . . . Leave me behind," Lirylah whispered, her breath

becoming ragged as she forced herself to lurch along with Victoire.

"No," said Victoire in a way that left no room for dispute. They were nearing the river, and there was the sound of a boat tied to a quay. The river lapped and rubbed at it, and occasionally the boat thudded against the pilings. "We go south here, I think," said Victoire, finding it difficult to speak. "Toward the village."

Another shot was fired, and this time the ball struck a tree close to them.

"They're coming after us," Lirylah whispered, doing everything to keep up. "Where is Murat?"

"Nearby, I pray God," said Victoire, and swore as she stubbed her toes on a length of wood left across the path.

The shouts of the men behind them were louder, and out of the corner of her eye, Victoire could see the bobbing light of a lantern. Hazlett's men had seen Lirylah's blood and were tracking them swiftly.

A third shot was fired, and this time found its mark, striking Lirylah high in the shoulder. The ball made a loud thump as it tore into the woman's flesh.

She screamed, stiffened, and then sagged in Victoire's grasp.

Victoire held on grimly and all but dragged the Egyptian girl along with her, praying that the next ball would not find her.

"They can't be far ahead," called out Hazlett, intending that Victoire should overhear him. "Bring them down."

Then, as all hope was about to vanish, Victoire heard the sound of hoofbeats, and recognized Roustam-Raza's distinctive voice raised to carry through battle. "Over here. There is something over here."

Hazlett's men faltered in their pursuit, looking to their leader for orders.

Victoire managed to pull Lirylah a few steps further, toward a stand of date palms.

"Where in the name of Belial—" Murat shouted from further off than Roustam-Raza.

"Here!" bellowed Roustam-Raza, who appeared suddenly on the narrow track where Victoire had stood the minute before. He was riding a horse Victoire had never seen, and he carried his scimitar at the ready.

The men with Hazlett saw him, too, and fell back as the Mameluke bore down on them.

A moment later Murat appeared on a spotted mare, sabre out and pistol ready. He was about to join with Roustam-Raza when Victoire called to him. He wheeled the mare and rushed back to the date palms where Victoire had tried to find some protection.

"It's Lirylah," she said as Murat hurtled out of the saddle. Now that she had begun, she did not know how to soften the blow. "I fear . . . she has been shot."

In the dark it was not possible to read his face, but his voice changed completely. "Shot?"

"There's a lot of blood," said Victoire, who had seen enough wounds in Larrey's service to realize that this one was very serious.

*"Jesu et Marie,"* he whispered. "Where is she?"

"Just here," said Victoire, and led him the few steps to where Lirylah sat at the base of a date palm, her back against the tree. Victoire stood aside as Murat went down on his knees beside Lirylah.

"You're here," she murmured as Murat touched her. "I knew."

"Oh, my God," he said in despair. He knew that sound of old; the sound of life fading from the body. "Lirylah, no."

"I said you'd come," she said on a sigh. "You would be here." She lifted her hand to touch his face. "You're here."

Murat crossed himself and reached out to pull her into his arms. As he touched the back of her *djellaba,* he felt the hot blood there, and tears welled in his eyes. "Lirylah. Lirylah." He said it as if her name could protect her; he stroked her hair.

"That's . . . so . . ." She smiled, then rested her head in the curve of his shoulder and arm.

"Don't, Lirylah," he urged her, trying to keep her with him a few seconds longer.

She looked up at him. "Stay here."

"Yes, yes, my love. Yes, little dove." His voice was thick with tears and grief.

Victoire moved a few steps away, afraid of intruding on them.

This time when Lirylah smiled, a line of blood trailed from the corner of her mouth. "It's almost . . ." She coughed once. "Done."

For more than two minutes, Murat remained completely still, holding Lirylah as if she were yet breathing. Then, very slowly, he started to rock her, cradling her close, gently. And as he rocked her, he wept.

It was more than an hour before Victoire could persuade Murat to release Lirylah. And when he did there was a darkness in his face, an implacable rage in his eyes. Heedless of the blood that dappled his clothing, he pushed past Victoire and strode to where Roustam-Raza had gathered Hazlett and his men together. He looked over them, something wild growing within him. "Who did it?" he asked in a voice so tight and rough that he sounded like a stranger.

"The Arab girl?" Hazlett drawled. "Or the French one?"

"Do you say it didn't matter?" Murat demanded, drawing his sabre as he started toward Hazlett. He did not wait for an answer, but struck down savagely, once, twice. Blood erupted from two deep, mortal wounds and Hazlett died before his body struck the sand. In three strokes, one of his men fell beside him.

By the time Roustam-Raza reached Murat and grabbed him from behind, a third man was dead and Murat was keening to the darkest part of the night.

Not long after the first morning call to prayer, Roustam-Raza buried Hazlett and his two men, and arranged for a proper burial for Lirylah. He went about his tasks silently, taking pains to avoid Murat, who stood at the edge of the Nile, staring across at the rising sun as if he wanted to drown it in darkness forever.

"Do you want anything?" Victoire asked him when at last she dared to approach him.

"Nothing you can do," he answered distantly.

Victoire did not bristle at the rebuke. "I wish I could say something for consolation, Joachim."

He wiped his eyes with the back of his hand. "You can't."

She wanted to remain with him, but the look in his brown eyes was cold and hard as rock. She moved a little distance away, noticing for the first time how very sore she felt all over.

Roustam-Raza was waiting for her now that he had returned from the village. "It is arranged," he said to Victoire. "Shall I tell Murat?"

"I don't know," said Victoire seriously. "Perhaps later, when he is not so filled with pain."

"That may be some time," said Roustam-Raza. "To feel such passion for one woman," he added. "It isn't the way of men to make such idols of women."

"It's the way of this man," corrected Victoire thoughtfully. "And I feel for him because of it."

Roustam-Raza shook his head. "There is food. We have to leave soon. Come and eat."

"Yes," agreed Victoire, knowing how sensible the suggestion was. "Find something we can carry downriver with us. Murat will not eat now, but later we must."

As he guided Victoire toward the open hut where the farmer had food waiting, Roustam-Raza said, "For a woman, she was very brave. Allah does not require much of women, but that they serve men and have many sons. But this woman, she was very brave."

Victoire realized that this was a rare encomium, and did not answer as sharply as she would had someone other than Roustam-Raza spoken them. "She *was* a brave woman. There are many Frenchwomen who would not have shown her courage had they been in her place."

They had reached the hut, and the farmer bowed before hurrying off to tend his goats. Two of his wives brought out trays of broiled chopped goat with onions, allspice, cinnamon, and pepper. Flat loves of bread were offered along with the meat, and Victoire made herself eat a good portion, expressing her thanks with every bite. When she was through, she drank two cups of the hot, sweet tea and watched as the farmer's two wives finished up the leftovers.

"Is that what they eat? What their husband and guests leave behind?" she asked Roustam-Raza as they made their way back toward the river, a sack of bread and sweetmeats slung over his shoulder.

Roustam-Raza looked down at her. "Of course," he said, as if that should be obvious to everyone.

"How very shortsighted," said Victoire. Her shoulders still hurt and she was very tired. For once she was looking forward to the afternoon nap that was part of life in Egypt.

"Murat is not himself," said Roustam-Raza as they neared the place they had left the bereaved Frenchman.

"And he will not be for some time, I fear," said Victoire. She shook her head. "It would have been easier if she had been his mistress. Not that he would have made her his mistress, you understand," she added quickly, "but if it had been possible, he would not be left with the emptiness of what they did not have."

Roustam-Raza shook his head in bafflement. "There are other women. Even Christians can have other women, can't they?"

"Yes," said Victoire. "But it isn't his faith that's injured—it is his heart." She looked ahead and saw that Murat had not moved; he still stood staring out over the river, his eyes fixed on a distant place.

# 11

THE DHOW WAS carrying wood from far up the Nile, beyond the limits of French exploration inland, and it made slower progress down the Nile than it would have with a lighter load. Murat had chosen it, claiming that he trusted the captain more than the others he had interviewed. With the scepter aboard, he wanted to be confident of the crew. Ordinarily he would fret at such a pace, but on this part of the voyage he made no complaint.

Victoire, watching him standing by the curve of the huge lateen sail, suspected he needed time to himself, to mourn Lirylah. She did not press him to confide in her, but made every effort to remain near at hand, in case he should wish to unburden himself.

She wrote to Vernet the first evening they were on the river.

> For, my dearest husband, I have never seen Murat in so bleak a state. He has endured disappointment and hardship with cheerful courage. In all our chasing and seeking, he has been the best comrade anyone could want. But the loss of that one girl—a girl he would not have been permitted to have as his own—has wounded him as no enemy fire could do. He does not even care how he looks, still wearing the same torn tunic he had on that night.
>
> Yet, for all the sympathy I have for his grief, I am also vexed with him, for in killing Hazlett, he has destroyed a witness who could have been most beneficial

to you. Hazlett would have provided the information that would have exonerated you completely. I fear that without the testimony of that Englishman, it will be a very difficult matter to discover who in the government has betrayed Napoleon, and you along with him. Roustam-Raza, who does not understand our way of laws, has suggested that the tongues be cut out of those who lie and we would have the truth soon enough. I cannot entirely object to his recommendation.

I ask again that you forgive my tardiness in writing to you, but the exigencies of this journey have made it impossible for me to entrust any correspondence to a responsible courier. I estimate that we should be back in camp before two weeks are gone; very likely less, barring any unforeseen developments. Now that we are coming close to Memphis, I await the chance to find a French courier once again who can bring me news of you. Until I started this letter, I could not admit how much I've missed you. Now that the words are before me, I long for you as a soldier with an empty sleeve must long for his arm. I have been at pains to think only kindly, happy thoughts of you, my love, to comfort me as we pursued the scepter. Now that we have it in hand, I can only trust that justice will be served, with or without Hazlett, and that we will be reunited before Easter.

Murat tells me that he does not regret killing Hazlett and his men; he would do it again a dozen times over and it would not avenge Lirylah. Poor man, to know his love only in her absence. I fear he will never again allow himself to trust to his emotions. Already he talks about making only a political marriage, one where he cannot be hurt.

I will write again soon, or add to this, as it happens.

On the sixth day they made Memphis, and Victoire handed the courier there a letter that had grown to fifteen crossed pages. At the French headquarters, two Carabinier captains waited for their general, the younger complaining that they had been there since before Christmas, and now, with Epiphany at hand, they were late joining the rest of the troop.

"Where are we bound?" asked Murat when his men presented themselves. He made no apology or explanation for his appearance, either his Greek clothing and haircut, or his remoteness.

"The army is going to Syria," said the older captain. "There are plans to move along the coast until we control all the land. Already our scouts have reached to the city of Acre. Berthier says it was the ancient key to all the Holy Lands. The desert between is full of enemies. You are to take your men and go south, joining with Kleber. There are Mamelukes still to be brought to heel." He noticed Roustam-Raza then and looked aside.

"If they are in need of learning a lesson, so be it," said Murat in the same distant way. "I relish the task."

The younger stared at him. "You . . . you might want to . . . find a fresh uniform, sir."

Murat looked down at his clothes, at the bloodstains that still marred the linen tunic he wore. "I suppose so." He straightened up. "I'll need a valet, if you can arrange for one. If not, then any steward you can spare will do." He looked around the villa the French had commandeered as their own. "I will want these clothes returned to me." He fingered his chin. "And I suppose I must have a barber. Arrange it." He was about to leave the withdrawing room when he noticed Victoire standing with Roustam-Raza at the far side of the chamber. "Madame," he said to her with a hint of a bow.

"General Murat," she replied, dropping him a curtsy and feeling very shabby in her worn hunting habit.

Reluctantly Murat came across the room to her, his face unreadable. "You were most diligent in our quest, and I have been a churl to you. You must accept my apology."

"Certainly," she said, more baffled than ever.

"I will have to file a dispatch on our activities. You may rest assured that you will receive credit for your intrepid devotion to duty and your husband." He sounded like a stranger, and she watched him more closely. "I am in your debt, Madame, however awkwardly I may discharge the obligation. Our cause would not have succeeded without you; indeed, there is every reason to suppose that we might not have lived to return. You may believe me at any time your most obedient servant." He took her hand and bowed over it in form.

He's saving my reputation, thought Victoire as she accepted this gesture with what grace she could muster. He is putting an end to gossip before it starts. "I am most highly complimented, Murat," she said, wishing she could speak frankly to him, offering the consolation of their friendship instead of this stilted good manners.

"I have given Roustam-Raza the thing we are returning to Napoleon, and I must rely on your devotion still further, to deliver it once again to Napoleon, or failing that, to Berthier. An account of how we came to reclaim it will be included in my morning dispatch." He looked at her, and for a few seconds tears stood in his eyes. "I have known many fine men who were less stalwart comrades-at-arms than you have been, Madame Vernet. Were you a man, you would surely have been elected an officer by now." His face remained impassive, but his eyes showed greater pain. "I must ask another favor, one I have no right to ask."

Victoire nodded. "I will send the message, Murat. It had better come from me in any case, I should think," she said, dreading what she would have to say to Kemal Nusair. "He would want to know . . ." She lost track of what she was saying. "Murat, you could not have anticipated," she said to him. "We knew there was a risk, but we could not anticipate . . ."

"I ought to have anticipated. I should have been better prepared. We knew the marine guard was butchered; the danger was clear. If one of us had to die, why, in the name of everything holy, did it have to be her?" His voice was very low, so that his men on the other side of the room could not hear him. He stared at her, his features like a skull. "I should not have permitted her to come with us."

"She wished to come, Murat," said Victoire as gently as

she could, and motioned to Roustam-Raza to distract the two captains on the other side of the room. "You didn't force her, and she knew that it might be dangerous to be with you; there is no reason for you to castigate yourself."

"Isn't there?" He shook his head. "I have tried to convince myself that it was only a fancy of mine, attaching myself to an Egyptian girl. I tell myself it is like the girls who captivated me while I was a seminarian, testing my faith with their loveliness. But it was not my vanity or my lust she touched; she touched my soul." He stared down at his worn, dusty boots. "How can I continue to live when she is dead?"

"She would not return to life if you died," said Victoire as gently as she could. "She would not wish you to make yourself less to no purpose."

"But would it be to no purpose?" He shook his head. "Don't bother to answer. I ask myself every hour and there is no answer."

"Then consider this, Murat," Victoire said more sternly. "An officer leading men into battle while he is seeking death is more dangerous to them than a field of enemy forces. You may not wish to live, but I suspect most of your men do."

He turned away from her as if she had slapped him, then looked back.

"You're right." He sighed, and briefly seemed himself again. "I wish I were going with you to return the scepter. I know that's foolish—it is safe with you and Roustam-Raza now that we are back in French territory. Yet I sense that something will be severed when you leave, and I regret that."

"It need not be severed on my account," said Victoire very carefully.

"Nor on mine," he replied, not meeting her eyes.

"Then I will look forward to that time when we meet again, Murat," she said, giving the appearance of good cheer. "And I will pray for your safety and swift return."

His desolate brown eyes met her blue ones. "I wish I could pray. But the words stick in my throat."

"Then I will do it for you," she said. "It may be unfashionable, but you know in what regard I hold fashion." She fingered the frayed lapel of her habit.

He attempted a smile and managed it a little better than before. "With such an ensemble. Yes, I surely do." He bowed once more, this time less perfectly, and stepped back. "I meant it, Victoire. Little though I may show it, I am in your debt."

"We will reach Cairo by sunset, if the wind does not pick up," said Roustam-Raza with satisfaction as he studied the banks of the Nile, his eyes shaded against the morning sun. Since they had cast off three hours ago he had been pointing out landmarks that were unfamiliar to Victoire. "Then it is a simple matter to present the . . . object to Berthier. He will have to reexamine the case against your husband." He came and stood next to Victoire. "He will do that, won't he?"

"I hope so," said Victoire, who was feeling more tired than she wanted to admit. Now that they were almost finished with their task, she had to fight off an unfamiliar lethargy that robbed her of purpose.

"There can be no doubt," said Roustam-Raza, one hand going to the hilt of his scimitar. "You have returned the scepter, they will return your husband with honor."

In spite of her own lowering mood, Victoire smiled at Roustam-Raza's naive assumption. "If the scepter is sufficient to convince them that my husband had no part in the death of the marine guard and was not the thief, then his honor will be restored. If Berthier permits it." She stretched, finding the morning sun burdensome on her burned arms. "I have to admit I miss Murat. And Lirylah."

Roustam-Raza said nothing for a short time, then pointed out a pile of rubble on the west bank of the river. "They say that was once a sphinx. But they say that about many piles of ancient rocks."

Victoire accepted this diversion and ventured nothing more about Murat and Lirylah, giving herself over to the pleasure of letting Roustam-Raza describe the various ruins along the banks of the Nile.

At midday, the felucca pulled to the shallows of the east bank and anchored there while the crew slept through the heat of the day. Insects droned over the water and in the reeds that stood along the banks, and small birds busied themselves catching them. Not far off two goats were tethered, bleating and occasionally butting heads.

"You should lie down, Madame," said Roustam-Raza, coming down the deck to where she stood. "It is going to be a very long day."

"Yes," she agreed quietly. "If we reach Cairo."

"They tell me it's certain," said Roustam-Raza, standing beside her. "And then we will find proper escort to return you to the camp."

"Yes," she said again.

Roustam-Raza regarded her closely. "What is it that troubles you, Madame?"

She shook her head. "I don't know. I have misgivings, but ... I fear that Berthier won't believe my account of how we recovered the scepter. I doubt he will accept any account of Hazlett. He might decide that this is nothing more than a clever ploy." She took a long breath. "It's foolishness to invite trouble, but ..."

"They will believe what you say, because I will say it as well," Roustam-Raza informed her. "They will have to believe what I tell them, for I will swear it with my hand on the Quran."

"I hope you prove right," said Victoire, wiping her brow with the remnants of her handkerchief. "It haunts me. I dislike puzzles when necessary information is held back. Why hold it back?" She made a gesture as if to shove her unpleasant thoughts away. "If only I could have learned who paid Hazlett."

"That is a misfortune," agreed Roustam-Raza. "But standing in the hot sun will not answer the question. You need to rest. You will need to be ready to present yourself to the garrison leader this evening, and if you remain here on deck, you will not be." He paused. "I will keep watch, and take my rest later, when we're under way again."

She allowed herself to be persuaded. "All right. I'll lie down for an hour. I suppose that means using that horrid little cabin?"

"And I will sit outside the door," said Roustam-Raza. "Open the window on the river side and you will feel a little cooler."

"That's not saying much," she remarked as she ducked down the narrow companionway. Here there was the pervasive smell of tar and wet wood, and the bitter-rich scent of the Nile. The passage was dark and narrow, just large enough for single file: Roustam-Raza walked behind her, his hand still on the hilt of his scimitar.

The cabin she had been assigned was not much larger than an armoire, with most of the room being taken up by the rope-sprung cot. A single lantern served to light the cabin at night. In one corner a worn canvas bag stood open, containing her night-rail, the *djellaba* Hazlett had provided her, and her other riding habit. Victoire was heartily sick of them.

On impulse she took off her habit and drew on the *djellaba*. It was cooler and less constricting than the habit. She decided she would sponge off the worst stains on the habit before she donned it again. No matter what I do, she told herself, I will not make a good appearance, not in those clothes. Disheartened, she opened the window and stared out at the bronze surface of the river fretted with deep blue. At another time, she thought, this would be pretty. She lay back on the cot and dutifully closed her eyes, convinced that she would not be able to sleep.

But she must have dozed, for a sudden scuffle in the passageway roused her, bringing her out of a fragment of dream where she was lost in an endless canyon, looking for someone or something that constantly eluded her.

Roustam-Raza shouted from the other side of the door. "Treachery!"

This brought Victoire to her full senses. She sat up, reaching toward the door to secure the bolt.

She was an instant too late. Roustam-Raza crashed into the room, his scimitar out, his dagger at the ready. He put himself between the three armed men who had crowded into the passage and Victoire.

"These are the Pasha's men, Madame," Roustam-Raza said breathlessly. "They have sent the crew away on the Pasha's orders."

"The Pasha sent you as well."

"I have sworn on the Quran to serve Napoleon. It seems this Pasha is unworthy and I could not serve him further even if that were not so."

Victoire closed her eyes in distress. Her own dirk was in with her clothes and useless to her now. "What do they want?"

"The scepter," said Roustam-Raza, falling silent as one of the men rattled off orders to them. "He says that if we will give him the scepter, we will be permitted to continue on our way. If we do not give him the scepter, he will kill us."

"He may kill us anyway," said Victoire somberly.

"Yes, that is very possible," said Roustam-Raza.

Another one of the Pasha's men was speaking, his tone angry and his words harsh.

"He says that the scepter rightfully belongs to the Pasha and it is necessary to return it to him." Roustam-Raza sneered. "They use a robber's excuse for stealing."

"The scepter rightfully belongs to one of the ancient kings if it belongs to anyone," said Victoire. "But we're honor bound to return it to Napoleon Buonaparte."

At the sound of that name the first of the Pasha's men spat and uttered what was clearly a curse. He brought his scimitar up as if he intended to use it on her.

"What do you think, Roustam-Raza?" asked Victoire, doing her best to remain calm though her pulse raced.

"I think we had best escape or expect to feed the Nile fish," he answered her. "They would be foolish to let us live once they have the scepter."

She looked startled. "Are you going to give it to them?"

"They will take it in any case," he said. "If I give it to

them, we may catch them off-guard." He then spoke to the men in Egyptian before adding to Victoire, "They grow suspicious easily and if I speak with you too often, they will assume we are conspiring."

"As well they might, since we are," said Victoire, finding the sweltering afternoon overwhelming. "What do you suggest?"

Instead of answering her, Roustam-Raza went on at some length to the Pasha's men. At last he said to her, "I will distract them, telling them that the scepter is in my quarters. As soon as their attention is diverted, dive out the window. I will meet you downstream where the asses are brought to drink."

"Dive?" she repeated. "Into the Nile?" All of Larrey's warnings about the danger of Nile water came back to her in a rush. The thought of the dangerous animalcules and effluvia all but stopped the breath in her throat.

"They will not be able to catch you." Roustam-Raza glared at her ferociously. "As soon as I go to the door."

She suppressed a shudder. "All right," she said, making up her mind. "And the scepter?"

"We will recover it later," he promised her. "Be ready." With that he said a number of terse things to her in Egyptian and then swung around, addressing the Pasha's men, indicating the door.

Victoire rose on her knees on the cot, feeling the ropes beneath the thin mattress dig into her knees. She hoped that she did not look suspect to the Pasha's men.

But those men were not looking at her at all, for it was disgraceful to look on a woman's unveiled face. They were relieved to give their attention to Roustam-Raza and spare themselves and Victoire the shame of their stares.

Roustam-Raza stepped through the door, the Pasha's men close behind him.

And Victoire stood up unsteadily and wriggled out through the window, dropping headfirst into the Nile.

The river was faster than she expected, and the water less clear than she had thought it would be. Her *djellaba*, loose though it was, was an encumbrance to swimming;

she floundered as the current bore her away from the felucca, tugging her toward the middle of the river. She kept her head up and gasped for breath, coughing as water splashed over her face and mouth. God and the Saints! what was she drinking? she wondered.

A face appeared in the window she had escaped through, and angry shouts followed her as she continued to slide further away from the boat. She realized that she must swim more strongly if she was not to drown and be swept down the river and her body out to sea. She paddled and kicked, rising up to get deep breaths every eighth stroke. Fighting the current sapped her strength at once, and the sun's glare made it hard to see the eastern bank clearly. With dogged determination she continued to paddle.

It seemed to Victoire that she had been in the river for hours. Whatever dreadful things lurked in the water, she was surely filled with all of them. She had swallowed more of the Nile than she had thought possible, and her garments were heavy with it. Her arms and legs moved automatically now, her will all but exhausted and only her persevering nature keeping her afloat. From time to time she looked for a herd of white asses. That was where Roustam-Raza said she should come ashore. She repeated those instructions over in her mind, trying to make sense of them, and all the while she continued to paddle and kick, paddle and kick, rising up for breath on every eighth stroke.

A lacy shadow of palm trees fell on the water, offering Victoire the first respite from the surface shine. She rose out of the water enough to look around, and was amazed to see that she was much closer to the shore than she had thought. With renewed vigor, she swam toward the palm trees, determined to ignore the exhaustion that was overtaking her. She was still drifting northward in the hold of the current, but she no longer felt caught in its inexorable grip, and she began to look for a place where asses drank.

In less than ten minutes she found it; she cried out in relief and surprise. Her arms trembled from the effort, but she continued on toward the shore, her waterlogged clothes dragging at her as much as the river.

Two brown Egyptian boys watched in amazement as she slogged out of the river, half-swimming, half-wading ashore. At last she stood unsteadily on the bank of the Nile, the two Egyptian boys and half a dozen white asses regarding her in bewilderment.

Victoire used one of the few Egyptian phrases she knew: "May Allah bring you riches, favor, and many sons."

One of the Egyptian boys made the sign against the Evil Eye, the other one started to run away.

"No," called out Victoire, though she knew they would not understand her. "I . . . I need help." She took a couple uncertain steps and watched the boys retreat. As soon as she reached the nearest palm, she leaned against it, hungry for its support. Her sodden *djellaba* enveloped her in yards of linen that now seemed unbearably heavy. Portions clung to her body, obviously embarrassing the youths. She could feel her hair, no longer confined in a fashionable knot on the crown of her head, cascade around her shoulders.

A short while later there was a thrashing in the reeds and low bushes just south of the palms. Victoire chided herself for having found no weapon, but knew she lacked the strength to use anything but a pistol. She moved around the trunk of the tree, hoping for better protection.

Roustam-Raza appeared, holding the two boys by the scruff of the neck. He was issuing gruff orders to them, shaking them as he did.

Victoire sighed, for the first time feeling that she was safe. "Over here," she called out, and then, to her intense embarrassment, she burst into tears.

The Mameluke released his small captives and rushed to where Victoire was hiding. "Where are you hurt?" he demanded.

She shook her head twice before she was able to say, "I'm not hurt. Just tired. And this is idiotic." Her own condemnation did not stop her tears.

Roustam-Raza folded his arms. "Yes, it is," he said emphatically. "There is no reason to weep if you are not hurt and you are safe."

"I know," she wailed.

He stared at her, shaking his head. "We ought to be gone from here soon."

She nodded, and made herself stop crying, swallowing hard against the sobs that still threatened to overcome her. "I'll be all right now," she promised Roustam-Raza, doing her best to stand up straight. She realized what a bedraggled sight she was, and checked her impulse to weep again.

"There is another boat, a small boat. We can ride it to Cairo, or so they have promised me." He watched her take a few steps. "You will be stronger shortly."

"Yes, I will," she said, in spite of inner misgivings.

He pointed to a path through the reeds. "There is a road not far from here. People will stare, but that should not concern you now. We must inform Napoleon that the Pasha has taken the scepter as soon as possible."

She nodded and tried to gather up the hem of the *djellaba.* "It will dry in the sun."

"And it will keep you cool while it does," said Roustam-Raza in approval. "Egyptian women could not do this, but you are French, as anyone who sees your hair will know." He indicated the path again. "I will go ahead. It isn't fitting for a man to walk behind a woman on the road."

"Of course," she said, thinking it was all of a piece. She squared her shoulders. "Lead the way, then."

With an approving nod, Roustam-Raza strode ahead of her through the bulrushes.

"It was fortunate that passage was so narrow," said Roustam-Raza a little later as they approached the square pier where a boat was tied up. "I was able to kick the leader back against the other two, and while they struggled to untangle themselves, I ran from the boat and hid by the shore. They did not bother searching for me; they had what they came for, and that was all that mattered to them."

"So you think they're taking the scepter to the Pasha?" asked Victoire as they stepped onto the uneven planking.

"That was their plan. Why should they not do it?" He called out a greeting, and was answered quickly by a convoluted blessing from the owner of the boat. "I have already paid the man," Roustam-Raza confided to Victoire.

"And you expected him to wait for you because of that?" Victoire guessed.

"Not necessarily. I expect him to demand more of us now that he is aware that I have gold." He gave a single, knowing nod to Victoire as he set foot on the plank that led to the boat. He reeled off a long series of good wishes and blessings on the owner of the boat, all the while gesturing to Victoire to come aboard.

Aching with fatigue, Victoire did just that.

Dusk had fallen by the time the boat tied up at the smallest of the Cairo docks. The owner of the boat made one last attempt to coax a few more gold coins from Roustam-Raza, then gave it up. He had already doubled his fee and was well pleased at the price he had got.

"I am going to find cloth for a veil, Madame," said Roustam-Raza as they left the boat. "Under the circumstances, it would be best if you covered your hair and face."

Victoire had recovered a little, and she realized that Roustam-Raza's suggestion was prudent. "Yes." She stayed close behind him as he started into the warren of dockside streets. For the moment she ducked her head and did her best to let her hair shield her face. It was a poor compromise, but it would have to do.

Three blocks later Roustam-Raza found a stall where lengths of silk were sold. He purchased one without much regard to its color, and handed it to Victoire. "Place it over your head."

She straightened up and did as he told her, feeling strangely safer now that she was not quite so clearly a foreign woman in these narrow streets. "We must go to the garrison at once," she told Roustam-Raza.

"To make our report," he seconded, and pushed his way through the crowd, motioning to Victoire to keep close behind him. "We have lost enough treasure for one day," he declared as they went.

"And you say that the men who took the sceptor were Pasha's men?" asked Captain Echevue, his manner making it very clear that he considered the whole tale Victoire had told him to be a fabrication.

"I say that they are," Roustam-Raza maintained, giving the captain one of his most murderous stares.

"And they took this treasure from you? The treasure which was taken from Napoleon's spoils after the battle?" His voice rose in disbelief. "Madame, I am sorry for whatever misfortune has brought you to this terrible state, but surely you must understand that I cannot ... How can I give any credence to a story so preposterous?"

"But it isn't preposterous," Victoire insisted, her voice almost breaking with emotion. "If he were here General Joachim Murat would vouch for me."

"And you had a letter to that effect, but lost it when you were forced to dive into the Nile," Captain Echevue finished for her. "Most intrepid, I'm sure."

Victoire wanted to scream, but she controlled the urge. "Would you rather I present you with a more credible lie? I am telling you the truth, and Roustam-Raza knows it to be the truth."

"A Mameluke's word ... well, it is an original notion." He was looking at Victoire and did not see the rage that crossed Roustam-Raza's features.

Roustam-Raza shoved his shoulder between Captain Echevue and Victoire, facing the officer as he said, "Bring the Quran and I will tell the whole story to you again, with Allah as my bond and witness. We were in the company of General Murat until he was ordered to join Colonel Kleber. Send a courier after him and obtain his testimony, if you must. Or send word to Berthier, and ask him to hear me out."

Captain Echevue was put off by this daunting assertion. He strove to put more distance between himself and Roustam-Raza, all the while trying to restore his own dignity with a deprecating cough. "I will send word to Berthier at once, you need have no fear of that. And I will detain you here until sense can be made of your story."

"In the meantime, the Pasha hides the scepter," said Victoire flatly. "I hope you will not have to answer for that."

Captain Echevue pursed his lips. "You tell me it is the Pasha who has arranged this. But Roustam-Raza is a Mameluke, the gift of the Pasha. Is it possible that he might have wanted to—"

He got no further. Roustam-Raza reached out and seized the front of Captain Echevue's pelisse. "I am sworn to Napoleon while there is breath in my body, and I am his man and no other's. If you doubt me, then make your claim where I may seek retribution for this lie you speak of me."

Now Captain Echevue was shaken. He managed to pry Roustam-Raza's fingers off his clothes. He did not speak for well over a minute while he neatened the front of his pelisse. "I will send word to Berthier at once. But I warn you: you had better have a good account to render. Berthier is not the sort of man to take kindly to deception." With that, he signalled the guard at his door. "See that these two have somewhere to clean up. And do something about that deplorable . . . thing! she is wearing."

Victoire plucked at the *djellaba*. No doubt the captain was right and she ought to have proper women's clothes. She rose from the upholstered bench where she had been sitting and addressed Captain Echevue as politely as she could. "Thank you. I have clothes in camp. So long as you are sending word to Berthier, perhaps you would be kind enough to ask Larrey as well if he could spare a moment or two from tending the wounded to arrange a valise of clothing for me?"

There was more caution in Captain Echevue's eyes. "How do you know Larrey?"

"I have tended wounded under his supervision, as most officers' wives do," she answered directly, and saw that at last she had scored a point.

But Captain Echevue was reluctant to concede it. "If it seems appropriate, I will."

Victoire studied him, then said, "Some arrangement of that sort must be made, or I'll have to continue to wear this Egyptian garment."

Roustam-Raza looked from one to the other, moving a step nearer to Victoire.

Captain Echevue capitulated. "Very well, I'll inquire about other clothes."

Victoire curtsied, knowing not to press her advantage. "Thank you."

## 12

Most of the garrison had retired for the night; only guards patrolled the darkened halls. On the second floor in a salon not far from the kitchen a few officers remained over hands of piquet; the rest had retired more than an hour before.

Roustam-Raza had established himself on a pallet outside Victoire's door, and was very nearly asleep when he heard a tap from the inside. He sat up at once, scimitar ready, and opened the door a crack. "Madame?"

"I need you to find me one of the page's trousers—preferably a pair that will fit, and nothing French." She gave him the instructions as if there were nothing odd about them.

"What?" he demanded, contriving not to raise his voice.

"I need a pair of page's trousers. I have the proper Greek shirt, but without the trousers ..." She did not wheedle—that would be useless with the Mameluke.

"And why would you want trousers, Madame, now that we are back in Cairo?" he challenged her.

"Because I want to see where the Pasha's men have gone. If we know they are at the palace, then we will know where to search for the scepter." Her voice was steady, as if her outrageous proposition were no more shocking than a stroll in the park.

Roustam-Raza swore comprehensively in Egyptian.

"I must do this, Roustam-Raza, and I will do it with or without your help. But it would be easier—and safer—if you were to assist me." She let him have some time to consider the implications. "Will you do this for me, Roustam-Raza?"

"No decent Muslim would help in such an insane and improper scheme," he told her. "What you suggest is appalling."

"My husband will be dismissed in dishonor if the scepter is not returned. I have it in my power to assist him. What else am I to do?" she inquired. "If I were a Muslim woman, I would not do this, but I am a Christian, and my duty is clear."

Roustam-Raza gave a long, slow sigh. "Trousers, you say?"

"I thought if I dressed like a Greek eunuch again, I might be able to get close enough to the palace to learn something," she said.

"More than you want to," Roustam-Raza pointed out. "Eunuchs of that sort are more preferred than women by many. If one of the Pasha's guards desired you, you would be doubly lost, and we would be helpless to save you."

It was Victoire's turn to sigh. "I've heard tales about the way these men are. If they attempted to . . . to detain me, I would reveal that I am a Christian woman."

"And you would be sent to the hareem, and would not be allowed out again, no matter what anyone said. Napoleon has no power inside the palace, and no woman who enters the hareem leaves it except as a corpse." He spoke bluntly in the hope that he could dissuade her.

"I will have to be careful," she said. "And I will be, Roustam-Raza. I am not a flighty girl, and I know there is danger."

Roustam-Raza turned his eyes toward the ceiling. "If I do not get the trousers you will find a way to do this mad thing, anyway, won't you?" He did not need an answer from her.

"I must, Roustam-Raza."

He knew he could not convince her to abandon her plan. "Give me an hour then. And do not leave that chamber until I return. If you do leave, I will not help you. Is that understood?"

"Yes." She sounded excited, and this made him wary.

"I'll come with you, as far as I am allowed. Now that I am Napoleon's man, I am not permitted to enter the palace, but with Napoleon himself." He sheathed his scimitar. "One hour, Madame Vernet. And I will do what I can for you."

"I'm grateful, Roustam-Raza," she said, and listened to the sound of his footsteps fading in the hall.

She then went to get her ewer and basin. She needed to bathe and wash her hair before Roustam-Raza returned. She would also need a little charcoal to pat onto her jaw and upper lip so that it would appear that she had a wisp of beard, as a few of the eunuchs did. This was one occasion, she thought, that she did not mind that her breasts were small, for it made her pose as a eunuch more convincing. She selected the rose-scented soap the garrison had provided her, and poured water into the basin, finding a sponge and a towel in the top drawer of the commode.

"How did you manage to persuade me to this," Roustam-Raza complained as they strode through the streets of Cairo not long after midnight. "Only thieves and murderers are abroad at this hour."

"And which are we?" she asked brightly, determined not to let his gloom touch her. "Thieves, I suppose, if we are trying to locate the scepter. Since the Pasha claims it as his own, and we intend to take it back, now or another time—"

"You are not to steal from the Pasha, Madame," said Roustam-Raza with force.

"No, certainly not." She said it much too willingly and too quickly for him to be anything other than suspicious. Sensing his reservations, she went on, "I wouldn't know where to find the scepter in any case, so the whole question is moot."

"I am pleased that you admit it," said Roustam-Raza, his stride loosening. "I will take you to near the kitchens. At this time of night it is the only place you can be safe, and my presence will not be noticed. I will not compromise my position, and you will be able to hear the servants and slaves gossip. That is your intention, isn't it?"

"I'd like to find the men who took the scepter," she reminded him. "But at this hour, that isn't likely." She changed from French to Greek. "From here on, this would be the wiser language."

"I do not speak it as well," said Roustam-Raza in that tongue. "But you are right."

They were nearing the palace now, and the surroundings were subtly grander: the streets somewhat wider, the housefronts in excellent repair, with more ornaments of worked iron and brass.

"The kitchens are opposite the stables," said Roustam-Raza, his Greek harsh and guttural, more Arabic than Greek in sound. "There are gardens between them."

"Very sensible," said Victoire. "Keep the midden away from the food. There are fewer flies on the meat. Although in this country, there are flies everywhere," she added as she considered the question. Little though she wanted to admit it, now that she was close to the palace, she was beginning to be scared. Roustam-Raza's warnings had taken on new credibility as they approached the imposing walls.

"Don't slow down," said Roustam-Raza as they reached the open square in front of the main gates. "The guards will detain you if they see you linger here."

"Yes," she said, permitting him to direct her around to the left, toward the kitchens. "I had no idea the palace was so large," she confessed as they walked.

"Keep that in mind," he recommended. "I would not think the less of you if you decide to put aside this venture."

"I would think the less of myself," said Victoire.

"Greeks," he said with heavy sarcasm, "are very proud."

"Indeed Greeks are," she answered in the same tone.

As they walked along the walls, Roustam-Raza told her, "It is not wise to look up. The guards could detain you for that, as well. They would say that you are spying on them."

"How absurd," she said.

"Isn't it. And when we reach the kitchens, remember that many of the servants and slaves know some Greek. And French." He walked a little slower. "You will need some pretext to be there."

"I suppose I will," she said, much struck.

"You might be carrying a message. You have delivered it and are waiting for a reply, or you have been sent to get a reply. Yes, that would be better. If you are waiting on one of the Pasha's advisors, it would be reasonable for you to remain in the kitchen area." He frowned. "A Greek eunuch might be the servant of . . . oh, any number of important men. Say you are the servant of a foundry master. You are waiting for official permission for your master to sell cannon to the Infidels." He rubbed his hands together. "There's enough of that going on, and it makes sense you being here at night."

"I'm the servant of a foundry master. Where is the foundry?" She glanced at him. "In case I'm asked."

"The foundry is in Ausim. That's close enough to Cairo, and to the French." He indicated two gates, one of which stood open. "If you go through that door, you are beyond me. Is that understood?"

"Yes, yes, I understand," she said with exaggerated patience. "But if I enter the kitchen yard, you'll be able to watch me, and I'll listen. It makes better sense for a messenger to be inside the gate, doesn't it? If I were going to stay outside, I might as well be at the front of the palace."

He glowered. "True enough." Although he was filled with misgiving, he nodded once. "The kitchen yard, and only the kitchen yard. If you are apprehended—"

"I know, I'm lost." She said it lightly enough, but the impact of it struck her at last. If she were caught inside the palace, she would have to remain there for the rest of her life. For a moment it was difficult to breathe, and then she recovered herself. "I'll be careful," she promised him.

He made a gesture that indicated he could not actually believe her. Ominously Victoire remembered how equally optimistic she had been at the start of their journey down the Nile.

She went to the gate, peering in to make note of the activity there. At this hour very little was going on. A girl with a scarred face—possibly Turkish—sat peeling onions at the entrance to what Victoire supposed was the pantry. Beyond her a thin young man was sweeping the cobblestones, his pleasant face vacant. Inside the kitchen there was some activity, but Victoire could not see it clearly. She nodded toward Roustam-Raza, and slipped through the gate.

She had not been in the courtyard for more than three minutes when a young man in palace livery came into the courtyard, calling out for one of the nighttime cooks.

"I want coffee," he ordered when one of the servants appeared in the hallway. "And something to eat. It is going to be a long night."

"It is always a long night," said the servant.

Victoire understood about half of what they said. Suddenly she felt much more vulnerable. If only she had taken the time to learn more Egyptian from Roustam-Raza. But her few phrases had seemed enough while he was with her to provide translations. She watched the kitchen servant, hoping that something in the man's manner would indicate how she should react to the elegant young man.

"They are making plans," complained the young man. "Something has pleased the Pasha and he has four of his ministers with him, and some of the commanders of his army."

"They have asked for coffee and sweetmeats," agreed the kitchen servant.

The young man caught sight of Victoire and gave her a single, penetrating look. "Who are you?" he demanded.

She answered in Greek, hoping that he would be able to understand her. "I am a messenger. From Ausim."

His Greek was passable. "To what purpose?"

"My master has a foundry. He wants to sell cannon to the French. I am supposed to bring him permission from the Pasha." She said it with all the confidence she could muster, but to herself she sounded patently dishonest.

"Part of the plan," said the young man, nodding. "Allah protect the Pasha and give him glory in battle."

"Allah is great," said Victoire in Egyptian, one of the few phrases she knew well enough to use. She went on in Greek. "I was told to wait for an answer."

"And well you might. We're all waiting tonight. The whole palace is filled with waiting men." He tossed his head. "The kitchen will never be cool."

"No, it won't," said Victoire, trusting that this was a safe answer.

"What is your name, and who is your master?" asked the young man. "I am Yousef."

Victoire had already invented. "I'm Perikles. My master is Abdel Hillet." It was an ordinary name, but not so ordinary that it would be grounds for suspicion.

"Perikles," said Yousef. "An auspicious name. Well, you could have a wait. You might as well come into the kitchen with me and have something to eat. They aren't going to finish any time soon."

Victoire managed to yawn. "Food might make me sleepy."

"The coffee will waken you. It's what the great ones are doing to keep awake." He nodded to the kitchen servant. "You can feed him, too, can't you?"

"Of course," said the servant, and started back down the hall.

Victoire followed along, trying to persuade herself that this was a stroke of good luck.

Yousef clapped his hands as they entered the main part of the kitchen and brought a dozen servants hurrying toward them. "Coffee. Sweetmeats."

The kitchen itself seemed a page out of history to Victoire, who had accustomed herself to the modern kitchens of France, with enclosed stoves and ovens. This kitchen was one of open hearths and tremendous spits, and only one old-fashioned griddle-stove. Huge chopping blocks and tremendous pastry boards made passage through the kitchen difficult.

Over their refreshments—which Victoire remembered to eat with the right hand only—Yousef, glad of an audience, regaled Victoire with his own knowledge of the current activities in the palace, embellishing with his own suppositions when he lacked information.

"Who are you supposed to see?" he asked when they were almost finished with their coffee.

"I don't know," Victoire confessed. "My master said that I would be given a sealed packet, and I was to bring that back to him."

"Your master is a prudent fellow, Perikles. Well you may thank Allah for his wisdom." Yousef pulled his insufficient beard. "I know a place you can wait that is less confusing than this one." He was proud to demonstrate his power to someone with less than he. "If you will come with me, I will take you to one of the waiting chambers."

"That would . . . that would be very gracious," she said, wishing she could get word to Roustam-Raza. As heartened as she was by the chance to get into the palace, she dreaded what would happen if she were caught.

"Then come with me," he offered, indicating one of the corridors beyond the kitchen. "The waiting chamber is on the floor above. It will not be incorrect for you, as a messenger, to wait there."

"That is . . . very generous of you, Yousef. I will tell my master of your service." She was fairly certain this was a correct response.

"Any words that will help my advancement are welcome, if Allah wills," he said, beaming at her as he led the way.

Victoire sat in the waiting chamber for the better part of an hour, every second fearing discovery. She heard men pass in the hall, and once the sound of angry voices drifted down from the floor above, but where the angry man was, or who, she could not guess. Her nerves were sensitized—she supposed that was the coffee at work—but that made her edgy. She paced the room until she knew every inch of it, and then she sat down on one of the two low divans there. She did not want to draw attention to herself, but she feared she would be forgotten until someone discovered her and exposed her.

At last the tension grew too much for her and she decided to explore. If nothing else, the room beyond was a meeting room. She might be able to discover something useful there. Yousef had told her that some of the Pasha's soldiers had been there earlier in the evening. They might have left something behind.

Very carefully, Victoire went to the connecting door and lifted the latch, hoping that no one would be inside, for she had no explanation for her actions that would not condemn her.

No one was in the room, which was lined with unrolled maps. Had the room been more brightly lit, she would have taken time to make note of what was displayed on them. But the single oil lamp did not provide enough illumination for her to do this. Very slowly and carefully she began to explore, noticing that the door to the main corridor was bolted, and the third door, the one leading to a chamber Victoire had not seen, was bolted also.

There were two trestle tables in the room, one with a dispatch case sitting on it. Very carefully Victoire worked the buckles loose and opened the case, knowing that if she was found out now, it would mean a quick and messy execution for her.

There was a letter in the leather case, one she did not give herself time to read thoroughly, although it was written in French. The handwriting was quite poor and the grammar hardly better. She noticed that there was mention of Napoleon having informed the Directoire that Egypt was now a French possession and asking for himself to be appointed governor. The letter was signed Tallyrand, though the signature was so smeared as to be almost unrecognizable. The seal on the letter was definitely that of the Directoire, she had seen one on Vernet's appointment as a major in the Gendarmes.

Victoire hurriedly returned the letter to the dispatch case, shocked at the enormity of what she had seen: that someone in the Directoire should send covert messages to the Pasha. Was Tallyrand truly the culprit, or was someone determined to destroy him as well as Napoleon? As she started to thread the leather straps through the buckles, she felt something shift inside the large dispatch case.

Curious, she opened it once again, shaking it and finding it much heavier than she had thought it was. On impulse, she felt the inside of the case and discovered a hidden latch. With trembling fingers she opened it, and found the scepter.

She stared at it for the greater part of a minute, astonished. Then she took it from the dispatch case and thrust it through the thick belt she wore, down the leg of her loose trousers. The gold was chill next to her skin, and reminded her again of the danger in which she stood.

Knowing that she was setting herself on an irrevocable path, Victoire slipped back into the waiting chamber. She smoothed her garments, doing her best to keep the scepter completely concealed. The head of the scepter actually added to her disguise, if she no longer claimed to be a eunuch. Her walk would have to be a bit more stiff-legged than usual, but she decided that she could manage it without becoming conspicuous.

Her heart racing, she went and opened the door, looking in both directions down the corridor. All she would need now was the opportunity to get back to the kitchens, and she would be able to slip out through the kitchen yard and back to the streets and Roustam-Raza's protection.

The thought of the Mameluke made her smile nervously. He would surely be out of temper with her when she returned. She hoped that the return of the scepter might mollify his anger.

She went down the corridor, just as Yousef had led her, looking for the ornaments that she had tried to memorize as they walked. But it was later in the night, and some of the oil lamps had been extinguished, which brought about confusion. Victoire knew that she had to get to the lower floor, and from there to the kitchens, but she could not find the staircase that led down. Resisting the panic that rose in her, she continued along the corridor, keeping alert for any staircase that would take her below. She was certain that she had come farther than Yousef had led her. At last she turned around, starting back along the corridor, trying to think what she would say if anyone came upon her.

Then she found herself before impressive doors, two guards standing with tremendous pikes.

Mère Marie, she thought, this is the hareem.

One of the guards started toward her, his voice tense, though Victoire did not understand the question.

"Your pardon," she stammered in Greek. "I ... I am lost, and—"

The guard was nearer, his pike pointed directly at her.

"There you are, you thankless young scamp!" bellowed a familiar voice behind her in dreadful Greek.

Victoire had never been happier to see anyone in her life, but she quailed obediently as Roustam-Raza came up to her and seized her by the collar.

He exchanged a few words with the hareem guards, and then lifted his hand as if to strike Victoire.

"If your master did not dote on you, I would beat you until you were blue all over," he announced, adding something to the guards in Egyptian that made the two men laugh unpleasantly.

Victoire cringed as Roustam-Raza grabbed her by the shoulder. "I did not know, great Mameluke. I never thought ..."

"You are a foolish boy, and you would not be able to find your way from one side of the Nile to the other without someone to guide you." He was enjoying hectoring her, harrying her toward the stairs she had not seen.

"Yousef brought me to a waiting room," she said, which was true enough.

"And you let yourself be lost instead of waiting. Praise Allah that you did not find your way to the Pasha himself!" They were almost to the kitchen now, and Roustam-Raza lowered his voice. "What possessed you to do that?"

"I thought it would be suspicious if I didn't," she explained.

"Not good enough," Roustam-Raza informed her. "You had no right to go beyond the kitchens. Where you should not have been." He shook his head and tightened his hold on her collar. "Think what could have happened."

This time her face was stark. "I did think. You may be sure of that."

He saw the fading fear in her eyes and relented a bit. They were at the door to the kitchens, and he shoved her ahead of him. "What am I going to say to your master about you? What would I have told them if you had done anything incorrect?" He looked toward one of the cooks and said something in Egyptian that Victoire realized was a curse on wayward youngsters.

"They grow older," said one of the cooks, which Victoire understood.

"This one might not," Roustam-Raza countered as he got Victoire to the pantry hall. "You will wait outside the main gates for your answer, youngster, and you will be grateful that nothing worse befalls you."

"Yes, yes," she said in Greek, pleased when they stumbled into the kitchen yard. The side gate was very close.

And then they were outside, and he forced her to move more quickly.

"I thought you were not supposed to enter the palace," panted Victoire as she strove to keep up with Roustam-Raza.

"When you disappeared inside and did not emerge, what was I supposed to do? I could not present myself to Napoleon to tell him that I had permitted a Frenchwoman to go disguised into the palace, where she was going to be imprisoned forever." He indicated a side street. "It will be dawn in another hour, and Muslims will be at prayer. You would surely have been found out then."

"And I tried to find a way out of the palace," she offered. "It is a very confusing place."

"It's supposed to be," said Roustam-Raza. "Only people who belong there are supposed to know how to find their way around it."

"Then they are very successful," said Victoire, whose leg was beginning to ache from the pressure and rub of the scepter against it. Yet she did not protest their pace. "I looked in one of the rooms."

"Allah show me mercy!" burst out Roustam-Raza. "There is more to your escapade?" He pulled her into a narrow doorway. "I should not lay hands on a Christian woman. But if I did not—"

"I take no offense, Roustam-Raza," she said. "And I know it was a great effort for you to go against your orders and enter the palace. Don't suppose I'm unaware of your danger as well as my own."

He stood a little straighter. "That is something," he conceded.

"And it . . . it was a gamble that was worth the risk." She was about to tell him of the scepter, then held her tongue about it. "I saw something in a dispatch case—"

"You opened a dispatch case?" he demanded incredulously. "They would have pulled the skin off you for that, had you been discovered. Flaying is the punishment for—"

"Stop," she said quietly. "Please."

He realized that she was more shaken than she had revealed before. "Very well. But you must give me your word—though it is the word of a woman and writ on water—that you will not return to the palace again, not for any reason."

"You have my word on that," she promised him at once. "I will not return to the palace of the Pasha for any reason." Had she not been worried about offending him, she would have crossed herself.

"I am a fool among fools, but I will take your word, Madame," he said gruffly. "What was it you found in the dispatch case that makes you believe your risk was acceptable?"

She shifted her shoulders and adjusted her rumpled collar. "I think, but I am not certain, I think that there is someone in France who is working against Napoleon. That was what the paper in the dispatch case indicated." She decided it was safe enough to tell him that much.

"How do you mean?" he asked, stepping back into the street and gesturing to her to follow. Now that they were out of immediate danger, he would not disgrace them both by touching her or her garments.

"There was a letter." She steeled herself to the discomfort of hiding the scepter and tried to match her stride to his. "I didn't have the chance to read it carefully, but it indicated that someone in Paris is working to Napoleon's disadvantage. I knew the name of the man who sent it, but I cannot tell if it is his signature or the signature of someone else who wishes to implicate the other man."

They were well beyond the area of the palace. The streets were narrower and Roustam-Raza drew his scimitar. "Would there be men who would do such a thing?"

"So it appears. There is much unrest in Paris. There is talk that a strong man is needed to guide the Republic. Many would see themselves as that man, others fear any who might be him. With so much at stake, it is surprising that ambitious men would try to end Napoleon's career in disgrace . . ." She stumbled and recovered. "I ask your pardon. I'm becoming very . . . tired."

Roustam-Raza shook his head and spat. "With all you have been doing, I am surprised that you have not fallen in the street. And do not tell me it is because you are a Frenchwoman. Not all Frenchwomen are as intrepid as you. For which I will thank Allah five times a day."

"Very well," she said, "it's not because I am a Frenchwoman, not entirely." Her eyes grew distant. "It is the fault of education, Roustam-Raza," she said sardonically. "I have always been curious, and my education gave me a direction and a method to use my curiosity."

"It is a mistake to educate women," Roustam-Raza stated. "But if someone must educate women, let it be you French, not good Muslims."

Victoire was too tired to rise to the bait. She hitched up

one shoulder. "I suppose it would be useless to ask where we would be if I had no education."

"We would not be here, running from the palace where you have committed a killing crime," he told her roundly. "Remember that, in future." He indicated another narrow street. "Cut through there. It will bring us to the south side of the garrison villa."

For once she complied without argument.

# 13

HER TENT NOW seemed a very ordinary place to Victoire. She sat down on the cot and looked at her things, which had been stored in trunks while she was away. On Vernet's cot there was another trunk, with his possessions neatly packed in it. That was the worst thing in the tent, she decided, that trunk of Lucien's things, for it made his absence all the more demanding to her. If only his side of the tent looked as if he were expected to return. As it was, she had to resist the urge to send his trunks on to Jaffa.

There was one leather case, not large but quite tall, used for carrying clothes brushes, boot trees, valet's supplies and such, that lay on its side under Vernet's cot, as ordinary and inconspicuous as a horseshoe in a farrier's tent. In it, wrapped in a length of worn canvas, Victoire had hidden the scepter; she would return it when she could give it to Napoleon himself, and no other.

She had put on one of her day dresses that morning and was startled to find that it was a little too large for her. She rose and looked in the small mirror set up on the largest of the chests. Yes, she decided, she had lost flesh. She sighed. She was more of an angular dab of a woman than ever. The sleek bosom of Pauline Foures and her elegant curve of arm and hip were not to be Victoire's.

There was a disturbance not far from the tent which attracted her attention, and then she heard Roustam-Raza call her name.

Knowing he would never come into her tent while they lacked a chaperon, she stepped outside, curtsying to him in form. "May Allah shower blessings on you, my friend."

The Mameluke was wearing a new set of clothes finer than any she had seen since the day he had arrived in the camp. The shirt was made of silk and embroidered with colored threads in intricate designs. His belt featured a large silver buckle, which he wore on the side. He smiled. "You are improving your Egyptian. Very good."

"With your help I will learn more," she said, and saw him frown. "What is it?"

He stared down at the sand between them. "I've been ordered to go to Napoleon and the army. I am to join the campaign in Syria." He looked directly at her. "I am sworn to Napoleon as his man for as long as there is life in my body. This is his command and I will obey it. I leave in the morning."

She nodded, feeling an unexpected desolation sweep through her. Not only was her husband gone, but she was to lose her friend as well. She brought her chin up. "May you have a swift and safe journey to Napoleon's side." That seemed insufficient to her, and she added, "I'm grateful for all you have done for me, Roustam-Raza. I'll miss you while you are gone."

His face darkened. "It is incorrect for a married woman to say such things."

"By now you ought to be used to my incorrectness, sir," she said, trying to smile.

"One should not grow used to such things. But I thank you." He coughed and spat. "It is dishonorable to think this, and more to say it, but I will miss you, as well, Madame Vernet."

She sensed the effort his admission cost him, and did her best to lighten the burden of it for him. "Oh, I think you may count on Napoleon to provide you with trouble enough that you'll not need me to add to it."

He did not smile. "Your husband will soon take your thoughts away from such folly."

Victoire met his gaze steadily. "I pray every day for his return. May God hear you."

They could not correctly embrace or even shake hands. They settled for a bow and a curtsy, then he turned away, pausing to add, "May you thrive, Madame."

"And you, my friend," she said, and watched him walk away between the row of tents.

Larrey was more irascible now than when Victoire had left. He gave her a long, condemning stare when she presented herself at his tent for tending the wounded.

"And where have you been, Madame Vernet? You asked for two weeks to go to Alexandria, and it is two months and more since we have seen you." He picked up a report and started to read it; his hands were shaking a little.

"It's a long story. When Murat comes back, you must ask him to tell you about it," she said.

"With Murat, were you?" His brows rose. "Your husband is in Jaffa."

"And I am doing all that I can to clear his name, since he cannot," she said. She hesitated, then said, "It was a difficult journey. There were many . . . hazards. I had to swim in the Nile. I would have been murdered if I had not."

This caught his interest. "Swam in the Nile! The day may come when you think you made a bad bargain, Madame Vernet." He rose and came nearer. "What have you felt? Are you ill? Have you had any headaches, severe ones, that cause your neck to grow very stiff?"

"No," she answered, surprised that he should seek to question her. "I believe that I am well."

"How is your digestion? Have you been liverish?" He reached out and took her jaw in his hand, angling her head so that he could inspect the white of her eyes. "No sign of yellow yet." He frowned, adding, "I wish I could say the same for some of the poor wretches we're tending here."

"My digestion is good, although I have—"

"Yes, I can see you have dropped flesh. Do you vomit after eating?" He pulled his stool closer and sat down directly in front of her.

"Not usually. I have when the meat has gone off." She cocked her head to one side.

"Have you had flux?" He opened her jaw and peered at her tongue so that she could not answer him at once.

"Yes, but not severely. Everyone here has the flux some of the time," she said.

"Lamentable and true," acknowledged Larrey, continuing his investigation. "Have you had nodules in your neck or under your arms? Painful ones?"

"No," she assured, feeling a stirring of alarm.

"Do you sweat in the night, or suffer sudden chills? Do you flush? Have you had the fever?" His questions came quickly, almost harsh.

"Occasionally I sweat in the night. How can I be chilled in this place?" She wanted to laugh but could not.

"And fever?" He placed his hand on her forehead and then felt the palms of her hands.

"Not that I know of. But crossing the desert, I might have had one; I would not have known it in such a furnace." Her voice was level but her apprehension continued.

"Crossing the desert." He regarded her thoughtfully. "Where on earth have you been, Madame Vernet?"

"We went up the Nile, as far as Medinet Habu. It's across the river from Thebes." She thought it was safe to tell Larrey that much, and enough to account for doing it. "We were following an Englishman."

"You and Murat?" Larrey asked, unable to conceal his condemnation of this irregular activity.

"And Roustam-Raza, and a very brave Egyptian woman. Roustam-Raza would not have gone with us without another woman so that we could chaperon each other. Muslims are very strict in that regard." She shook her head slowly, thinking of Lirylah.

"God's Teeth!" whispered Larrey, growing truly astonished.

"Much of the food we had was not of the first quality, and though we took care to drink from wells, I don't know that all were pure. But Roustam-Raza is well, and

General Murat . . . had no illness when I saw him last." Except sickness at heart, she added to herself. She looked down at her hands, pleased that unlike Larrey's, they were steady.

Larrey sat more rigidly. "I will want to observe you carefully, Madame Vernet. Report to me regularly, and if there is any change in your health, no matter how minor, tell me at once. If you have taken any infection, I will want to treat you immediately. You are to inform me at once if anything irregular—"

"It was my plan to do that," she interrupted. "I have no wish to contract foreign fevers."

"No one has," said Larrey very seriously. "Yet it occurs with regularity. You will find that we number many fallen to illness now, more than when you last worked with the wounded. You must treat them carefully so as not to take infection from them." He swatted at the mosquito that landed on his arm and considered the little patch of blood the insect left behind. "We are out of oil of citron, and the mosquitos are everywhere."

"The flies are worse, too," said Victoire.

"Yes. Flies are inescapable in Egypt." He stood up abruptly. "You may work half a watch today, in order to reacquaint yourself with our procedures. By tomorrow I will want you for a full watch. Unless you feel ill." This last was a specific warning, and she responded to it at once.

"If I become ill, I'll send you word of it at once, as you have instructed me." She, too, rose and started toward the tent where the wounded lay. "Is there anything else?"

Larrey's eyes grew distant. "In Thebes. They say there are temples as grand as Chartres. Is it true?"

"I don't know," said Victoire candidly. "We did not cross to the east side of the river. But I saw columns and the front of a tremendous and ancient building near Medinet Habu, and a few fallen statues of formidable size. It may have been a temple."

"Ah," said Larrey, indicating she could leave.

\* \* \*

Without her allies to aid her, Victoire found it difficult to watch Berthier more than a few hours a day. Each morning and most evenings she lingered near his tent, making note of everyone who visited there, including the lovely Pauline Foures, who was trying to arrange for passage to Syria, ostensibly to be with her husband.

On those occasions when Berthier left the camp, Victoire tried to discover where he went, and for what purpose. She could not pursue him very far, for she was on foot and Berthier rode, yet she watched when he came and went, and tried to find out the reasons for his various expeditions.

She looked at what she had written to Vernet and shivered in spite of the heat.

For Tallyrand—if it is truly Tallyrand who has betrayed Napoleon—must have supporters here in Egypt. If the purpose is to destroy Napoleon, who better to do it than Berthier? So far I have discovered nothing of importance, but I am convinced, my dearest, that it is only a matter of time before he gives himself away, and then we will expunge forever any blot on your reputation, and fix the blame where it belongs. More is at stake here than your career in the army: the fate of Napoleon himself may lie in uncovering the identities of those who have implicated you. You have my whole account of everything I have learned thus far, and I beg you to keep it safe in case any misfortune should befall me; I will not give them the satisfaction of concealing their crimes with my intimidation.

Berthier is a cautious man, not one to make foolish mistakes. I do not underestimate his capacity for deception and wickedness. But I am a patient and determined woman, and I will persevere. I am determined to confront him when I am certain of how he has accomplished his sedition; he will not be able to hide behind a mask of ignorance when he is formally accused. Be of good cheer, treasured husband, and trust that while justice may be blind, she is not stupid. We will win through.

There was very little else to tell him; the letter she handed to the courier that evening was only two crossed pages.

Berthier nibbled the cuticle of his thumb, having run out of nail to chew. He looked over at Eugene, who was still pale and weak from a recent bout with swine fever. "If you are tired . . ."

"A little," his secretary conceded. "But for a time I can continue." In demonstration he took another sheet of paper from his portable desk and reached for his pen.

"This is not a letter, or not yet," said Berthier, the line between his brows deepening. "It is Madame Vernet."

"She is still watching you," said Eugene.

"Persistently. I could bring myself to admire her if she were not so inconvenient." He stared across the tent, his eyes fixed in the middle distance. "I have not yet received word from Murat. I want to know about the scepter. She claims it was taken after they recovered it. I am not willing to accept her word, but Roustam-Raza agreed; I must evaluate the worth of the Mameluke's story."

"Surely you don't doubt him, do you?" asked Eugene, trying to follow Berthier's train of thought.

"I d-don't know. The scepter is Egyptian. He is Egyptian. Would he lie about it because of that? Have they struck a bargain between them, whereby he gains the scepter for Egypt and she falsely exonerates her husband for his treason? Would she be able to sway him?" He tapped his fingers together. "Would Roustam-Raza lie to protect Madame Vernet? That is another question. Muslims are not given to protecting women beyond locking them up. Is it possible that he would defend her?"

"The scepter is Napoleon's," said Eugene. "The Mameluke has sworn lifelong fidelity to him. Surely he would not take the property of his master."

"I wouldn't have thought so," said Berthier. "If he is as

honorable as he seems." He shook his head sadly. "She is in it somehow, Eugene. She and that husband of hers, they are at the heart of this plot. She reeks of it."

Eugene nodded. "How will you discover her duplicity?"

"I have not yet hit upon a plan," Berthier said slowly. "But I can see that I must."

"Is she the instigator or—" Eugene began, only to be cut off.

"Oh, not she. It is her husband and she is his accomplice. No woman would concoct such a plan. She is an unusual female, but she would not tolerate a murder." Then his face darkened. "There are women aplenty who watched the heads fall, seven years ago. Some of them even held the bags of spent grain to receive them. That was retribution, and those women were not the daughters of prosperous merchants. This is not some gutter woman from Paris, but the educated daughter of a Rouen merchant. Could she tie the marine guard thoroughly and cut his throat like a sheep? That takes the cunning and strength of a desperate man. Three officers knew about the treasure, and of those who did, all can account for their time, save one. Vernet is the man responsible, I am certain of it."

"Does she truly think he is innocent?" asked Eugene, fascinated by what Berthier conjectured.

"Who knows? She is not foolish. But women are curious creatures where their husbands are concerned. They believe more nonsense about them than nuns believe about the Holy Ghost." He pinched the bridge of his nose. "I do not want to confine her, but if she continues to watch me, what other choice have I got than to order her to remain in her quarters?"

"Would that be prudent, sir?" Eugene inquired very deferentially.

"Probably not," Berthier admitted. He leaned back on his stool, taking care to maintain his balance. "You'd better get the rest of my dispatches ready. The courier will be here shortly."

\* \* \*

It was more than a week later when Berthier rode into camp from Cairo only to find Victoire waiting for him at his tent. He stared at her in his most daunting manner and was surprised when it had no effect on her. As he swung off his horse he confronted her.

"You are growing very bold, Madame Vernet," he said coolly.

"No more than you," she answered, giving him an opportunity to speak.

"How is that, Madame?" he inquired with spurious courtesy. He whistled for a groom to come and take his horse.

"Last night I observed you hand a dispatch case to a marine guard. He, in turn, delivered that case to a corvette. There is no official record of any dispatches from you, and no record in the camp of the ship landing." She met his gaze unflinchingly. "Would you like to discuss this further? May I suggest we speak inside your tent?"

The groom arrived and took the reins from Berthier.

"What I do is no concern of yours," said Berthier, attempting to push past her.

"If it compromises my husband and endangers the campaign, it is very much my business—and the business of every other Frenchwoman in Egypt," she declared. "When a man of your position sends covert messages, surely there is reason for sensible people to be dismayed."

Berthier rolled his eyes upward. "Come into my tent, then, and let's get this over with."

"Thank you, General Berthier," she said, following him through the flap. She stood very straight, remaining near the door.

He drew up his camp stool and sank down onto it; his back ached and his eyes were reddened. He thrust his hands into his coat pockets. "All right. You seem determined to drag me into your conspiracy. I can understand why you wish to keep your husband from danger, but I do not know why it must be at my expense. Find another officer. What of Desaix? Or Lavallette? Aren't they equally culpable?"

"The others are not sending secret dispatches, or striving to throw blame onto Vernet, as you are. From the first you have been determined to fix the guilt on my husband, and have been at pains to point all suspicion at him and away from you. I'll not permit you to ruin him." She stopped abruptly, as if revealing so much exposed her.

"It would be damnable of me, if he were innocent." His features were forbidding and his voice was hard.

Victoire refused to be daunted. "You will not succeed in your plan. When it is known that you are sending covert dispatches, that you have concealed important information, you will no longer be able to make honorable officers your victims." She planted her feet and stared him down. "Your perfidy will not go unanswered."

Berthier was on his feet, his hands closed into fists. "Breath of God, you go too far, Madame!" he thundered. "I have troubles enough without your meddling in matters you cannot understand."

"I understand betrayal well enough," she answered, taking one step back. "Threaten me all you wish—it will only add credence to my argument."

That struck home. Berthier rocked back on his heels as if she had struck him. "If that is to be your game—"

"You're the one who has created the game. I'm only doing what I can to counter your moves before you bring on the destruction of my husband." She shook her head. "Do you think I cannot see how you are at work? When I left here in November, morale was good and our men were filled with enthusiasm. Now they are distressed and disheartened. Everything has deteriorated. There are desperate rivalries among the officers and the men do not treat one another as comrades. Who has brought this about? Surely not Napoleon, for he is in Syria. Who has been entrusted with this camp, with the maintenance of the army? Who has been in the best position to loot and pilfer?" She folded her arms. "Or do you think that Vernet did that as well, from Jaffa?"

Berthier locked his hands behind his back so that he would not be able to throttle her. "If you were a soldier, you would be in a cell, Madame Vernet, and if you persisted in these calumnies, you would be shot."

"An admirable way to silence embarrassing questions," she said. "I am preparing a report. I want you to know of it. I don't want you to claim that you were unaware of the suspicions of others, and that you have been taken advantage of." She looked toward the door of the tent. "Your motives are known, General Berthier. And your associates in the Directoire are known as well. You are no longer hidden."

"What are you talking about?" he demanded, for the first time truly confused by what she said.

"I saw the dispatch." She nodded once. "You thought that was a secret still, didn't you? But I know. And I have already informed Vernet of it. If you take any action against me, there are others who will accuse you." Her face brightened. "Did you think no one would find out?"

"I don't know what you're talking about," he complained.

"As you know nothing of the scepter, or the death of the marine guard." She wanted to laugh but could not. "Or do you claim ignorance of that, as well?"

"When it comes to the scepter, you have more to answer for than I, Madame Vernet," said Berthier curtly.

She was prepared for his attack. "It must reassure you to think so," she said.

Berthier pursued the point. "You were the one who went in search of it. You were the one who claims to have found it and lost it. Losing it is very convenient, Madame Vernet. Very, very convenient."

"How do you wish me to interpret your implication?" she asked sweetly. "There are so many ways you could intend offense."

Angry enough to speak more than he might ordinarily, Berthier said, "I think you found and kept that scepter. I think you have it now. I think you took it to make your husband rich, just as you intended from the f-first."

Victoire had gone pale with rage. When she spoke her voice was very quiet. "If I had the scepter, you may be certain I would not be foolish enough to entrust it to anyone but Napoleon himself." She turned on her heel, about to leave, when Berthier stopped her.

"If you have that scepter and do not give it to me at once, it is certain proof of your husband's guilt. And yours." He intended it as a parting shot.

She was prepared for it. "And if I had it to give to you, how could I account for its disappearance, since you would certainly insist that you never possessed it. As you claim to know nothing of a conspiracy in Paris." Satisfied that she had shaken him, she left his tent, stimulated and frightened, and feeling very much alone.

By nightfall Larrey was so exhausted that he could not sleep. He sat in his tent, the last of the brandy he had brought with him open on the leather trunk beside his cot. Two large tots had not been enough to release the tension of fatigue that held him in its grip. He regarded Victoire with an ironic shrug. "Are you sure you do not mind taking the night watch again, Madame Vernet?"

She watched him with concern. "It is no trouble."

"Of course it is," he protested, but without much heat. "Who wishes to tend these men in the night? It is thankless." He put his long, large-knuckled hand to his forehead. "It is almost as thankless by day."

"But they must be tended or they will be lost." She smoothed the front of her dress, thinking that it would need mending again soon. "We've had too many die already."

"Yes. The wounds mortify, and the flux does the rest," he said, the end of his words slurring. "This is a terrible place to be."

Victoire was not certain whether he meant the camp, the hospital tents, or Egypt itself. "The army goes where its leaders take it," she said, as she had heard Vernet say many times.

"This is still a terrible place." He filled his cup again and drank from it greedily. "The food is inedible, the water is contaminated, the heat is ruinous, and we are being cut off from retreat." He shook his head. "Even with the additional troops sent to Syria, how can we prevail?"

"What additional troops?" asked Victoire, who had been hearing rumors for more than a week. "Who's being sent?"

"Murat, for one. He's been gathering all the cavalry together. That can only mean Napoleon expects a battle. There will be more wounded, more ill." He tipped his head back. "I'm drunk."

"You're tired," she added. "You need sleep."

"And I can't sleep," he admitted. "I lie down, so worn that my bones hurt, and I remain awake. Every minute I suppose that in the next minute there will be another emergency, and I will have to be awake for it. And the whole night is gone." He had another long sip of the brandy. "When this is gone, I don't know how I will manage."

"Some of the men have taken hashish," said Victoire.

"They are fools; hashish drives men mad." He fixed his gaze on the single leaf of flame from the oil lamp. "Did Murat use it, when you went upriver?"

"Not that I know of. I suppose Roustam-Raza must. He does not touch strong drink. His religion forbids it." She frowned. Thinking of Murat troubled her.

Larrey waved in the direction of the hospital tents. "You'd better go and relieve Madame Vendrai. She doesn't like to remain after her watch."

Victoire rose at once. "Certainly. If there is need of you I'll send word. In the meantime, sleep if you can."

"If I can," echoed Larrey as he helped himself to a few more drops of brandy.

For the first hour of her watch, Victoire was distracted by thoughts of Murat. She had not heard from him but once since they parted near Memphis, and the tone of that letter had not reassured her. With his continuing silence, she began to fear that his promise of support might not be as reliable as she had first supposed it would be. Although he had corroborated her account of their recovery of the scepter, she was now convinced that she could not depend on his advocacy.

The moans of a soldier suffering from a putrefying spleen claimed her attention, and from then until her watch ended after midnight Victoire had no more opportunity to bother herself with unhappy conjecture about Joachim Murat.

# 14

IT WAS AUGUST and the Inundation was finally retreating, giving the Delta its precious annual gift of water and soil. In the sweltering heat the land became fecund and rich. The French camp had lost many of the Egyptian servants who had worked there through the winter and spring; now planting demanded their presence in the fields and the tasks they had performed were left to the women and recuperating men.

The arrival of the troops returning from Syria brought the greatest excitement to the wives who had been left in camp. For the first time in months many of the women were animated; even those who had avoided Victoire because of the implication of scandal attached to her now treated her as a friend and confidante, sharing the joy of reunion. The afternoon when the men returned, all the women were sisters.

There was a shout, and the waiting ranks broke apart as the men started forward into the camp. Many of the wives went toward them, but a few hung back, some of them looking confused or troubled.

Victoire remained at the edge of the camp center, her eyes restlessly scanning the faces of the men as they surged into the place. At the instant the men were released from muster, she had to fight an irrational fear that swept through her—after all these months apart, would she be able to recognize her husband? She shivered and made herself take several long breaths to calm down. Where was Lucien? She wanted to call his name, but there was already so much noise, such whoops and cries, that she knew she would never be heard above it all. She had to find him. Vernet was tall. She ought to be able to pick him out by his height. His eyes were gray-green, a color like the ocean. He had a square jaw and dark hair.

What if he had not been sent back, after all? The question echoed in her mind like the remembered fragment of a bad dream. What if they had changed their minds? What if he had been detained by Berthier, or one of his agents? She clasped her hands together.

And then she saw him: he was coming toward her with long, purposeful strides. She lifted her hand and almost waved.

He stopped a little more than an arm's length from her. "Victoire," he said.

"Lucien."

For a short while they stared at one another, the world narrowed down to the space between them.

Then he closed the distance and gathered her into his arms, heedless of the others around them. No matter how improper it was to embrace so passionately in public, neither of them cared.

Vernet's cot sagged under their double weight. Victoire, straddling his supine body, tucked her head into the hollow of his chin and throat. They were both slick with sweat, and her fair hair stuck to her face and his neck. They were both exhausted and both wanted more of the other.

"Lord of the Prophets, how I have missed you," Vernet whispered, one hand looping her ringlets through his fingers. "I forgot how much I missed this. And this."

Victoire kissed the point of his collarbone and smiled. "I dreamed about you . . . and this." Her fingers began to trace enlarging arcs on his chest, the center of the circles growing lower. He began to respond, despite the hours of lovemaking already past.

"Dreams are not good enough, not nearly good enough," he said, his free hand roving down her back as if reassuring himself that she was really there. "I never want to be away from you so long again."

"Not ever," she agreed, wishing that she weren't quite so luxuriously tired. But Vernet was finding new energy and she would never deny him, not after so very long.

"I worried about you every hour." He kissed her languorously, as if released at last from his concern. "Those weeks you were gone ... When no word came, I was frantic."

"It couldn't be helped," said Victoire, doing her best not to squirm as his hand searched along her leg. "Without couriers, there was no safe means to—"

"I know." He smoothed the damp tendrils back from her brow. "I know." Then for a long time there was no need to talk.

"I worried about you, too," Victoire said dreamily a while later. "With you so far away making sure the supply lines stayed open, I had no means to discover what might be—" She stopped, determined not to let the anxiety that still hung over them to ruin this night together.

"It wasn't as bad as all that." He smoothed the side of her arm. "Jaffa was boring, most of the time. The rest of the time, there was too much happening. I didn't have to think about it, not the way you did."

"But you could have been killed," she said, and felt a flash of anger that he could be so careless of someone she loved.

"So might you, while you were gone." He looked at her, staring into the depths of her eyes. "I would never have forgiven you, if you'd been killed."

"Nor I you," she said.

"No," he said.

"No," she concurred, and yet again let her body say the rest.

An hour before dawn, as they sponged one another with the limited amount of bathing water permitted, Victoire at last revealed everything she had learned to Vernet.

"But what you're saying is monstrous," he insisted.

"When I read your letters, I couldn't believe what you wrote to me."

"I didn't want to believe," she reminded him. "You had to be warned, no matter how great the risk in writing. But what else could I do? Someone in Paris is attempting Napoleon's fall; he has an accomplice here, someone high in the chain of command. From all I have been able to discover, that man must be Berthier. Who else is in a position to do so much damage?"

Vernet paused before emptying a small amount of water over her shoulders. "You're very convincing, but . . . Why would he support Paris when he has made such a place for himself with Napoleon?"

"Perhaps because he has been promised Napoleon's place," said Victoire, giving the reason that seemed most sensible to her. "A man in his position might grow envious; he could hanker for command."

"But Berthier—" Vernet reached for her towel and held it out to her. "Berthier isn't that sort of fellow. Look at him. If he hadn't a commander, he'd come all to pieces."

As she wrapped the thick cotton around her, she cocked her head. "You do not think he is well-suited to lead? That may be, but it would not stop his ambition." She stared at him as he finished his own ablutions. "It's his ambitions that trouble me, not his abilities."

"I pray you're wrong," he said, taking the last of the water in the ewer and pouring it over his head. "If you're not . . ."

"It isn't only my assumption because I . . . I dislike him. Berthier is sending dispatches in secret. I've followed him. I have seen his secretary hand them to marines. A corvette has landed unofficially and carried his reports for him." She watched him bundle himself in his towel. "I've kept a record of the occasions."

He nodded. "And I have your letters. You say he knows about it?"

"Yes. I told him. It was necessary. I wrote to you about what happened. I haven't approached him since. I thought it would be wisest—I told you." She unfastened her hair and let it fall around her shoulders.

"That you did," he said, his mouth grim. "If I had been here, I would not have allowed you to approach Berthier."

"If you had been here it wouldn't have been necessary." She sat down on her cot. "There is a conspiracy, Vernet. And it reaches very high."

He sat down opposite her. "You've convinced me of that." He reached out and took one of her hands in his. "What are we going to do?"

"I don't know," she said softly. "Wait for Napoleon to come back, I suppose. After that . . ."

He nodded.

"How was it?" she asked, eager to talk of something else.

"It was hard going. I spent the first weeks establishing guardposts along the supply route. Twice we were attacked by large numbers of mounted men. Fortunately they could not stand up to disciplined musket fire. Then we arrived at Acre. The siege was terrible. The walls were thick, and the first attack cost us heavily."

"Yes," Victoire agreed. "We received many casualties from that attack."

"Then we settled into a formal siege. It was my job to make sure no one infiltrated the camp. It wasn't meant to be a long siege, but the English intervened. They captured the siege train, all the big cannons. We held on longer than I thought we would. Then the Ottomans finally sent an army after us. We left as an army, at our own pace. It all cost us many lives. Men I left on picket disappeared and I fear they did not die easily."

Victoire saw that Vernet was almost shaking as he recounted what happened. Gently she took his hand and stroked the top of it with her fingertips. After a few seconds he seemed to calm down.

"Well, as we marched away they attacked, but the divisions formed large squares and drove them off. The ground was covered by their dead. We marched on, dogged by those dreaded desert horsemen. Most didn't even have muskets. They followed us with a fleet. Less than a day's march from here they landed. Then Murat gathered the cavalry and drove them off. He had been in a funk since Napoleon recalled him to the army. No one knew why. It was something to watch. He seemed happier after the battle, more willing to talk to the rest of us. The others moved slowly back to Acre. We hurt them badly, but couldn't take the city. The rest of the army was only a few hours' march behind me. I'm glad to be out of it."

"And I am thankful you're here, and safe." She did her best to smile again.

"If we are safe," he reminded her.

"If we are," she echoed.

Napoleon rode through the camp to cheers; they were not as joyous as when the French had first landed in Egypt, but everyone pretended not to notice until Napoleon was once again in his command tent.

"How has discipline become so lax?" he demanded of Berthier once he had dismissed everyone but his senior staff. He sat at the trestle table with Roustam-Raza at guard behind him. "I expected better from you, Louis."

"It has been very difficult here," said Berthier, coloring to the roots of his frizzy hair. "Our morale is not good, and with the number of sick and wounded, many of the soldiers here have lost their . . . devotion."

"It should not have happened," said Napoleon, watching the rest of his officers nod. "How did it come about?"

"I didn't want it to," said Berthier. "I have been trying to reverse the decline, but so far without results." His face clouded as he sought some means to escape from the condemnation of his hero. "Supplies have been short, and the Egyptians have been charging terribly high prices for their goods. Much of the treasure we took was on the *L'Orient*. Most of the troops here feel their inactivity and it chafes on them. Soldiers sour if they do not have battles to test their valor. And from that idleness grow rumors and discontent. They feel isolated, too far from France, and they are losing their purpose. If there weren't so much suspicion and deception among those remaining here, I would have been better able to uphold your standards, General."

Napoleon scowled. "You speak of rumors. I've been hearing rumors. Some of them do not redound to your credit." He tapped his fingers on the trestle table where he sat. "Very well. You might as well tell me the worst now. I don't want this coming back to haunt me."

It was Berthier's intention to lead gradually to his accusation, but with this clear opportunity, he spoke directly. "The worst has been Madame Vernet. Not content with throwing dust in our eyes with the intention of protecting her husband from the consequences of his acts, she has implicated me in his treason, so that it would appear that he was the innocent one and I the one to betray you." He realized that all the officers were staring.

Roustam-Raza took a single step forward. "I know Madame Vernet, and what you say of her is not like the woman I know."

"She is very clever," said Berthier, his back stiff. 'If Murat were here, he would tell you. He was her supporter once, but he is not so willing to take her part now."

"Murat knows her as well as I do, and he will say nothing to her discredit," said Roustam-Raza, and there was such candor in his manner that none of the men sniggered or winked. "This woman would not act against you," he said to Napoleon.

"Indeed she would," Berthier insisted. "She has done nothing but conspire against our cause since the marine guard was killed and her treachery was thwarted."

"She sounds formidable," said Napoleon drily. "We'd better have this paragon in—and her husband with her—before we continue. Whatever the truth of the matter may be, it won't be obtained without questioning her." He motioned to Roustam-Raza. "You know her. Fetch them."

Roustam-Raza bowed. "At once."

Napoleon signalled to Lavallette. "I'll want Larrey here later for a report on the wounded. Desaix, find out how our horses are holding up. The farriers will tell you. I give you all half an hour to bring me a first report. And while they are gone, you, Berthier, may explain how it comes that we have been robbed of so many medical supplies."

Victoire stared at the figure in the door of the hospital tent, not quite willing to trust her eyes. She put a fresh bandage on the young dragoon's smashed hand, then rose, smoothing the front of her dress as she did. "Is that you, Roustam-Raza?"

"May Allah favor the cause of your husband and give you many sons," he said formally, bowing to her deeply.

She curtsied. "And may you bring honor to your house and to your master," she said, her Egyptian marginally improved in the last few months.

He studied her face. "It is good to see you once again, madame. I would have liked it if this were a happier errand. I have been ordered to bring you to Napoleon."

Color rose in her face. At last! she thought, grateful that she could finally be relieved of the burden of the scepter. "I'll inform Larrey at once," she said, and started toward the far end of the tent.

"Lavallette will visit him shortly," said Roustam-Raza. "For a preliminary report."

"I wish it could be better. There has been an increase of illness in the camp." She did not mention her own spasms of flux that afflicted her from time to time, doubtless the result of her swim in the Nile.

"That is unfortunate. And so is the cause for this summons: it appears that Berthier and you have trouble between you," said Roustam-Raza as he followed her.

"That would be a fair estimate," she answered as she pulled back the door to Larrey's quarters. "Monsieur Larrey," she called, "I must leave for a time. Napoleon has summoned me."

From behind a screen Larrey answered, "Return when you are finished. We're shorthanded."

"Very well," she said, and gave her attention to Roustam-Raza. "I will need to stop at my tent before I present myself."

"I'll have to remain at your side," said Roustam-Raza.

They moved away from the hospital tent, taking the most direct route to her quarters. "There are many questions you must answer for Napoleon."

"About Berthier, no doubt," said Victoire. "That I will, as soon as I have given the scepter to Napoleon to demonstrate my good faith."

"Ah," said Roustam-Raza with a slow nod. "You have it still. I guessed as much."

"Yes," said Victoire. "I wanted to be certain it didn't . . . fall into other hands again. I've had my fill of searching for the thing."

Roustam-Raza shook his head. "May you never find yourself in such a coil as you did at the Pasha's palace again. I've thought of that escapade many times, and the memory is shocking."

"I couldn't leave the scepter in the Pasha's hands." As they reached her tent, she regarded Roustam-Raza gravely. "Yet, if I had not been in the Pasha's palace, I would not have seen that dispatch and we would know nothing of the plot being hatched in Paris. In that sense, I must be grateful for the chance that brought me to the palace."

"Yes," said Roustam-Raza. "But we are no nearer to finding out who is at the heart of the conspiracy, and that, I fear, will not look well for you."

"And that may not be completely an accident," said Victoire as she ducked into the tent and pulled the leather case from under Vernet's cot. Very carefully she opened it and drew out the canvas-wrapped scepter. She paused long enough to drag a comb through the loose curls by her face, then she signalled Roustam-Raza, who waited in the door. "All right. I'm ready."

Vernet was waiting at Napoleon's tent, his uniform still dusty from his short ride. He glanced at Victoire, then at Roustam-Raza. "Do you know why we've been called?"

"To answer questions, or so Roustam-Raza has told me," she said, her attitude unflustered. "It provides us an excellent opportunity to—"

Vernet nodded toward the canvas wrappings. "Yes. Thank goodness."

Roustam-Raza escorted them into the tent where Napoleon and his officers were waiting; most of them regarded the new arrivals with curiosity, but Berthier's reaction was blunt and angry.

"I expect an apology from these two," he said to Napoleon. "If it weren't for their meddling, I would have been able to execute my duties more regularly."

Victoire curtsied to Napoleon, pointedly ignoring Berthier. "Before we do that, General, I have something that belongs to you; something that I want to return to you with witnesses present so that there can be no questions concerning my actions." She glanced at her husband and went on, "I and two of your men have been at pains to recover this and keep it safe." With that she held out the canvas-wrapped bundle.

Napoleon signalled to Roustam-Raza to take it. "What is it, Madame Vernet?"

"The ancient scepter," she said blandly, enjoying the general excitement that ran in whispers through the tent. "The one that was stolen when the marine guard was so hideously murdered."

"Is it?" Napoleon motioned to Roustam-Raza to open the wrappings.

"Roustam-Raza was with me when I recovered it. He can vouch for my actions." She stood very still as Roustam-Raza let the canvas drop before he handed over the golden flail.

Napoleon took the scepter carefully, weighing it in his hand. "Murat told me about the English spy."

"Who claimed he had been paid by the French," Victoire reminded him at once. "And Roustam-Raza can tell you how it was taken from us after Murat departed. For that matter, he was with me with I found it again." She wanted to take Vernet's hand but dared not. "I have reported everything to my husband. He has kept my letters."

"Is this true?" Napoleon asked Vernet as he put the scepter down in front of him on the trestle table.

"Yes," said Vernet. "At your request, I will produce the letters."

"I will wish to see them today; all of them, and any journals that record the events," said Napoleon. "I will also want an explanation why you held the scepter, Madame Vernet, instead of giving it to Berthier, whose work it is to deal with all such items." He folded his arms. "I trust there is an explanation."

"Berthier has all but accused my husband of treason," said Victoire. "Whether or not Berthier acts for you, he certainly acts against Vernet. Therefore I decided it was best to deliver the scepter into your hands, and your hands alone. There is another factor: through a dispatch I discovered in the Pasha's palace—"

"The Pasha's palace?" Napoleon said. "Very enterprising."

"Roustam-Raza will describe it to you," said Victoire, not wanting to be distracted from her purpose. "Through a dispatch discovered there, I came to believe that there are those high in your staff who may be working with men in Paris who are anxious to break your power. I didn't want to provide any of them with a weapon to use against you, such as that scepter." It was as close as she dared come to making a direct accusation.

"So you withheld it from Berthier," said Napoleon. "Isn't that a little beyond your authority, Madame Vernet?"

"Yes, it is," said Victoire at once. "It was my decision. If I have erred, it was in the hope of preserving you and the army. And my husband's reputation and honor, as well."

Napoleon glared. "And did your husband approve of this?"

"My husband was in Jaffa, on your orders. I wasn't able to ask him for advice." She fixed her eyes on the scepter. "If he had told me to deliver the scepter to Berthier, I would have done so at once."

Vernet spoke up. "I stand by what my wife has done. She is a woman of excellent good sense. I trust her judgment."

"I see," Napoleon muttered. He swung around to look at Roustam-Raza. "What do you think? Is this a clever ploy?"

"Madame Vernet does not deceive you," said the Mameluke. "For a woman she shows much honor."

Napoleon nodded once. "But she suspects my faithful Berthier."

"As he has suspected her and her husband," said Roustam-Raza.

"True." Napoleon drummed his fingers again. "Well, I appreciate the return of the scepter. But I am not pleased that this disagreement should have become more important than the campaign in Egypt." He rose. "Murat will be back tomorrow or the next day. I will consult with him, and I will make a decision at that time."

"General Buonaparte," Victoire dared to intervene. "What of my husband and me? And what of Berthier's actions?"

Napoleon stared at Victoire: they were much the same height, which was unnerving for both of them. "Berthier does not need to account for his actions to you."

"But he must to you," she countered. "And given all that is transpired, I think that an account must be rendered. Don't you?"

Berthier gave a put-upon sigh. "There is no reason to keep the secret now that Napoleon is back. But I dislike having my hand forced, Madame Vernet. Everything you have done has made my work more difficult than it needed to be, which has endangered far more than my position. I have been given a task that requires the utmost discretion, a discretion that you have been determined to compromise, Madame Vernet. A select number of Napoleon's staff are about to leave Egypt to return to France. As you say, there is trouble at home, and it cannot be ignored."

"And you have been arranging their departures?" Vernet asked, surprised.

"Of course," said Berthier.

"On my orders," said Napoleon.

"Of course," said Berthier again. "We are being trapped

here by English ships. Nelson is still out there with over a dozen men-of-war. If that were not enough, the merchants say that the blockade has been extended to cover Toulon and Marseilles. There is no way we can again pass an army through the Mediterranean. Yet it becomes vital that Napoleon return home, with those he can truly trust. I have had the two surviving frigates wait in the harbor at Alexandria. They could slip past the English." The aide stared at Vernet as he ended his explanation.

"I see," said Vernet, glancing once toward Victoire. "It is a reasonable precaution, my love. Berthier is doing what any responsible man in his position must do when the enemy is near."

"I'm pleased that one of you grasps that simple fact," said Berthier harshly.

"Our hour for departure grows near," said Napoleon. "We are waiting on the final arrival of a dozen more officers, and then we must move, or risk being driven back into the desert." He made an energetic sweep with his arm. "There is still a chance to surprise the English, and we must do it. And we must surprise those traitors in Paris, before they can do any more damage."

The officers in the tent growled consent.

Victoire listened. "Then only a few of your staff will go with you," she said thoughtfully. "The rest will be left behind?"

"Theirs is a rear-guard action. They can hold this land against the Ottomans. Further, it will force the British to send an army to recover his land. That will cost them gold that can't be used against France herself. And there is always the chance we will prevail before the English can raise an army to fight them." Napoleon rose and paced as if unable to contain his energy any longer. "We have work ahead of us if we are to preserve our cause. There are those who long for the days of Madame Guillotine and the sound of tumbrels in the streets. I say this will not happen. The Revolution has brought us to this, and if we return to the excesses of eight years ago, we will eventually ruin all we have achieved."

This time the officers cheered him, and Desaix had to wipe his eyes.

Berthier took advantage of this moment to rise and bow to Victoire. "I very much regret, Madame Vernet, that due to the circumstances of our withdrawal, you and Inspector General Vernet will not be accompanying Napoleon. I am certain you understand?"

"Louis, for mercy's sake, not now," said Napoleon.

"I'm not stupid, General of the Division Berthier," said Victoire, curtsying to him. "I understand perfectly."

Roustam-Raza dozed in the shade of Napoleon's tent; most of the camp observed the midday rest, and those few people who could not lie down through the heat of the day went about their work lethargically.

Victoire, returning from the hospital tent, made a point of going to speak to her Egyptian friend.

"Allah shower blessings upon you," she said as she sank down on the sand beside him.

"May he advance your husband and—"

"I know; give him many sons," Victoire finished for him. She folded her hands in her lap. "I hear that Murat is back."

"Early this morning," said Roustam-Raza. "He looks very thin."

"Poor man." She watched Roustam-Raza for some clue to how Murat had acted. "Have you spoken to him?"

"Nothing more than a few words. He was tired. They rode most of the night." The Mameluke pulled at his moustache. "You are concerned for what he will tell Napoleon."

"Yes," she said. "I thought he would be a champion for . . ." Her words trailed off. "When Lirylah died . . ."

"He bleeds for her. Deep inside him the wound is not healed," said Roustam-Raza, his large eyes bewildered. "Why that should be so, when she was only a woman . . ."

"He mourns her," said Victoire.

"You fear he will not defend you to my master because

the girl died," said Roustam-Raza. "That would not be honorable."

"No, it wouldn't," Victoire agreed. "But grief does strange things. It's possible that Murat could come to believe that somehow I was at fault, for I was with her when she was shot. If he thinks that, then he will turn away from me, and Vernet and I will be lost."

"I have given my account to Napoleon already," said Roustam-Raza.

"And for that I thank you, and so does my husband." She wiped the sweat from her brow with the tips of her fingers. "I wish I had a proper bonnet still. This"—she fingered the round straw hat she wore—"is terrible."

"You will have more in France," said Roustam-Raza.

"If ever I see France again." She kept her eyes on her hands so that Roustam-Raza could not see the tears there.

Roustam-Raza started to speak, then fell silent. After a short while, he said, "I will speak with Murat."

At that she met his gaze steadily. "I couldn't ask it of you, my friend."

"Nevertheless, I will speak with him," said Roustam-Raza.

# 15

LARREY ROLLED DOWN his bloodstained sleeves and watched Victoire with bleary eyes as she began the thankless task of preparing the dead soldier for graves registration. "He was too weak. If he had not had the flux, he might have survived. But when pernicious pus comes and the flux as well, no physician on earth can save—" He turned on his heel.

"Yes. He was too weak," said Victoire steadily. She watched her hands go about their tasks as if they were no part of her. "He didn't have sufficient strength to fight, even had there been no pus. The flux had taken its toll."

"No, he hadn't any strength left," said Larrey. "I had hoped that I would not have to write many more of the letters ... You know how difficult it is, telling a father or mother or wife or brother or sister that ..." He motioned the words away.

"You have saved many others," said Victoire, wanting to keep her thoughts away from what she was doing. "There are hundreds who are walking the earth who would be under it, if not for you. Be consoled with that, Monsieur Larrey."

"I'll do what I can," said Larrey, rubbing his face and jaw, heedless of the faint smear of red he left on the stubble of his beard.

She was almost finished with what she needed to do. "Do you want me to write the report, or will you?"

"Oh, I'll do it. You've been doing more than your share here these last two days." He glanced her way. "I gather from your presence that everything is the same. Still no change on Berthier's part?"

"You mean in regard to our returning to France?" She saw him nod. "Nothing. He's obdurate. I think he would bury us here if he could find an excuse for doing it."

"And there is no lessening of the animosity he has for you?" He fixed the cuff latches and gestured to her to come away from the dead man. "Leave him alone now."

"Very well," she said, willing to be finished. As she moved between the ranks of beds, she said, "What will become of these men, once Napoleon is gone?"

Larrey caught his lower lip between his teeth before he answered. "I'm not certain. Once the staff leaves, any who recover will be needed back with their battalions. In the many battles or through illness almost half the men who first came here have been lost. Pressure will be greater, once it is known that Napoleon has left. Though after the Ottoman's recent defeats, so long as the army stays together, you will be safe. If the Pasha or the Ottomans return to power here you will all be killed out of hand. I wish there was something I could do. It seems pointless to save a life, only to strand the same person in this thankless land. It's out of my hands; that troubles me as much as it removes a burden from me."

"But they won't simply be abandoned," said Victoire anxiously. "It's one thing to leave the able-bodied behind—if we must fend for ourselves, we will—but the wounded and ill, they're at the mercy of everything. I fear for them, Monsieur Larrey."

"Well you should," Larrey said as he lifted the flap leading to his own quarters. "Someone must concern themselves with their welfare or none of them will live." He looked over at Victoire. "Is that what you want me to do before I leave? Do you want me to make guarantees?"

"No," she said, a bit uncertainly. "But there is something I want you to do: I want a last opportunity to speak with Berthier."

"With Berthier? Your dealings with him have always been disastrous. Why would you want to bring his wrath upon you again?" He pulled up a stool and sank onto it. "Isn't it bad enough now?"

"That's why I want to speak with him. I'd like him to understand. I want him to know why I came to suspect him. It wasn't caprice, Monsieur Larrey. If he can grasp that, he might reconsider Vernet's position." Her hands were caught together, her knuckles white.

"It's possible," said Larrey. "But it could make matters worse between you. Have you thought of that?"

"I have." She pulled her hands apart and they clung to the folds of her skirt instead. "But I must make the attempt." She faltered. "If you asked it of him, he might listen to me."

"Very well," said Larrey. "I'll do what I can. I owe you that much. Come back at eight this evening, after everyone has eaten. If I can persuade him, he will accompany me. If I can't, then—" He made a gesture of capitulation. "I wouldn't do this for most of the women who have tended the wounded. They are competent nurses, most of them, but they are timid and unobservant. You are not cut of that cloth; you are determined and you are constantly alert. You have never hesitated when you thought the welfare of the patient was at risk. For that, for the men who are alive because of you, I will do this."

Such praise took Victoire by surprise, and she stared at Larrey. "I didn't do this to have . . ."

"No, you did not. You have never tried to turn your work here to your advantage until now. And I share your sentiments. So I will make an attempt." He indicated the door. "I think it would be best if you will leave your husband in your quarters. Berthier might agree to talk with you, but not the two of you as a united pair. He is not satisfied that you were not simply following Vernet's orders." He caught a glimpse of himself in his shaving mirror and shook his head. "And I had better do something before I present myself at Napoleon's mess."

Victoire curtsied before she left the tent. "Thank you, Monsieur Larrey. I'm very grateful to you."

Larrey muttered a response as he reached for the sliver of soap that remained and his shaving brush.

Berthier's eyes were flinty as Victoire came into Larrey's quarters; it was a quarter after eight and the camp was thrown into the last eager activities of the day as dusk swiftly surrendered to night. "Madame Vernet." He gave a movement that might have been a bow. "Larrey has been your advocate all through our meal," he said without any courtesy. "For the respect I bear him and in order to put an end to this, I have agreed to hear you out, Madame Vernet. And let that satisfy you."

It was not a very promising beginning, but Victoire did not argue with him. "If that is how you will have it, I will accept it," she said. "And so will Inspector Vernet."

"He is working with General Marmont tonight, as I recall," said Berthier. "Preparing for tomorrow's departure."

"Yes," said Victoire. "Earlier today he was with Desaix and Kleber." She hesitated, then said, "The Egyptians will miss Desaix."

"His duties keep him at Napoleon's side," Berthier said sternly.

"Of course," said Victoire. "But the Egyptians prefer him to Kleber, and admire his demeanor. His conduct suits them and they admire his courage. That was all my remark intended." She glanced at Larrey, hoping to find some encouragement in his eyes.

Berthier selected one of the two stools in the tent and sat down. "How is it that you are inclined to study such things as what the Egyptians approve?"

"We are in Egypt, General Berthier. It is wise to know how to go on here." She did her best to keep the challenge out of her tone. "This isn't France, and we are mistaken when we suppose it is. When I went in search of the scepter, I learned a great deal."

Berthier snorted, but for once said nothing. He regarded her steadily, giving her the obligation to speak.

She gathered her courage and began. "I realize I was mistaken in my assumption that you were the officer acting against Napoleon. For that I apologize again, and assure you it was never my intention to embarrass you. I didn't have sufficient information at my disposal—or, rather, I did, but did not realize it. You appeared to be the one who acted against Napoleon when I examined the facts as I knew them. I did not arrive at that conclusion without cause." She pressed on, trying to ignore the forbidding countenance Berthier turned on her. "I've wanted to tell you how I came to believe this dreadful thing of you, so that you will not leave here convinced that I was attempting to impugn your honor without cause." Now that she had cleared that first hurdle, some of her terror faded. "I am very pleased that Monsieur Larrey is willing to listen to this, so that you and I will both have the protection of a witness to our remarks."

"Go on," said Berthier, no change in his condemning expression.

She presented her arguments just as she had ordered them in her thoughts. "It was the death of the marine guard that began this whole terrible episode. His death must be marked as the point where the actions of those opposed to Napoleon took form. Until then there may have been those who wanted to bring Napoleon to heel, but they had no opportunity to put their desires into action. With the death of the marine guard, matters changed. This was not clear when the crime was discovered. It was assumed at the time that the entire purpose of the murder was to permit the thief to steal the scepter."

"Yes," said Berthier. "What other reason could there be?"

She met his eyes. "Silence," she answered. "If the guard had not known the thief, there would have been no reason to kill him. He could have been bound and gagged, and the thief could have taken the scepter. But the guard was murdered, and the murder was deliberately brutal."

"It was," said Berthier. "On that we will agree."

"Thank you," said Victoire at once. "The thief wanted to leave a warning to the other marine guards, the ones set to watch Napoleon's treasure. Which implies that they, too, would recognize the man if they saw him. There was no way to anticipate they would all be killed on the *L'Orient*."

Berthier pursed his lips. "It is possible. There is some merit in what you say."

"I have had a long time to think about it," said Victoire. "And much reason to examine the case." She looked toward Larrey, but the physician had not altered his neutral expression. Victoire resumed her argument. "Who was aware of the treasure and the guards? You were one, General Berthier. My husband was another. So was Murat. The other two were Desaix and Lavallette. And, of course, the guards who stood watch."

"Yes?" said Berthier impatiently. "What is there new in—"

"Therefore one of you had to have been the thief. The rest of the camp was not aware that the treasure was stored here, or how it was guarded. Whoever murdered the guard had to know those things. Murat was on patrol when the murder was done, and so it was not he. Desaix is accounted for, and so is Lavallette. That leaves my husband, you, and the guard himself." She stared at Berthier. "I know that my husband did not do it. So who else could I suspect, if you not you?"

"A very loyal posture for a wife to take," said Berthier, but his tone was softened a little.

"Bear with me, General Berthier. Whoever took the scepter was able to contact the Englishman Hazlett, either directly or indirectly. This meant that the thief had to be in a position of power, or be the tool of someone very high, or he would not have been able to search out Hazlett without discovery, let alone send the man so far up the Nile for the purpose of concealing the scepter. And Hazlett was willing to do it, instead of stealing the scepter for himself. From that I've concluded that he was aware of the man in Paris ordering the venture, and was convinced that he must be obeyed." It was very difficult not to pace as she spoke. "If Hazlett had succeeded in concealing the scepter so that it could be found later on, by those who had reason to know where to look, then the political importance of the scepter becomes greater than its material worth. You will allow that a scepter of solid gold is worth a great deal."

"I will allow that," said Berthier, not quite so stiffly as before.

"Therefore, I had to conclude that the theft was political and not motivated by simple greed. If greed were the only issue, the scepter would've been out of the country and in the hands of anyone with sufficient money to pay for it." She went very carefully now. "Roustam-Raza holds the scepter in high respect. Speak to him about it if you doubt what I tell you. For the Egyptians it is a symbol of the link from the ancient kings to the Pashas. Therefore if the thief was Muslim, there would have been no reason to employ the Englishman. The scepter would have been returned to the Pasha and that would have been the end of it. So I must conclude the thief intended to use the scepter against Napoleon, otherwise why go to so much trouble?"

Now Berthier appeared a bit more interested. "You have some sense in your supposition."

Victoire was too caught up in what she was saying to be distracted by this near-compliment. "If the theft of the scepter was part of an attempt to compromise or discredit Napoleon, and the thief known to the guard, then it followed that the actions of the thief were part of a larger plot. The actions of the thief were much too complicated to be accidental or the whim of the moment. Hazlett had been paid and expected to earn more. That means that the murder and theft were not isolated, but part of a larger scheme." She took a deep breath. "I saw a dispatch that was signed by Tallyrand, or someone who wanted to implicate him. In it he states that there are those close to Napoleon who are committed to bring him down."

"I read your report on the dispatch," said Berthier.

"With everything else I had found out, how could I not believe that you had a role to play in this conspiracy? Vernet was not part of a plot—for if he were, I would know it."

"That I am coming to believe," said Berthier, looking once toward Larrey, then back at Victoire.

"Murat was not the conspirator, or he would not have gone up the Nile with me, searching for the scepter. And as we've agreed, he was not in camp at the time of the murder. Desaix is loyalty itself, and his life is the army. He does not strive for advancement beyond what he has, nor for political position. If he were part of a conspiracy, it would be one within the army, not one centered in the Directoire. Therefore Desaix is not the man implicated. Lavallette was out of touch when the dispatches were being sent. He could not have received them, and had he received them, he could not have acted upon them. Therefore Lavallette is not implicated. Who does that leave?"

"I take your point." Berthier coughed once. "Very well. I concede that you had some reason to assume I was part of the conspiracy. But so long as you are making accusations, who else is there who might have done this? You have accounted for everyone."

"Yes, that's what I thought for some time. If you were not guilty, then who could have done it? Everyone was accounted for. That assumption was my greatest error. In fact, there is one man left. Something I just realized a few hours ago." She took great satisfaction in answering Berthier's puzzled frown. "The officer in charge of the marine guard."

Berthier stared at her. "What?"

"The marine officer. The man who was with you when the treasure was secured, the one who explained what the schedule of the guards was. We tend to discount those who do the actual work, and so not even Vernet thought of him." She saw that Larrey was also giving her his full attention. "Think, General Berthier. The guards who stood their watches over the treasure would recognize him, probably more readily than they would recognize any of the generals. He would have the means of finding the Englishman Hazlett, and if he was the agent of someone in Paris, he would have money enough to corrupt half the country, and go about it unnoticed." She played her last card now. "And Vernet told me that the marine guard who was killed was tied up, the knots were so strong that the ropes had to be cut to free the body."

"Sailor's knots?" said Berthier, and did not wait for an answer. "Yes. That would be it."

"If you are not the conspirator who murdered the marine guard and stole the scepter, then that marine lieutenant has to be." She wanted to shake Berthier, to force him to endorse her deductions.

Berthier frowned, but this time it was not directed at Victoire. He stammered a bit when he spoke. "I . . . I must find out what has become of th . . . that marine. I remember seeing him in camp after the disaster in the bay, so he must have survived." He looked at Victoire. "You're very persuasive, Madame Vernet. It may be that you have stumbled on the solution to the whole thing."

At another time Victoire would have protested Berthier's choice of words, but she was too relieved to cavil now. "Find out who that man is, and where he is assigned. Most of the remaining naval personnel were assigned to the merchants or frigates that survived. If he is near Napoleon—"

"Yes. You have followed my thoughts." He rose and bowed to Larrey. "I did not suppose when I accepted your invitation that I would be in your debt for listening to Madame Vernet, but I am." Then he turned to Victoire. "If what you have told me is as accurate as you make it appear, you will have my thanks in spite of all you have done, Madame Vernet."

"Then I am more than satisfied," said Victoire, not quite honestly.

"I will leave you." Berthier went to the door of the tent. "And in the morning, first thing, I will expect you to present yourself at my quarters, Madame Vernet."

This puzzled her, but she said, "It will be my pleasure, General Berthier."

"We'll want to consult you before we question this marine." With that as a parting shot, Berthier was gone.

Larrey watched Victoire for a short while. "Quite an impressive display," he said to her. "I didn't realize you had such skill in reasoning."

"It was part of my education," said Victoire.

"You appear to have turned your education to your advantage," said Larrey.

She could think of nothing to say in response. She took refuge in good manners. "No matter how this ends, I am in your debt for what you did tonight."

"Let us pray that you are right about the guard, and that he can be found before the first ship leaves." Larrey indicated the door. "Your husband can take pride in you tonight."

Victoire answered slowly. "That would be premature, I fear. Until the marine lieutenant is apprehended, danger remains."

Dawn was an hour away, but Berthier was dressed and shaved, watching as two corporals prepared his belongings for loading on the waiting ship. At his feet were two large leather cases he would not permit the soldiers to touch: they contained the shrine he kept to his beloved Giovanna.

Eugene, pale and drawn, stood at Berthier's side, his portable desk ready. "It appears that Madame Vernet may be right," he said, handing two sheets of paper to his superior. "The search was worth it."

"Armand Fellisse. He's from Provence. Formerly attached to the *L'Orient* at the last minute. No one alive remembers why. Papers show that he was assigned to guard Napoleon aboard ship after Malta." Eugene's expression grew more somber. "Here is his appointment." He handed over another sheet of paper.

Berthier read it, filled with a combination of horror and gratitude. "Appointed by Tallyrand. That's Tallyrand's signature," he said as he handed it back to Eugene. "There's no doubt about it. He is not someone's dupe, but at the center of it. If only it can be proved."

"It is a personal appointment, too," said Eugene.

"Never mind," said Berthier, motioning to Eugene to

close his desk. "I believe you." He smiled. "As I am coming to believe Madame Vernet. I thought she had ventured too far and assumed too much, but with all this, I can't deny that she is now in the right."

"She is a very persuasive woman," said Eugene.

"Probably because she is intelligent." He moved aside so that the two corporals could haul off two of his trunks. "I hope Vernet knows what he has. She will be a better ally than the patronage of half the Directors in Paris. And if ever he plays her false, she will make his life the inner circle of hell."

"Jealous women—" began Eugene only to be cut off.

"She isn't jealous, not the way most women are. Hers is not the loyalty of lapdogs but of tigers. She is like a good officer, ready to tolerate many things if they do not compromise the campaign. But dishonor the regiment, or put the gain of a moment ahead of the goals of the—" He broke off as the flap of his tent lifted and Victoire Vernet presented herself.

"You asked me to be here, General Berthier," she said cordially, giving no sign that she had overheard anything he said.

"Yes. I am pleased to see you, Madame Vernet. Eugene has been busy during the night, and it appears that your deductions are correct. The marine lieutenant, Fellisse, may be the man we are seeking." Berthier hesitated. "If we can find him. And we must find him very soon."

"Oh?" said Victoire, coming into the tent. "Why do you say that?"

"Because he has been appointed to guard Napoleon while he is aboard ship. If everything you have told me is accurate, then we are delivering Napoleon into the hands of his greatest enemies." Berthier shook his head. "I have sent him word, but my messenger hasn't returned yet. There is such confusion, and . . ." He lifted his hand to show his frustration.

Victoire understood the problem at once. "Vernet will be delighted to help you," she said at once. "He has never faltered in his loyalty to Napoleon. Let him demonstrate that now."

Berthier regarded her, then shrugged. "If I say no, you will probably set him on the task in any case, won't you?"

"It's likely," she admitted. "It is more likely that with or without my suggestion he would do it himself."

At last Berthier gave in. "All right. I can't interrupt the preparations for departure to search for the man personally. I don't want to see him alerted by pursuit. And if I send men after him now, he would be warned and might flee or try something desperate. So. You will have your chance, Madame Vernet, you and your husband. Fellisse will not be expecting you, and will pay no notice. Find Napoleon and warn him about this Fellisse. Your husband might recognize the man, though it is a year since he saw him." He looked at his cot where open cases stood, waiting for the last of his books, maps, and clothes.

"We will do what we can, General Berthier, and will send you word when there is anything to report." She dropped him a curtsy and hurried out of the tent, making way through the busy pre-dawn bustle of the camp to their tent.

Vernet was rubbing wool fat into his boots, taking extra care where the leather was starting to crack. Other than his boots, he was in uniform and ready for muster. He looked up at her. "Well? What did he have to say?"

"He said there is a marine who may be intending to harm Napoleon," she answered, barely able to conceal her excitement. "And he's given us permission to stop him."

The staging area was full of small carts, stacks of trunks and cases, and men busily loading these things aboard the boats ferrying them out to the *Murion* and *La Carrière*.

Searching through the chaos, the first man Victoire recognized was Joachim Murat, who had just arrived to deliver his trunks to the sailors. He glanced at Victoire, then looked away. "I was sorry to hear that you would not be coming with us, madame," he said formally.

"Under the circumstances, it is to be expected," she answered, adding, "Vernet and I are looking for Napoleon. Have you seen him?"

"Not this morning. Have you tried Madame Foures's tent?" His tone continued to be distant.

"Yes, but neither of them are there," she answered at once. "He is not taking breakfast and I am running out of ideas where to look for him."

"What does Roustam-Raza say?" asked Murat.

"I haven't found him, either," she answered. "That's the one thing that relieves me—if Roustam-Raza is with him, Napoleon is protected." She cocked her head to the side and regarded Murat. "Are you well?"

"Perfectly well, Madame," he said as if speaking to a stranger. "I trust you, too, are well, Madame Vernet?"

"Not just at present," she said with asperity, wanting to throttle Murat for his infuriating remoteness. "And time is very short for action. I fear that an assassin is going to make an attempt on Napoleon's life. That's why I want to find him."

"An assassin?" asked Murat. "What assassin?"

"The same one who killed the marine guard last year," she said. "The one who stole the scepter. The one who caused all else to happen. He is still at liberty, and therefore Napoleon is in danger."

Murat's brown eyes were hooded but there was light in them now, and anger. "Are you certain of that? That it is the same man?"

"Certain enough to be searching for Napoleon with Berthier's blessing," she said. "If you have any suggestions where I might find him, I would be grateful for them. As would my husband. He is with Desaix at present."

A little of the animation Murat had shown six months ago stirred in him. "If I am not mistaken, he will be on his way back from the Pyramids. He said last night that he wanted to see them once more before he left Egypt. They fascinate him, the Pyramids, and the Sphinx."

"Ah," said Victoire. "And is he alone?" she asked urgently.

"Probably. He is sad having to abandon for a time his

dreams for the Orient. But there will be an escort waiting for him at the river, including Roustam-Raza. He would have to be returning now. The morning is already too hot for riding very far."

"But if he is there, how can I reach him? I haven't the right to order a courier, if one could be found, and ..." She flung her hands in the air. "The assassin will strike when he can do so with impunity. And what better place than near the Pyramids? It would serve his purposes very well to have Napoleon a victim of Egypt." Her eyes opened wide as one more hideous thought occurred to her. "The assassin might intend to cast blame on Roustam-Raza. He has already tried to implicate Vernet and Berthier." She stared at Murat. "Who is with Napoleon?"

"I'm not sure. Probably his marine guard." Murat stared at her. "What is it, Madame Vernet?"

"The marine guard." She felt cold in the heat. "And Roustam-Raza?"

"He is making his farewells. This is his land. He may even have family here. He has never said. He is supposed to meet Napoleon when he returns from the Pyramids." Murat grasped her fear. "The marine guard! He was there as well." He signalled to one of his men. "You. Grossante. Keep watch on these things for me. And you. Donerien. Carry a message to Inspector-General Vernet. You'll find him with Desaix." He glanced at Victoire. "You join your husband. I know where to find Roustam-Raza, and I'll attend to it at once."

Donerien saluted. "What message, General Murat?"

"Tell him to meet his wife at the foot of the road to the Pyramids. As quickly as possible." Murat motioned him off, and said to Victoire. "Let's go get a horse for you. You'll have to push the beast, but there's no help for it." He started away from the staging area back to where the horses were stabled.

Victoire strode along as fast as she could, holding her skirts higher than propriety allowed. "Will it take you long to bring Roustam-Raza?"

"No. I must reach him, but he will come at once when

he knows the reason." He increased his pace so that Victoire had to break into a slow run beside him. "Was this your work, Madame?"

"If you mean did I piece it together, yes. But there are many others who could have done so," she said.

"After Napoleon was murdered," said Murat grimly, the darkness that held him still possessing him. "When it would do no good."

The mare was flagging but Victoire spurred her on, forcing her to an extended trot that covered the ground handily; sweat darkened her coat and foam rose on her neck and flanks. Victoire felt the weight of the sun and knew that the mare would not be able to stand much more.

Ahead on the plateau the Pyramids sat, seeming small because of the distance, and the fine ribbon of road leading down from the tremendous monuments appeared to be empty. Victoire shaded her eyes, but the glare was too fierce and she could not see clearly enough. She glanced backward, but there was too much dust from her mare's hooves for her to be certain that anyone was behind her. What would she do if she arrived alone? Warn Napoleon perhaps. He was a soldier and said to be brave. At least he could then fight for his life. If the marine didn't kill her as she approached. She offered a brief, fervent prayer that Murat's man had reached Vernet quickly.

She was near enough to the junction now that she pulled her mare in and gave her some respite from the hard pace. At a fast walk the mare's panting was more apparent, and Victoire patted the water-skin she had brought with her, knowing that the mare would need it all as soon as she was cool enough to drink safely.

Then Victoire could see a lone figure waiting on a horse at the junction of the main road with the track leading up to the Pyramids. Even at this distance, she was aware that it was the marine guard, and that he carried a pistol in his belt, though she could not yet see it.

Where was Napoleon? Victoire scanned the road again, and finally made out a horse and rider coming down the narrow trail. They were more than halfway down from the plateau, and descending at a good pace.

Victoire cursed herself for not insisting on a weapon. The worst she could do was run her horse into the marine guard's, assuming the fellow could be taken by surprise by the action. Considering how nervous he must be, more likely he would shoot her as she approached. Though that might warn Napoleon as well. The general might even think the marine was protecting him from her. She urged the mare back into the trot and considered throwing the water-skin at Fellisse, the marine officer, when she got close enough. But she was not certain she would be able to hit him squarely, and that would not be enough. She had to stop the marine guard or warn Napoleon of danger.

This last goaded her to action. She struck off the road, cutting through the fine sand toward the road where Napoleon rode, hoping to cut him off before he came into range of the marine guard's pistol. If Napoleon saw her coming, he might realize something was wrong, she decided, and pressed the mare harder.

She was nearing the trail when the marine guard became aware of her, and shouted something. He rose in his stirrups, then put his horse into a canter, set on chasing her down.

On the trail, Napoleon reined in.

Victoire forced her mare into a gallop, holding her together with firm hands as they raced over the sand.

And then there was another horse coming up fast, aimed right for the marine guard's mount. Victoire recognized Vernet, and her dread began to lift as she hurtled toward Napoleon.

Napoleon kicked his horse to a slow trot, as fast as he dared on the steep, slippery trail.

Vernet managed to cut Lieutenant Fellisse off, swinging his horse around to block the trail.

Victoire reined in, and shouted to Napoleon, "He's armed."

Vernet, paralleling him now, urged his horse ahead just as the marine aimed his pistol. At the next instant there came a shot as Fellisse made one desperate attempt to kill Napoleon. "Liberty! Equality! Fraternity!" the lieutenant shouted before wheeling his horse and heading at a flat-out run back toward the French camp.

Vernet lurched in the saddle and bellowed in pain as the ball intended for Napoleon struck his upper arm. He had been so close to the discharging pistol that the cloth in his jacket smoldered.

Victoire pulled her mare around and rode to her husband's side as the marine guard became a speck in a distant dust cloud.

"The ball went through," Vernet said through clenched teeth. "It isn't too bad."

Despite the countless wounds Victoire had dressed and tended without turning a hair, she now felt queasy and a trifle faint at the sight of Vernet's injury. "I . . . I'll bind it for you," she said, tasting bile at the back of her mouth. She set about tearing her petticoat while her mare sobbed for breath.

A short time later Napoleon came up to them. "That was either very reckless or very brave, madame," he said to Victoire. "And you, Vernet—to take a ball for me. Quite an impressive act."

"It is my duty," said Vernet as Victoire busied herself in wrapping lengths of petticoat cotton around his injury.

# 16

❧

ROUSTAM-RAZA ARRIVED IN camp an hour after Napoleon returned with Lucien and Victoire Vernet; he led an exhausted horse with an unconscious man bowed, tied, over the saddle. Streaks of blood ran down the gelding's dappled flanks.

Victoire was the first to look up as he approached. "You caught him," she cried out in relief.

"Of course," said Roustam-Raza, and drew in his horse to dismount. "I should have gone to the Pyramids with Napoleon," he said to her as she came nearer. "He was in danger because I wasn't there."

"But you couldn't have known," said Victoire reasonably. "And you may never see your brothers again."

The camp was returning to full activity after the midday nap, an activity made more hectic by the preparations for departure that night. In the bustle of activity, Roustam-Raza was unharried. He looked at Fellisse and spat. "I should have been with Napoleon, not my brothers; I have sworn to guard and protect him," Roustam-Raza said stubbornly. "I must never compromise my oath again."

Vernet, the sleeve cut off his uniform and his arm impressively bandaged, said, "You could have helped us catch the rascal sooner, before he could fire."

"He is caught now," said Roustam-Raza, his voice very hard. "That is some consolation."

"Not to him, I'd wager," said Vernet. Now that the worst of his pain was over and the desperation of their acts had passed, he was strangely euphoric, as if all this had happened elsewhere, and was made of the stuff of legends. "Not that he doesn't deserve—"

"He deserves worse than I can give him," said Roustam-Raza, adding, "He talked. It took a little time, but he talked. Murat has the record of what he said. He's taken it to Napoleon."

Victoire, recalling the Englishman at the villa near Alexandria, felt slightly faint as Roustam-Raza said this. She made herself look at Fellisse long enough to make a quick assessment of his condition.

The Mameluke noticed her glance. "This man was a traitor. He's alive for a little while yet. He won't last much longer. Waste nothing on him. He has lost his honor.

"Oh, yes, he's alive to breathe; but there is no skin on the palms of his hands, or his fingers." He paid no attention to her shocked expression. "He was determined to resist, and so I had to use stern measures." The Mameluke looked at her. "He tried to kill Napoleon and he wounded your husband, and would have killed him if his aim had been better. He would surely have killed you, and his men tried more than once. He slaughtered the marine guard and he is responsible for the death of Lirylah, because he ordered Hazlett to follow the two of you. He deliberately implicated your husband in treason. How can you balk at returning to him a little of the pain he has given to others?"

"It ... it isn't ..." She was going to tell him that the French didn't do such things, but that would be less than the truth. Not very many years ago France was an abattoir.

"I must report to Napoleon, now that Murat has delivered our account of the questioning. And it would be best to find a guard for Fellisse. He may regain consciousness before he dies." He patted the neck of his horse. "And the animals need water. I'll send a groom."

"Yes," said Victoire, with the odd sensation that Roustam-Raza was leaving her on guard with Fellisse. She glanced at the traitor but could not look at him for very long; she had worked with the wounded and knew what approaching death was like.

Vernet, watching from the stack of their belongings, now hastily stored in trunks and cases, said, "I'll guard him if you want to find Larrey."

She shrugged. "I suppose I ought to. But I don't suppose—"

"No," said Vernet, cutting her off. "I don't suppose, either."

Two privates emerged from their tent, a large trunk between them. "Is this the biggest?"

"I think so," said Vernet, not trusting himself to be certain. The aftermath of his pain left him unable to concentrate for very long. Often he found he had to lean on Victoire in order to stay upright.

"Yes," confirmed Victoire. "That and the clothespresses are the largest, and the rest are as you see."

One of the privates sighed. "It will take another two hours before it is all stowed aboard. The ships will leave in three. You're cutting it very fine."

Vernet answered for them both. "We weren't aware we were going until a short while ago. Napoleon just informed us a few hours ago that there was space available and requested that we prepare to leave at once."

"Well, the ships sail on the night tide. You'd better make certain that all your gear is packed. Otherwise it will be left behind." This second private was rangier than the first, and had a roving eye.

"My wife will inspect the tent to be sure everything is packed," said Vernet, making this minor observation a warning. "Rest assured."

The privates lugged the trunk in the direction of the staging area.

Victoire saw a groom approaching and her gloom lifted. She held out the reins of both horses to the groom, saying, "Give them water, and then find out what Napoleon wants done with that . . . offal."

The groom paid no heed to her outburst. He patted the neck of Roustam-Raza's horse, then ran a critical hand over Fellisse's, paying no attention to the man bound to the saddle. The word that the marine was the thief and also a failed assassin was all over camp. "It's a bad business, punishing horses like this. I'll do what I can for him, but he might have lost his wind."

"Do what you can," said Victoire, and stepped back to allow the groom to lead the horses away.

Vernet got unsteadily to his feet. "I'd better find another pelisse. This one is ruined. Napoleon might not be a stickler for dress, but a missing sleeve is more than he'll tolerate in proper dress." He wandered into the tent, looking for the clothes case where his second uniform was stored.

"I have it," said Victoire, coming after him. "I took it out for you earlier, once Larrey cut the sleeve." She helped him out of his ruined pelisse, then gingerly eased his arms into his second one. As she fastened the lacings up the front, she went on, "The dress uniform is in the case. It will be in our cabin aboard ship, in case you need it. You can order new ones when we get home." It was strange to say these things, and the words felt unwieldy in her mouth. All at once it was an effort not to cry.

"Come now, Victoire," said Vernet as she pushed her fair head against the braid of his pelisse. He put his good arm around her and held her close. "We're through it now, my love; it's behind us."

"That's why I'm crying, you idiot." She sniffed, then wiped her eyes. "I never fail when there is trouble. It is afterward that I'm useless." Her gruff apology brought a smile to his mouth.

"Better after than during," he said, and kissed her forehead.

She glared at him. "If you are teasing me, I'll—"

"I'm telling you the truth," he protested. "Word of honor."

"Oh." She relented. "I should've warned you: I'm impossible when the worst is over."

"And unstoppable while it is going on," Vernet confirmed. "I must count myself a fortunate man. Most wives, from what I have seen, run counter to you."

She decided that he had given her a compliment; when she smiled, tears welled in her eyes again and she dashed them away in exasperation. "I'm truly not such a ninny as I appear."

"No one has ever said you are," Vernet told her softly. "Except you."

Murat was not much taller than Napoleon, although this was only noticeable when the two men stood close together, as they did now. The ruddy glow of sunset flooded the staging area, casting long shadows from the few remaining trunks and cases, and turned the faces of both men into brilliant masks.

"I've read the report," said Napoleon. "Enlightening. So it was you and Desaix they wanted to compromise, with the intent I would not deploy my troops widely for fear of mutiny." He watched Murat closely. "A good thing Fellisse didn't know about your night patrols, or there could have been just such a mistake made."

"It was Vernet's bad luck to be the one who could not account for his time," Murat added.

"Fellisse must have expected the supplies to be brought ashore that night, with the activity to cover his crimes. Did he reveal anything about it?" Napoleon asked. "There was nothing in your report."

"He didn't say, and there were other, more pressing questions we had to ask. Roustam-Raza didn't think Fellisse would resist as long as he did. I thank God we learned so much," said Murat, deliberately keeping his voice low. "Treachery on that scale—"

"I should have anticipated it," said Napoleon, with a quick, admonitory glance at Murat from his dissimilar eyes. "Those ambitious, greedy, venal cowards who clutter the seats of power in Paris—"

"I've been telling myself the same thing, that I ought to have realized the enormity of the treason," said Murat. "But how could I? Or anyone?" His face was bleak. "If I had suspected the truth, matters would have gone differently. As it was, I underestimated the gravity—"

"I'm fortunate that Vernet is not a vengeful man," Napoleon interrupted him. "He would have good reason to leave my service after what he has been through. He's a capable officer and would prove useful to those engaged in international trade."

"Vernet isn't that sort; he won't leave the gendarmes," said Murat. "More to the point, his wife would not advise it."

"A formidable woman, you tell me." Napoleon waited for an answer.

"Yes," said Murat, his tone measured. "Yes, she is formidable in her way. But more than that, she is knowledgeable."

"Ah?" said Napoleon. "Why do you remark on that?"

"Because she thinks. It makes her quite . . . quite unpredictable." Murat still did not smile readily, but amusement brightened his brown eyes. "After courage, she is certainly Vernet's most valuable asset. And all your soldiers have courage."

"Interesting," said Napoleon, rubbing his lower lip with his forefinger. "Well, I suppose it would be best to promote him, then, or something of the sort. I want such men around me. There are so few I can trust." He sighed. "I want to have a staff meeting tomorrow morning. Tell Vernet he's to be there, will you?" He started away from Murat, then stopped a moment. "Berthier's cooled down. I don't think he'll set himself against, um, Gendarme Colonel Vernet again. Or Madame Vernet, for that matter."

Murat nodded. "Was that his idea or yours?"

Napoleon only chuckled as he resumed his steady, rapid stride.

In the brisk wind the *La Carrière* leaned on a tight reach in choppy seas. The crew went about their routine work with zest—whether it was because Napoleon was aboard or because they were at last leaving Egypt, no one stated—as the morning wore on.

The main cabin of the ship was crowded as Napoleon's officers gathered for their staff meeting. Berthier, sitting on Napoleon's immediate right, carried Eugene's portable desk, a pen with a fresh-trimmed nib held at the ready.

"I am certain you are all aware of the attempt that was made on my life yesterday," said Napoleon without preamble. "That attempt was thwarted by Colonel Vernet, one of the Gendarme officers who came to guard our supply lines. General Murat and my Mameluke, Roustam-Raza, apprehended the would-be assassin and questioned him. It seems this man was in the hire of my enemies. Not the English, but someone in Paris. Further, he must have been more than a mere marine officer. He showed too much initiative in taking the scepter.

"This Fellisse, if that was his real name, hired some renegade Englishmen to do his filthy bidding. They are the ones to whom he passed the scepter. It seems that his plan was to plant the symbol and then have the Pasha find that it had been 'miraculously' restored as a sign that they were to throw off the foreign oppressors, us. We very nearly had to face a full-scale revolt by millions of Egyptians. If it weren't for Murat and Roustam-Raza's fine work, we would certainly have been trapped between the two forces at the battle near Akoubir fort.

"So we have thwarted the plot here. The scepter is safely in my cabin. The assassin's bullet was taken by Vernet. It will take the English time to rally their forces and retake that forsaken country. Unless luck deserts us, we will be back in France within two weeks. Thus we leave one set of hazards in Egypt for another set in Paris."

Berthier cleared his throat. "Each of you will be asked to report any attempts to suborn you or your staff by anyone holding power in Paris. We will be using only trusted men in the future. Those who are proven in their loyalty must work twice as hard until we are in an unassailable position. We, once betrayed, have no choice.

"Each man in this room is trusted. Look about you, remember who is here. Should anyone else try to suborn you, contact Vernet here. He has bled to save Napoleon and will watch for further conspiracies in the future. He has many assets, some you would not expect."

The newly promoted Gendarme colonel nodded at the compliment, meeting the aide's smile.

Napoleon heard him out with occasional nods. "Yes. We must end this blight before it ruins all we have worked to achieve, for our tasks have just begun. I have determined that there is no choice but for us to seek power in Paris. I, we, or my family can never be safe so long as those who currently rule in Paris are in a position to do us harm."

The short, simply dressed general looked around the room. His voice grew louder, riveting every man's attention. "France is being poisoned from within. When we should be carrying the Revolution to the rest of Europe, we bicker and waste our resources. Europe has struggled too long under the heels of monarchs. Wasted too many of her best men in fruitless wars. I see a day when all the world lives without war, each man enjoying the benefits of liberty, fraternity, and equality."

Napoleon had begun pacing. The other officers in the room sat, barely breathing, watching him pass by and waiting for his next words.

"The strength of France is her army. And we, gentlemen, can make ourselves its masters. Then, safe from the meddling of politicians and bureaucrats, we can turn our efforts outward. Unite Europe in a 'Pax Napoleon' that could last a hundred years." The dark-haired Corsican stopped by his desk, a few feet in front of Lucien Vernet. "Join your fate with mine, gentlemen, and we will unite the world."

Vernet regarded Napoleon directly. "If that is what you seek, General, then it is our duty to do all that we can to help you achieve it." The other officers in the room moved toward them to join Vernet in swearing their loyalty to Napoleon and his dream.

Victoire stood on the afterdeck, her eyes fixed on the spreading wake. Apparently she was preoccupied, for when Murat came up to her, he had to speak her name twice before he claimed her attention.

"You're sorry to be leaving?" he asked, waving to the south-southeast, where Egypt lay.

"In a sense, yes," she said, still surprised that he had approached her. "It is a very mysterious place. I never really understood its people."

"It is a very dangerous place," Murat corrected her.

She nodded. "I don't mind leaving the danger, but I hate to lose the mystery."

"Until it is solved?" he suggested.

"Yes," she admitted, wondering why he had come to speak with her.

Murat said, "I told Vernet I wanted to have a word with you; I don't want you to think otherwise."

"This isn't a clandestine setting," she said, thinking of the weeks she had been cut off from the world with Murat, Roustam-Raza, and Lirylah.

He narrowed his eyes at the horizon. "I have it on very good authority that Vernet's due for a change of duties, to something very important." He turned to her as she stared at him. "It's not official yet, but I thought you'd like to know."

"That's very kind of you," she said, keeping her voice level in spite of her urge to cheer. "May I tell him?"

"Leave that to Napoleon," Murat suggested. He was silent again for a short time. "Roustam-Raza has given Berthier an account of our search for the scepter. He's also given a copy of it to Vernet. It's official, not confidential."

Victoire blinked. "Why official?"

"It's part of the exoneration of your husband. But it has bearing on you, and—" He stopped, and when he spoke again, his voice was softer. "I've been surly, Madame Vernet, and for that I wish to make amends."

"You lost someone dear to you," she said. "It was your hurt speaking."

He looked at her. "No. I've permitted myself to believe that, but it isn't true. I ... I could not bear my guilt. So I thrust it upon you."

Her face reddened. "Murat, you don't need to say this to me."

"Yes, I do," he countered. "Not for your sensibilities, Victoire; for mine." He hesitated. "I have been detestable.

You would be right to repudiate me. But I pray ... Are we ... Is it possible for us to continue as friends?"

She managed not to laugh. "Yes, Joachim. It's not only possible, it's welcome."

He nodded twice, decisively. "Good. That's good. What will your husband say?"

"He will no doubt find a pleasant respite from our previous difficulties with Berthier in having a powerful general and hero as an ally," she said with a wicked grin. Her amusement faded. "You will never find him against you. He knows that without your help I would be dead."

Again he nodded, this time watching his hands flex on the rail. "Tell him for me that if he ever abuses you, he will answer to me, and damn the propriety."

Victoire cocked her head to the side. "Unlikely. I think though, perhaps, that last should remain between you and me."

"You're probably right," he concurred. He slapped the rail lightly several times, then said, "Are you looking forward to returning to France?"

"I suppose so," she said. "It will certainly be calmer."

He waited, and when she said nothing more, he turned toward her. "But?" he prompted.

She nodded. "Ah, yes. But."

"Well, what is it? What worries you?" He regarded her with concern. "Is it money? Position? What?"

At last she admitted the one thing that had troubled her since she and Vernet had stepped aboard the *La Carrière*. "Oh, Murat, you'll think I'm very, very silly."

"Tell me," he urged her.

"I'm so afraid I'll be bored," she confessed, and wondered why Murat burst out laughing.

# TAUT, SUSPENSEFUL THRILLERS BY EDGAR AWARD-WINNING AUTHOR
# PATRICIA D. CORNWELL
## Featuring Kay Scarpetta, M.E.

### BODY OF EVIDENCE

71701-8/$5.99 US/$6.99 Can

"Nerve jangling...verve and brilliance...high drama... Ms. Cornwell fabricates intricate plots and paces the action at an ankle-turning clip."

*The New York Times Book Review*

### POSTMORTEM

71021-8/$4.99 US/$5.99 Can

"Taut, riveting—whatever your favorite strong adjective, you'll use it about this book!"

Sara Paretsky

*And Coming Soon*

### ALL THAT REMAINS

71833-2/$5.99 US/$6.99 Can

Buy these books at your local bookstore or use this coupon for ordering:

Mail to: Avon Books, Dept BP, Box 767, Rte 2, Dresden, TN 38225     C
Please send me the book(s) I have checked above.
❑ My check or money order— no cash or CODs please— for $_____is enclosed (please add $1.50 to cover postage and handling for each book ordered— Canadian residents add 7% GST).
❑ Charge my VISA/MC Acct#_____Exp Date_____
Minimum credit card order is two books or $6.00 (please add postage and handling charge of $1.50 per book — Canadian residents add 7% GST). For faster service, call 1-800-762-0779. Residents of Tennessee, please call 1-800-633-1607. Prices and numbers are subject to change without notice. Please allow six to eight weeks for delivery.

Name_____
Address_____
City_____State/Zip_____
Telephone No._____PDC 0293

# ELLIOTT ROOSEVELT'S DELIGHTFUL MYSTERY SERIES

## MURDER IN THE ROSE GARDEN
70529-X/$4.95US/$5.95Can

## MURDER IN THE OVAL OFFICE
70528-1/$4.99US/$5.99Can

## MURDER AND THE FIRST LADY
69937-0/$4.99US/$5.99Can

## THE HYDE PARK MURDER
70058-1/$4.50US/$5.50Can

## MURDER AT HOBCAW BARONY
70021-2/$4.50US/$5.50Can

## THE WHITE HOUSE PANTRY MURDER
70404-8/$4.50US/$5.50Can

## MURDER AT THE PALACE
70405-6/$4.99US/$5.99Can

## MURDER IN THE BLUE ROOM
71237-7/$4.99US/$5.99Can

---

Buy these books at your local bookstore or use this coupon for ordering:

Mail to: Avon Books, Dept BP, Box 767, Rte 2, Dresden, TN 38225          C
Please send me the book(s) I have checked above.
❏ My check or money order— no cash or CODs please— for $_____is enclosed (please add $1.50 to cover postage and handling for each book ordered— Canadian residents add 7% GST).
❏ Charge my VISA/MC Acct#_____Exp Date_____
Minimum credit card order is two books or $6.00 (please add postage and handling charge of $1.50 per book — Canadian residents add 7% GST). For faster service, call 1-800-762-0779. Residents of Tennessee, please call 1-800-633-1607. Prices and numbers are subject to change without notice. Please allow six to eight weeks for delivery.

Name_____
Address_____
City_____State/Zip_____
Telephone No._____ROS 0892

# FOLLOW IN THE FOOTSTEPS OF DETECTIVE J.P. BEAUMONT WITH FAST-PACED MYSTERIES BY J.A. JANCE

**UNTIL PROVEN GUILTY**  89638-9/$4.50 US/$5.50 CAN

**INJUSTICE FOR ALL**  89641-9/$4.50 US/$5.50 CAN

**TRIAL BY FURY**  75138-0/$3.95 US/$4.95 CAN

**TAKING THE FIFTH**  75139-9/$4.50 US/$5.50 CAN

**IMPROBABLE CAUSE**  75412-6/$4.50 US/$5.50 CAN

**A MORE PERFECT UNION**  75413-4/$4.50 US/$5.50 CAN

**DISMISSED WITH PREJUDICE**  75547-5/$4.99 US/$5.99 CAN

**MINOR IN POSSESSION**  75546-7/$4.50 US/$5.50 CAN

**PAYMENT IN KIND**  75836-9/$4.50 US/$5.50 CAN

### *Coming Soon*
**WITHOUT DUE PROCESS**

### *And also by J.A. Jance*
**HOUR OF THE HUNTER**  71107-9/$4.99 US/$5.99 CAN

---

Buy these books at your local bookstore or use this coupon for ordering:

Mail to: Avon Books, Dept BP, Box 767, Rte 2, Dresden, TN 38225                                C
Please send me the book(s) I have checked above.
❑ My check or money order— no cash or CODs please— for $_____ is enclosed
(please add $1.50 to cover postage and handling for each book ordered— Canadian residents add 7% GST).
❑ Charge my VISA/MC Acct#_____Exp Date_____
Minimum credit card order is two books or $6.00 (please add postage and handling charge of $1.50 per book — Canadian residents add 7% GST). For faster service, call 1-800-762-0779. Residents of Tennessee, please call 1-800-633-1607. Prices and numbers are subject to change without notice. Please allow six to eight weeks for delivery.

Name_____
Address_____
City_____ State/Zip_____
Telephone No._____

JAN 0193

# Meet Peggy O'Neill
## A Campus Cop With a Ph.D. in Murder

## "A 'Must Read' for fans of Sue Grafton"
### *Alfred Hitchcock Mystery Magazine*

# Exciting Mysteries by M.D. Lake

**AMENDS FOR MURDER** 75865-2/$4.50 US/$5.50 Can
When a distinguished professor is found murdered, campus security officer Peggy O'Neill's investigation uncovers a murderous mix of faculty orgies, poetry readings, and some very devoted female teaching assistants.

**COLD COMFORT** 76032-0/$3.50 US/$4.25 Can
After he was jilted by Swedish sexpot Ann-Marie Ekdahl, computer whiz Mike Parrish's death was ruled a suicide by police. But campus cop Peggy O'Neill isn't so sure and launches her own investigation.

**POISONED IVY** 76573-X/$3.99 US/$4.99 Can

**A GIFT FOR MURDER** 76855-0/$4.50 US/$5.50 Can

*And Coming Soon*
**MURDER BY MAIL** 76856-9/$4.99 US/$5.99 Can

---

Buy these books at your local bookstore or use this coupon for ordering:

Mail to: Avon Books, Dept BP, Box 767, Rte 2, Dresden, TN 38225     C
Please send me the book(s) I have checked above.
❏ My check or money order— no cash or CODs please— for $_____ is enclosed
(please add $1.50 to cover postage and handling for each book ordered— Canadian residents add 7% GST).
❏ Charge my VISA/MC Acct#_____ Exp Date_____
Minimum credit card order is two books or $6.00 (please add postage and handling charge of $1.50 per book — Canadian residents add 7% GST). For faster service, call 1-800-762-0779. Residents of Tennessee, please call 1-800-633-1607. Prices and numbers are subject to change without notice. Please allow six to eight weeks for delivery.

Name_____
Address_____
City_____ State/Zip_____
Telephone No._____

MDL 0493